Dear Diary, I Have A Mate

By: Abbie Lynn

BLVNP

ISBN: 978-1-68030-955-3

Table of Contents

Please feel free to send me an email. Just know that my publisher filters these emails. Good news is always welcome.

Abbie Lynn – abbie_lynn@awesomeauthors.org

Sign up for my blog for updates and freebies!
http://abbie-lynn.awesomeauthors.org/

About the Publisher

BLVNP Incorporated, A Nevada Corporation, 340 S. Lemon #6200, Walnut CA 91789, info@blvnp.com / legal@blvnp.com

DISCLAIMER

Praise for Dear Diary, I Have A Mate

This book is absolutely one of my favorite books of all time, it was actually wonderful to see the main character develop throughout the story. It was just so heartwarming and brought tears to my eyes and let me just say I'm pretty sure I've read this book more than like 25 times and I plan on doing it many more.

-Ishita Rana, *Goodreads*

This was such a good book. Definitely one of my favorite werewolf books

-Nyaluak, *Goodreads*

I first read this book on wattpad, and the story line was just amazing. This book is so good and I would totally advise anyone who hasn't read it yet to read it. It's not one of those clique werewolf books that you read. The first time I saw this, I was wondering how it would come along and by the time I finished it was amazing. Abbie did an amazing job on this story and I advise her to keep on writing because I will read all the books.

-Sophia Brunetti, *Goodreads*

I love this book. Abbie did such a great job with the plot, character development, and keeping the romance alive without it being too cheesy.I have read this book 13 times and counting. I hope that this book does really well.

-Alli Zier, *Goodreads*

DEDICATION

This book is dedicated to my brilliant Wattpad fans. Without their love and support, this book would have never been finished.

FREE DOWNLOAD

Get these freebies and MORE when you
sign up for the author's mailing list!

abbie-lynn.awesomeauthors.org

Prologue

June 2

Dear Diary,

I have a mate. What is a mate? I don't know. I think it means friend.
I don't have friends. I don't talk to anyone, besides you. I don't even write in school. People think I'm stupid. It's him, Diary. It's Tyson. I don't know what it is about him; well I guess I do know. It's everything about him. Everything he does makes me smile. It's him—he makes me want to talk. He makes me feel like me again. I want to talk to him, I really do, but I have to do what's best for me. He might even be what's best for me. I'm lost Diary… I need help or maybe a friend. If I had a mom I would ask her. If I talked I would ask Ty what he wants with me. If I showed emotions I would show everyone that Arrabella James Middleton is a real person with real thoughts and feelings. However, Diary I don't talk. I haven't talked since I was eight years old. You're the only person I talk to, or write I

suppose. I don't know where I stand anymore; I'm just so confused...

~Aria

Chapter 1

3 Months Earlier

I walked up to my house and looked at it for a minute. Sure it looked nice on the outside, but the inside was a hellhole.

I took a breath and walked in. My father lay passed out on the couch. I rolled my eyes and prepared dinner. I set it on the table so that when he woke up it would be there, maybe then he would appreciate me.

Then again, I had been making him dinner ever since my mom went to rehab, and he never once said thank you.

"Arrabella?" I heard him ask.

I turned and looked at him.

"You start school tomorrow," he reminded. I shrugged my shoulders. He got up, and I flinched back.

"Calm down, I'm not in the mood to waste my energy on you," he sleepily spat.

I nodded and then headed upstairs. I don't like school. Then again what teenager does?

I sighed to myself and thought about all the strange looks, and same questions I would be getting tomorrow.

I stopped talking when I was eight. That was nine years ago. I just stopped. Who just stops talking? Well me, but I have my reasons. I wasn't being heard anyways.

People thought I was weird or deaf. I didn't write or talk, I just occasionally nodded so that they knew I wasn't stupid. I'm not stupid. I'm actually quite smart. I only write in my diary. Otherwise I don't write, talk, or even laugh.

* * *

March 3

Dear Diary,

Today is my first day of school. I'm a little nervous. I guess we'll see how it goes.

~Aria

I got up when my alarm rang at six in the morning. I don't mind waking up early; I just wouldn't do it if I had the choice.

I pulled on some jeans and a simple pink hooded sweatshirt. I went into the bathroom and washed my face. I brushed my teeth and combed through my hair. My brown hair was straight and simple. Besides who was I trying to impress anyways?

I walked on the path my dad directed me to, and I was off. I hope I can get through the day without getting noticed. I walked up to the school and noticed a lot of eyes on me. I hate when people stare at me.

I looked down walking and continued towards the office; it was a small school, so I don't think I could get lost.

I opened the door to the office, and the lady behind the desk gave me a warm smile.

"Are you Arrabella?" she asked. I nodded and gave her a small smile.

"Well here is your schedule. Don't stress about your first day. Just be yourself and I'm sure you will fit right in," she encouraged.

I nodded and then waved. She waved back and I went in search of my locker.

"No, but I hear there's a new girl, so you better check her out." I heard someone demand.

"Hey I think that's her. I won't mind checking her out," he replied.

I don't think they knew that I could hear them. I also heard the first guy growl a no.

I put some of my stuff in my locker and then I turned around to head to my first class of the day, English.

I walked in and sat by the window. I was one of the first ones there so I sat down and started reading.

"Twilight?" An amused voice said from beside me.

I looked up slightly startled.

"I didn't mean to scare you." He chuckled, sitting down next to me. I couldn't take my eyes off of his vibrant light brown ones. He was gorgeous, and I just wanted to run my hands through his dark brown silky looking hair.

I shoved my thoughts away and then nodded. This boy was a god compared to my boring brown hair and green eyes.

"What's your name?" he asked.

Arrabella. I thought. How do I tell him that? I pulled out my schedule from my backpack and pointed to my name.

"Arrabella?" He read.

NO! I almost shouted. How do I tell him to call me Aria?

I shook my head and smiled.

"No, how about Bella?" He suggested. I shook my head no again, pointing to the Twilight book; I don't want the name of a girl who for some reason picks a dead guy over a werewolf.

"Aria?" He tried. I smiled. Well that was easy.

"Where did you go to school before?" he asked.

Why is he so interested? I sighed not knowing how to tell him.

"What? Was it that bad?" he asked.

I smiled and shook my head no.

"So I need to know something: werewolves or vampires?" he asked, pointing to my book.

I rolled my eyes and then opened the book and pointed to Jacob's name.

"Werewolf." He grinned.

I nodded.

"Um, can you, er, talk?" I froze. I could but that's not technically what he was asking.

I shrugged in response.

"Oh so you can. You're just being difficult," he teased.

I shook my head. There is no way I can play this game with him; I need to stay away from him.

"You can hear me, right?" he asked.

I nodded.

"Just say one word," he pleaded.

I used my hands to make a can't motion.

"You can't?" he guessed.

I nodded.

"Sorry."

I shrugged and faced forward. When the bell rang I shot out of my seat and headed outside. I had a break after that hour.

I sat with my back against a tree, continuing to read my book.

I heard some people approaching so I looked up.

"Hey Aria," the boy greeted. He had some other guys with him this time.

I stood up and was about to leave when he begged, "No, don't leave."

I shook my head, trying to tell him I wanted to leave.

"You can't?"

I shook my head again.

"Listen just stay," he pleaded. I sighed and then looked behind me; it was stupid, but it was a habit. No one's watching I told myself, sitting back down.

"Were you looking for someone?" he asked.

I shook my head no.

"Well I kind of forgot to tell you in English, but I'm Tyson." He smiled. It didn't really matter to me; I was never going to call him that.

"This is Carter, Jason, and Alex." He smiled, pointing to each of the boys who had also sat down with him.

I nodded.

"Arrabella," someone called from my left. I looked over and saw the lady from behind the desk.

I smiled and waved.

"Can you fill this out?" she asked, handing me a clipboard.

I took it from her and looked it over.

"You can turn it in at the end of the day," she added.

I nodded and then looked at it again.

I checked the female box, the white box, and the numbers for my birthday; I couldn't fill out the others though. If I did it would be talking in writing form, and I can't, not when people are watching.

I set it aside and sighed.

"You didn't finish it." Tyson stated, pointing to the unanswered questions.

I did the same signal for can't as I did earlier and he nodded.

"Do you want me to help you?" He offered.

I shook my head no.

"I'm going to help you." He grinned, grabbing the clipboard and scooting to sit next to me.

"Do you have any allergies?" he asked.

I nodded.

"Really? What?"

I pointed to Alex's sandwich.

"Peanut butter," Tyson growled.

"Throw that away and go wash your hands!" Tyson demanded. Alex did it without a second thought.

I sighed, shaking my head.

"How bad is it?" he asked.

I shook my head back and forth to tell him it wasn't too bad. He nodded and then wrote down so-so. I almost laughed, but I held it in.

"What is your full name?"

I took out my schedule and pointed to it.

"Arrabella J. Middleton?"

I nodded.

"What does the J stand for?" I turned red and smiled.

"Is it embarrassing?". I nodded. My middle name was James! A boy's name, but hey what can I say? My father wanted a son.

"I'm going to figure it out," he teased.

I shook my head.

"Okay let's see. I know you are a senior and let's see what else is there? Oh, previous school?" he asked.

I took out a penny and pointed.

"Lincoln High?"

I nodded.

He laughed and then nodded.

"Team work," he added.

He handed it back to me, and I put it in my backpack.

I stood up; I might as well take it to the office now.

"Are you going to take that to the office?" Tyson asked.

I nodded.

"I'll walk with you."

I shook my head no, but he ignored me and kept walking beside me.

I handed it in the office and then went to my locker.

The warning bell rang and I started to walk towards our English classroom because I remember that history was near that.

I waved to Tyson and walked in.

I sat in history and barely listened to the teacher.

Tyson is so different. He's just so friendly? I can't even explain it. I wish I could talk to him. Maybe even call him Ty. Yeah, Ty is a cute name.

The bell rang so I stood up and walked over to the science hallway. I walked into chemistry and sat down.

"Hey Aria." Ty beamed.

I nodded and continued to doodle on my notebook.

"What are you drawing?"

I shrugged. I wasn't drawing anything. In fact I was just scribbling.

"So I had an idea."

I raised my eyebrows in interest.

"Whenever you want to say something, you can write it down." He smiled, pulling out a notepad.

I shook my head.

"Can you write?"

I shrugged.

"Is that a yes?"

I sighed. He wasn't going to let up so I smiled and then I put the notepad in my backpack.

He seemed content with that so I continued to doodle in my notebook.

I could feel his eyes on me, but I didn't want to get lost in his eyes again, his amazing brown eyes, so I kept my head down.

When the bell rang I sighed; it was lunchtime.

I grabbed my bag and headed outside. I had no lunch money.

I sat down and pulled out Twilight.

"Hey Aria." Ty smiled, sitting across from me. I smiled at him but then frowned when I saw him sitting down.

"What's wrong?"

I sighed; he should be sitting with his friends.

I pointed over to where Jason and Carter were sitting.

"Do you want to sit over there with them?"

I panicked, shaking my head and pointing at him.

"I should, oh I should be sitting over there."

I nodded.

"Okay, let's go." He shrugged.

I shook my head and went back to my book.

"Aria," he sighed.

"Arrabella."

I looked up and raised my eyebrows at him. What does this kid want from me?

"Either you come with me over there or I stay here with you." He shrugged.

I stared at him like he was crazy.

"Don't give me that look." He chuckled.

I shrugged and then smiled at him, actually smiled.

"Aren't you going to eat?" he asked concerned.

I shook my head.

"Why not?"

I sighed. It's hard not being able to talk to him. I want to talk to him, to ask him what he thinks he's doing, but if I do that I will have to explain why I act the way I do. It will lead to endless questions that I will be expected to answer and I can't do that. I will remain mute even if it kills me a little every day. Hell, it's killed me a little every day since I stopped, since it happened.

"Are you okay?" Ty asked, making me snap out of my thoughts.

I nodded. Why isn't he sitting with his friends?

"You don't look okay," he added.

I sighed. This is going to be a very long day.

After I stopped responding to Ty he would just tell me stories about him.

I liked his stories.

Once school was over I walked home and up to my room.

Dear Diary,

My first day was, not what I expected. I think I made a friend.

If you could talk Diary I would ask you for advice...but you are just paper. I wonder if Ty thinks I'm stupid? Or maybe he's just making fun of me. I don't know I think I will just stop everything, once he realized I'm not going to respond he will probably ignore me like the others.

~Aria

Chapter 2

Dear Diary,

Last night was bad to say the least. Dad came home drunk again or maybe he was high, or both. It was just bad....I'm sore and tired. My bruises will be difficult to cover today mostly because it's sunny 75 degrees, and I'm going to be wearing long sleeves, jeans, and a scarf.

~Aria

I arrived at school and sighed when everyone was in shorts and tank tops. If I had friends they would ask me what the hell I was doing in jeans and long sleeves. I walked into English and sat down by the window. I gazed out into the parking lot and held back the tears as I remembered last night.

"Why don't you do anything right?" Kick in the gut.

"I swear, Arrabella your mother doesn't need rehab."

"She didn't even have a problem until you were born," he screamed and threw a beer bottle against the wall.

"Then you stop talking and she blames me," he went on.

"Clean this up dammit!"

"Aria," a soft voice pleaded.

I slightly jumped and then remembered I am in English.

I focused in on Ty's worried face.

"I didn't mean to startle you." He apologized.

I shook my head trying to tell him I was okay.

"You do know it's like eighty degrees outside?" he asked amused.

I shrugged.

"At least take that scarf off, you are going to overheat." He said while reaching towards it.

'Don't you think I would if!' I could I screamed in my head.

I shook my head at him.

"Okay but take it off if you get hot," he replied.

Ugh if I take it off you would be able to see my father's fingerprints around my neck when he attempted to choke me last night.

I sighed sometimes I don't even know why I was born onto this planet.

"Are you okay?" he asked.

I nodded.

"Hey I didn't mean anything by it."

I smiled trying to let him know it wasn't his fault.

"You should smile more, you have cute dimples." He grinned.

I grinned at him while feeling heat rise up my neck, was I blushing?

"Oh is that a blush I see upon you cheeks?" I almost laughed at his failed attempt at an accent.

I shook my head and put my head down.

He reached over, placing his hand gently underneath my chin and tilted my head up so I was looking at him.

"Never hide your face from me. I like it when you blush babe."

I slapped his hand away and mock glared at him.

"You're cute when you're mad." He laughed.

I stuck my tongue out at him just because I didn't have any other way to express my feelings to him.

He just laughed more.

The teacher finally decided to show up and I tried to pay attention but Ty kept looking over at me and smirking!

I kept hitting him when the teacher wasn't looking.

"And that is what your appositive sentences should look like," she kept going.

Another smirk, this time I brought my hand up and was about to bring it down insanely hard but instead of me hitting him he grabbed my hand in his.

I looked over at him and mock glared.

"I didn't want you hurting your hand." He shrugged.

I smiled and then looked to the front of the room, my hand still in his.

I have never had a boyfriend. I used to have a lot of guy friends when I was little, but after it happened I lost all my friends.

The bell rang and I took my hand back from Ty.

UGH, stop smirking! I wanted to yell at him.

"You know you sure do yell at me a lot in your head," Ty remarked.

I stood there frozen and watched as he walked out of the room. What the hell just happened?

The rest of the day dragged on.

I didn't sit with Ty at break. As a matter of fact, I hid from him.

I went into the girl's washroom and sat in a stall for the entire twenty-five minutes.

When I heard the bell ring I raced into history and sat down. I looked up during my lesson and saw that Ty was in the doorway. The teacher had his head towards the chalkboard. He kept skimming the desks until his eyes landed on me. Relief flashed over his face. He smirked at me, waved, and then walked away.

I sighed; I think he's clinically insane.

After history I walked to chemistry, another class I have with Ty.

He was sitting where we sat yesterday, bouncing his leg anxiously in his seat.

He hadn't noticed I had walked in yet; he started drumming his long fingers against the desk. I walked over and placed my hands on top of his large one, making tingles shoot through my hand and up my arm.

His head snapped up and he jumped out of his seat and gave me a gigantic bear hug; I haven't been hugged since I was seven, ten years ago.

"Aria where were you during break?" he asked as we both sat down in our seats.

I looked at him confused.

"Arrabella." I looked everywhere but his face.

"Here draw a picture or write it down. I can help you spell it."

I almost laughed out of anger. *I can spell! I can spell damn well. He thinks I'm stupid.*

I shook my head.

"You can't," he said.

No I can, I won't.

"Why?" he asked.

I sighed and then got up and walked out of the classroom. I walked over to my locker and shoved my backpack inside. I walked to the doors of this damn building and walked out. I couldn't go home, so I walked to the park. I sat on the swing and kept pushing off with my feet. I kept getting higher, and higher. The swing was frantically swerving, but I don't care.

Higher and higher.

All of a sudden it rammed into the other swing, sending me flying forwards. I tried to use my hands to brace my fall but I could only get my left one in front of me fast enough.

I heard a snap and I screamed in pain.

I quickly shut my mouth and tried to move.

I couldn't though. I just lay there and let the darkness take over.

"ARIA!" I heard a voice scream.

"Don't you dare shut your eyes." The voice demanded.

"Come on, stay with me!" the voice pleaded again.

Is that Ty?

I felt the ground disappear from underneath me.

Where is he taking me?

The pain was too much I slowly let myself drift further and further into the darkness.

* * *

"She's fine," a female voice reassured again.

Are they talking about me?

Wait, where am I?

"Why isn't she waking up?" A deep voice growled.

Ty?

"She is waking up," the female voice replied.

"Aria, are you awake?" Ty asked.

I felt him grab my hand. I squeezed my eyes shut and then opened them.

"Aria," he gasped.

I looked over at him and then down at my arm that was now in a cast.

Great, why am I in a cast?

"Are you okay? What happened?" he questioned.

I pointed to my left arm that was now covered with a cast.

"You broke your arm," he said.

Dammit my dad is going to be pissed. If I have a cast on my arm then that means I went to the hospital. Wait is that where I am right now?

"Aria please, how did this happen?" he asked again.

I looked down at my sheets.

"I heard you scream."

I ground my teeth together.

"So I know that voice in there works," he added.

I never made any assumption that I couldn't talk.

"Why won't you use it?" he asked.

Can't, I motioned with my hand.

"Physically you can." He pushed.

I pointed to my brain.

"Mentally," he guessed.

I nodded.

"Aria I know that you aren't stupid, in fact you are quite smart."

I shrugged.

"Just draw a picture."

I took the piece of paper drew a swing and then handed it back.

"You fell off the swing?" he asked.

I nodded.

"Okay." He smiled.

I sighed I'm going to be killed if I don't get home. I looked around for a clock; there was one on the side table that said it was two.

I looked down and noticed my scarf was still on. Good because the last thing I needed was for him to question me about that.

"Are you too hot?" he asked.

I shook my head even though I was.

"You shouldn't have worn long pants and sleeves today."

Yes, I'm aware.

"Do you want to spend the night here?" he asked.

I quickly shook my head and started to get out of bed.

"Hold on." He panicked, wrapping his arm around my waist and helping me.

I held back my groan; I had a huge bruise on my hip from last night.

"What hurts?" he almost growled.

I pointed to my arm even though I could barely feel it.

"She gave you medicine for the pain," he said mostly to himself.

"Do you want more pain relievers?" he asked.

I shook my head and smiled, trying to show him that I'm fine.

"School will be over in an hour."

I nodded. I didn't want to go back to school.

"Okay. Should I drive you home now?"

I shook my head and went towards the door.

"No?" he asked.

I walked out and started walking to the sidewalk.

"Wait," he called, jogging up to me.

"You aren't going to walk home." He insisted.

Oh aren't I? I always walk home; damn this guy is going to get me in so much trouble.

"Come on my car's right there." He prompted, pointing to the black Mercedes, damn.

I shook my head again and then started walking.

"I will carry you." He threatened.

I backed away in fear.

"Come on Aria." He ordered.

I didn't look up at his face.

"Arrabella."

I walked around him and then started on my path again. He muttered something about stubborn and I smiled at that. Then I felt a presence next to me and he put his hand in mine and started walking with me. I pulled my hand from his and shoved his chest.

"I'm walking you home." He shrugged. A smile was playing at his lips.

I stopped walking, no way that could happen. I shook my head and pleaded with my eyes for him to just walk back inside.

"Arrabella get in the car or I am walking with you."

I looked up and studied his face. He wasn't kidding. I sighed and then walked over to the car. I know he was smiling, so I flipped him off over my head.

"Did you just flip me off?" he asked in mock anger and amusement.

I shrugged.

"I didn't think you were that kind of girl."

I held in a laugh and covered it with a cough.

"You pointed at the stop sign," he roared with laughter.

I was smiling like an idiot. He did not understand I was telling him to slow down, not turn!

I pointed at a house that was about six away from mine.

"This one?" he asked.

I nodded.

"Okay," he replied. It seems like he knew I was lying.

I smiled and waved.

He didn't leave so I walked around to the back of the house and then started sprinting. I ran all the way to the backyard of my house. Then I walked to the front of my house and walked in. I sighed in relief when I realized my dad wasn't home yet, well better safe than sorry.

I started on dinner and then waited for the demon to arrive home. I heard the garage door open and I flinched, waiting. He walked in and grunted at me. He sat down at the table and I stood off to the side and waited to clean his dish.

"I heard something that didn't quite sit right with me today."

I looked over at him.

"ARRABELLA COME OVER HERE WHEN I TALK TO YOU!" he roared.

I walked over and waited.

"Greg said that he's seen you 'round with some boy," he continued. Shit.

"What are you doing with some boy Arrabella?"

"Ain't I tell you how many times girl." He shot up from the table.

"WHO IS HE?" He demanded.

He punched my stomach until I fell to the ground, his foot replacing his fist.

The last face that flashed on my mind before I completely blacked out was Ty's.

Chapter 3

Dear Diary,

I can't be seen with Ty anymore. My black eye is too black and blue to be covered.

He's going to ask me what happened. He's going to ask me to draw it.

I can't keep lying to him; it hurts too much.

The only thing I can do is save him.

I know how to save him but it might be hard.

I need to stop almost laughing when he's around, stop smiling, and just be the mute freak.

I most stop becoming friends with him.

~Aria

I walked to school and sat down in English.

"What happened?" Ty asked. He grabbed my face with his hand and rubbed his thumb over my swollen eye.

Stay strong Aria.

I shook my head.

"Draw it right now." He forcefully insisted.

I sat there looking down and playing with my hands. Why can't he just leave me alone?

"Arrabella," he growled.

He took his hand and grabbed my jaw and forced me to look up at him. It didn't hurt but I flinched back anyways.

"Draw it."

I looked at him emotionlessly.

Whenever we touched I felt this weird tingling through me. I just need him to get his hand away from my face!

He groaned in frustration and grabbed the pencil on the desk and shoved it in my hand.

I held onto it, waiting to see what he would do next. He put the piece of paper in front
of me.

"Draw."

He really did think I was stupid. That bothered me more than it should, but I held back the tears and threw the pencil at him.

"Everyone, take a seat," the teacher whose name I still don't remember announced.

Finally, I need to stop getting here early. Ty sat down, looking furious. The whole class he would shift in his seat and sigh every once in a while. He would glance over at me as well, but I never looked back.

The bell rang and I got out of my seat, grabbed my backpack, and left.

I don't really know why I'm in school.

I fail all my classes except math. I'm good at math and with numbers. I can write numbers—numbers don't hurt to write; numbers don't make me remember…

I felt two strong arms grab me and I almost yelled in shock. I turned around to see Ty had pulled me into an empty classroom. He shut the door and then stood in front of it with his arms crossed. I tried to go around him but wouldn't budge.

"You aren't leaving until I know who did that," he said, referring to my black eye.

I backed away from him and sat in one of the desks. *I don't need this!* He doesn't realize how hard he is making this for me.

"Aria who did this to you?"

My dad did!

I shrugged.

He walked over to me and grabbed my hand. I tried to pull it away but he wouldn't let go.

"Please tell me."

I sighed and then grabbed a pencil from my bag and my notepad. I pulled my hand from his and then drew a door.

"You ran into a door?"

I nodded.

"When?"

I drew a moon.

"Last night?" he asked. He didn't believe me I could tell.

"Are you sure?"

I looked at him and then glanced down and nodded.

"Okay thank you for telling me." He smiled, but it wasn't a real Ty smile, more like an I-know-you're-lying-to-me smile.

Now I feel like crap. I promised myself I'd stay away from him and now I'm lying to him. I stood up and then pulled the door open and walked out. It's bad enough that I have this cast on my arm and now I have a black eye. I also always have to wear a scarf because my father's fingerprints won't go away.

I walked into history and sat down at my desk. The class goes by in a flash when the entire period you're thinking about Ty's broken smile. The bell rang and I headed to chemistry.

Ty was already in there waiting for me. He smiled when he saw me. I felt bad for what I was about to do but I had to do this. I walked by his table and sat down at a table in the corner.

I didn't dare look back at him though he was basically burning a hole through my head with his stare.

I watched the clock the entire hour and when the bell rang I nearly sprinted out of the room.

I went to my locker and then I sat outside by my tree.

I pulled out Twilight and began to read to distract myself from how hungry I am.

"Hey," a familiar voice greeted.

I looked up to meet Carter's pale blue eyes. I smiled and gave him a small wave.

"So, you should come sit with us?" he asked.

I looked over and saw Jason and Ty sitting at a table.

I shook my head.

"Are you and Ty in a fight?" He joked but he seemed like he knew that something was wrong.

I shrugged. We weren't in a fight and we aren't really even friends.

"You two should um work it out."

I shook my head.

"Why not?"

I pointed to my arm.

"I'm not following you." He sighed. His eyebrows were scrunched together like he was trying really hard to understand me, like it's his job or something.

I sighed back and then pointed at him and then the table Ty was at.

"You aren't going to come with me, are you?" he asked in defeat.

I smiled and gave him a thumb up.

"Alright well if you change your mind we'll be over there," he added before walking away.

I shook my head.

Dear Diary,

Today was hard.

I failed.

Ty heard me scream... he knows I'm capable of talking. He makes me want to talk and laugh. I'm lost. We will both end up getting hurt in the end so why can't I seem to get him out of my mind? Why does he even talk to me?

My dad is home... I'm scared. Why does he have to hurt me?

~Aria

Chapter 4

Dear Diary,
I don't know if I can take any more pain...
~Aria

I woke up the next morning feeling sad.

Today all I have to do is stay away from Ty and avoid his friends. How hard can that be?

I walked into English, arriving just before the bell rang.

Ty was sitting in his usual spot, looking well besides the obvious, incredibly adorable but he also looked tired. His brown hair didn't look as silky and soft as it usually did. In fact, it was kind of all over the place like he just rolled out of bed and came to school.

I sat down in my seat next to him and faced front.

I didn't look at him.

I didn't even acknowledge the fact I had seen him when I walked in.

After English I went on break. Today I sat on a bench away from my tree and away from Ty and his friends.

"Hey," a boy from my math class waved.

I gave him a small smile and waved back.

"Do you think you can give me the homework from last night?" he asked.

I nodded and wrote it down for him. I can write numbers for him; no words, just numbers.

"Thanks, Arrabella." He smiled, walking away.

Surely there had to be someone else he could have asked. *What is it with the guys at this school?*

What was his name anyways? Damon, Dustin, Dlake? Wait. Dlake? Is that even a name?

"What did Drake want?" Ty asked, sitting down next to me.

DRAKE! Yes, thank the lord. That would have bugged me.

"What's that smile for?" he asked.

I shook my head and then wrote down the math assignment again.

"He wanted the homework." He nodded, understanding.

"So why does he get to call you Arrabella?" He smirked.

I rolled my eyes.

"I'm curious," he admitted.

I drew a cat on my paper.

"Oh curiosity killed the cat?"

I nodded.

"Well I'm not a cat, am I?"

I laughed.

It just came out.

Like a quick ha.

I slapped hand over my mouth in shock. Ty looked at me with mixed emotions. I got off the bench and bolted, leaving my backpack in panic. I sprinted until I reached the pond near my house.

I swear Ty is going to be the death of me.

Dear Diary,

Ty did it. He made me laugh for the first time in nine years.

~Aria

"Aria the last time you ran you broke your arm," Ty shouted at me. I was sitting near the pond with my arms wrapped around my legs.

I glanced up at him; he had my backpack in his hands.

I nodded.

"You have an amazing laugh." He sighed, sitting down next to me.

I shook my head.

"Why, why is laughing so bad?"

I lowered my head so he couldn't see me.

"Don't hide your face." He demanded.

What the hell, Aria. I was supposed to be avoiding him. But no here I am sitting next to him just about two blocks away from my house.

I looked up at him.

"I want to help you," he said.

I am not a charity case!

I stood up and grabbed my backpack.

"Not like that, I mean I want you to trust me. I want to be friends," he added, but he stumbled on the word friend.

I shook my head.

"No."

I began to walk away.

"Aria," he called.

I looked back at him.

"I guarantee I am more stubborn than you, so challenge accepted." He grinned.

I looked at him as if he were crazy. Wait he is crazy.

I narrowed my eyes at him.

"Don't give me that look," he scoffed.

I flipped him off once again and then walked away.

* * *

Ty is all that's been through my head since I've been home!

UGH.

Today I woke up happy.

It is Saturday.

My dad leaves me here alone on Saturdays; he goes golfing, I think.

I got up cleaned the entire house and then went to my pond. Once I got there I smiled remembering the last time I was here. I can't help but be a little scared though. I mean what did Ty mean by challenge accepted?

"Fancy meeting you here," an amused voice called.

I looked up to meet Ty's face. I glared at him.

"Cute," he smirked.

I shook my head in response.

"Well the doctor, the one you saw a few days ago, wants to check your arm," he informed.

I shrugged.

"Is that a yes?" he asked but it sounded like it didn't matter what I implied.

I shook my head; I can't keep going out in public with him.

"It's really not an option, Aria, you have to see if it's healing right." He sighed. It sounded like he was explaining this to a small child.

I sighed.

"Come on." He grinned, grabbing my hand and pulling me to the parked car.

I got in and we rode to the doctor's in comfortable silence.

We arrived and it was weird because I can kind of remember the doctor's from when I was little but I don't remember it looking like this.

"This is my house," he said.

I stared at him like he was crazy.

"The doctor inside is a family friend," he added.

I nodded I guess that's better than being at a real hospital where someone could tell my father that they saw me there.

I got out and Ty led me back into the small white room.

"Hello, Arrabella. I am just going to check your arm," the same lady who attended me before smiled.

I flinched away from her. Ty sat next to me and held my other hand. I sighed, letting her take the cast off. I clenched my teeth together as she started to poke at it.

"Hurry," Ty growled.

"Yes sir."

I almost cussed out loud at the pain shooting through my arm. I buried my head into the side of Ty's arm.

"It's okay." He soothed.

The lady put the cast back on and I lifted my head from Ty.

"Another two weeks."

I nodded.

"Thanks," Ty muttered, leading me out of the room.

We went out to what looked like a living room.

"Do you want to watch a movie?"

I nodded.

"Okay." He beamed, rushing over to the television.

He popped in one of the movies. Ty was laughing out loud at the movie. I almost laughed because his laugh was contagious but I swallowed all of them down. I love hearing him laugh.

"Come on. This is hilarious." He chuckled again.

Wow, he is trying to get me to laugh.

"You know you want to."

I smiled at him but shook my head.

"Aria," he sang.

He then started tickling me!

I am a ticklish person however this hurt like hell. I have bruises all over my ribs and hips, which is exactly where Ty was pressing on. I pushed his hands away.

"I'm sorry. You look hurt, is it your arm?"

I shook my head.

"Aria, I'm really sorry." He apologized again.

I stopped him, holding up my hand. I pointed at the clock and then got up.

"You have to go?"

I nodded.

"Okay I'll drive you." He smiled.

I nodded.

He drove me back to the house that wasn't actually my house.

I waved to him and then once again ran to my house.

Dear Diary,

Ty.

He isn't like Dad.

Maybe all guys aren't the same...

~Aria

Chapter 5

Dear Diary,

Today I woke up happy.

I would say maybe my life is turning around or someone is really watching over me, but I know the truth.

It's Ty. He may just be good for me.

~Aria

Sunday's always dragged on.

I woke up and cleaned the rest of the house, and now I'm at the grocery store.

I walked down the cereal aisle in search of my dad's favorites. Since I was barely allowed to eat food, I couldn't pick up anything I like.

"Aria," a voice called out.

My body instantly felt at ease, telling me it was Ty.

I looked up and waved at him. He came racing over and gave me a hug. I flinched back at first but then I melted into him and hugged back. He beamed at me.

"Are you here alone?"

I nodded.

"Grocery shopping?"

I smiled and kept walking.

Now why is he here? I pointed at him and cocked my head to the side.

"Why am I here?"

I nodded. He looked a little embarrassed.

"I needed to pick up a few things." He shrugged. He was lying, I think.

Why would he come all the way to this market when there was a convenient shop like a block away from his house? Oh my, is he following me? No. Why would he be? It's not like two people can't be at the same place at the same time.

"What are you thinking about?"

I smirked and then grabbed some cereal and tossed it into my cart.

"Oh, you aren't going to tell me?" he mocked as he started walking with me to the meat section.

I shook my head.

"Really?"

I nodded.

"Hmm, well I guess I could always kidnap you," he teased.

I punched his arm.

"Ow okay you're tough, but I could take you."

I shook my head.

"I'm just saying," he said defensively, putting his hands up in mock surrender.

After we both checked out we headed outside.

"Are you walking home?"

I hesitantly nodded.

"I will drive you." He almost demanded.

I shook my head in protest. It was too late he already took my bags and put them in his car. I walked over to take them out.

"Aria, I will take you home or walk you home." He ordered.

I sighed.

I bet I could outrun him.

I was about to take my bags when Ty pulled me away from the car. He opened the door to the passenger seat, pushed me in and buckled me up.

He then got in his side. I punched him when he got in.

"Yeah I knew that was coming." He laughed.

He drove me to my fake house. I got my groceries out of the back and then waved to him. I walked to my house and then started to put the groceries away.

* * *

Monday mornings are usually the worst, but not this Monday. I combed my long brown hair and changed my outfit three times. I looked at myself in the mirror and my usual dull green eyes were a little brighter this morning.

I walked into English and sat down next to Ty.

"Well someone's happy this morning." He observed.

I raised my eyebrows in surprise.

He shrugged and I smiled.

"Tyson," a girl called, walking up to him.

"What, Claire?" he asked sounding annoyed.

"What are you doing hanging around with this shit?" Claire sneered.

"What did you just say?" he growled.

"People are starting to talk, Tyson." She clicked her tongue in anger.

"Let them talk." He shrugged.

"You're going to throw everything away for some mute freak? She doesn't talk because she wants attention," she almost yelled.

How dare she!

"Claire," he warned.

"I'm serious, Tyson. I hear she's deaf too. Watch her. She stares at people's lips when they talk."

"Claire," he growled. She flinched back and flipped the both of us off.

"Sorry about her."

I shrugged. She was right. Why is Ty hanging around me?

"Are you okay?".

I nodded and smiled.

"Good because you are beautiful and important. Never let anyone tell you different."

I looked at him in awe; no one has ever told me I'm important. I smiled and then reached out and hugged him. He seemed surprised but he instantly accepted it. He sighed and I swear he said I love you, but I know I'm just hearing things.

Once English was finally over Ty and I walked outside to my tree. I saw the woman from the office approaching us.

"Arrabella, your father is here. He says he needs to take you to an appointment."

I froze.

"He's waiting over there," she added, pointing to the parking lot.

I peeked over and saw my dad leaning against his car watching me carefully. I nodded at the lady.

"Are you okay?" Ty asked.

I pointed over to Carter and Jason.

"What?" he asked confused.

I shoved him slightly.

"Aria, Aria, calm down. What's wrong?" He panicked.

I shoved him and then started to walk away.

"Aria," he called.

He grabbed me and looked into my eyes.

"Are you going to be okay?"

I nodded.

"Is that your dad?"

I nodded again.

"Stay here, with me." He suggested but ordered it at the same time.

I shook my head. He is getting me in so much trouble right now.

I shoved at his chest and then walked away.

My dad was glaring at him and then his eyes snapped to me as I got into the car.

"Who is that boy?" he roared, pulling out of the parking lot.

Maybe I should tell him that he bullies me and makes fun of me?

"Arrabella, I'm done with this I don't talk act."

Is he serious? Hes did this to me!

I stared at him to see if he was joking.

"Speak to me girl dammit!"

I cleared my throat.

"He, he bullies me," I spoke softly.

"Bullies you?" He almost laughed.

"For, for not talking," I whispered.

I started shaking. It was too much.

I can't deal with this. Talking is hard; it brings back too much.

The last thing I remember was my dad pulling up to our house and slamming the door, leaving me in the car.

Chapter 6

Dear Diary,

I spoke.

My first words in so long.

*It hurts when I talk like he's going to do it again—take
away my voice.*

I want to talk to Ty, but I can't.

*This is my life. I will always be broken and Ty deserves
better.*

I'm done. I'm checking out.

~Aria

I woke up and walked slowly to school.

My head was pounding.

When I arrived at school I walked into English and
saw Ty sitting impatiently at his desk.

I almost smiled but then I remembered that I was done dragging him down with me.

"Hey," he greeted.

I glanced over and nodded in his direction.

"Really Aria just a nod?" he joked.

I shrugged.

"About yesterday," he started to say.

I held up a hand to stop him.

"I'm sorry if your dad doesn't want you hanging out with guys or something."

My dad doesn't like me associating with anyone.

Ugh why am I even here?

"So I talked with Sherry, the doctor at my house, and she said she can check your arm and take off the cast today." He smiled.

I'm pretty sure my dad broke my arm again last night.

I shook my head.

"You can't come?"

I nodded.

"Why?"

I shook my head again.

"Draw it, Aria." He sighed.

I took out my notepad and threw it at his face.

He caught it and then placed it back on my desk.

I picked up my arm to slide it off but Ty snatched it off my desk and sighed.

"Fine, be stubborn."

The rest of the hour I ignored Ty, which was easy because he was ignoring me as well.

He didn't even follow me out for break so I sat alone.

Maybe he finally realized that he was hanging out with a mute, might as well be talking to a wall.

I put on my headphones and listened to some Kesha. I took them out when there was about three minutes left of break. I finally looked over for the first time all break and I was sorry I did. I saw Ty sitting with Jason and Carter, however Claire was on Ty's lap. My heart clenched and I looked away and stood up.

I glanced over one last time to see Claire attacking his face! I ran and grabbed my chemistry book from my locker. This is what I wanted: for him to be happy and find someone better, but Claire is not better!

I sat down in chemistry and drummed my fingers on the desk. Ty came strolling in a minute later, looking pissed yet nervous. When he saw me, his expression changed to hurt. He walked over and sat next to me. I thought I could handle it but I couldn't. I got up and was about to leave when Ty pushed me back down into my seat.

I held back the tears and tried to stand up again, but he once again pushed me back into my seat.

"Aria, I'm so sorry."

Why was he sorry?

"Just please sit here," he begged.

I rolled my eyes and stood up once again. This time Ty followed me out of the classroom. I turned around and shoved him and pointed at the classroom.

"I'm not going back in there without you." He shrugged.

I sighed.

"Are you going to go back in?"

I shook my head.

"Great, let's go." He smiled, grabbing my hand and pulling me outside of the school.

I let him take me to his car but stopped when he was opening the door and telling me to get in.

I turned around to go back to class when Ty grabbed my hips and hugged me.

"Please come," he pleaded.

I kicked him in the shin, and he didn't even seem affected.

"Go ahead. Hit, punch, and kick me. I deserve it."

I sighed.

"Please, Aria," he pleaded.

I shook my head.

"Aria," he whined.

I flipped him off and then got into the car.

I am not good at not following demands. When we arrived at his house I became nervous. We walked in, and Sherry took off the cast.

"Oh my," she said.

"What?" Ty asked.

"Aria, what happened to your arm?" she asked.

I looked at her, acting confused even though I knew what she meant.

"It looks like it got broken again," she noted.

"Aria, what happened?" Ty asked.

I shrugged.

"Sherry?" he asked.

"Well I'm not sure but it seems as if it just snapped in half again."

"Leave," he ordered, and she left immediately.

"Aria," he demanded.

I looked anywhere but his face.

"Arrabella, what the hell happened?" he growled.

I peeked up at him and his eyes grew darker. They were no longer their usual cheery light brown color; they were more of a chocolate color.

I flinched back and looked away.

"Arrabella, I'm not going to ask again."

I looked up and gave him a blank stare.

"I will find other ways to find out."

I sighed and then drew a car.

"A car?" he asked, obviously frustrated.

I drew a tree.

"The car hit the tree. Wait you were in a car accident?"

I nodded. It wasn't true of course but what else could I have drawn?

"Aria, I know you weren't in a car accident." He sighed.

I shrugged.

"Just tell me what happened, who did that?" he roared.

He sounded like my dad. It wasn't directed towards me as much but I was still scared. I ran out of the room and out of his house.

"Aria?" a familiar voice asked.

I looked over to see Carter. I ran over and hugged him.

"Oh hey," he laughed.

"What's wrong?" he asked.

I wiped my tear away and got out a piece of paper. I drew my house on it with a question mark.

"Whose house is this?" he asked.

I shook my head and then drew a car.

"Oh, you want me to take you home?"

I nodded.

"Yeah I can do that." He smiled.

I smiled back as he led me to his car. He got in and I pointed the way. I pointed to the house that I told Ty was my house just in case it was ever brought up. I smiled at him and waved.

I then ran to my house. My dad wouldn't be home until later. I blasted some music, lay down on my bed, and cried.

Dear Diary,
Ty hates me. I kind of hate me too.
~Aria

Chapter 7

Dear Diary,
I'm tired of feeling like this.
~Aria

I walked to school, feeling sick.

I feel like I'm going to cry and puke at the same time.

When I arrived at school I trudged into first hour, dragging my boots on the floor. Ty wasn't here yet. I guess he has better places to be.

He didn't come at all. I waited, and when the bell rang my heart just sank even more in my chest. I walked out to my tree and sat against it. I felt a presence in front of me so I opened my eyes to see Ty.

"Can we talk?"

I shook my head.

"It's not really an option, Aria."

I looked away from him.

He sighed and then lifted me off the ground, threw me over his shoulder and carried me to his car! I squirmed and punched his arm but it was no use. He then placed me in his car, buckled me in, and then he got in and drove off.

Where are we going?

He pulled up to his house and I sighed. He got out and was opening my door before I even got my seat belt off. I stepped out and followed him in. He sat down on the white couch in his living room and I sat next to him.

"Look, I'm sorry I yelled at you yesterday. I just feel very protective of you and when you didn't tell me the truth I just snapped," he explained apologetically.

I nodded.

"You've lied to me a lot," he added.

I didn't lie.

"I know you didn't get that black eye because you ran into a door, that you didn't get into a car accident, and that you live about six houses down and I drop you off at a random house every time."

I stared at him in shock. Was he some kind of stalker?

"I need you to stop lying."

"You can trust me," he added.

Trust him? I barely know him. I stared at him for a long time.

"Tyson, do you know why—," Carter started to say as he walked into the room, but then he stopped when he saw me.

"Oh sorry. Hey, Aria." He waved.

I smiled and waved back.

"It's okay Carter just tell me later," Ty replied. *Wow, he didn't even say hi to him.*

"Okay have a nice chat." Carter smiled but then stopped once again.

"I mean talk or write or…" he stuttered.

I smiled at him. I mean it's not his fault he doesn't know what to say, at least he tried.

"Draw," Ty corrected.

"Oh you draw right? I just thought you liked to write since you always write those little notes in your notebook." He shrugged.

I froze. When did Carter see me writing? I thought back to one of the first days I started. So it was last week, Wednesday.

I was in math with him and I did write something in my notebook! I wanted to transfer it over to Diary. I was sitting in the corner at the back. I didn't think anyone saw me.

Ty said something to Carter that made him leave.

"Aria," he pushed.

I snapped my head up at him and then got off the couch.

"Nope you owe me a lot of answers." He demanded, lightly pushing me back down.

He got out a notebook and pencil and pushed it towards me. I stared at it for a moment and then wrote my first thing to him.

'I'm sorry.' I scribbled down.

"Just tell me what's going on," he begged.

'Can't.' I wrote.

"Why?"

I looked away and tried to control my breathing.

"I know this is probably hard for you but I want to help you so bad," he pleaded.

I pointed to the "I'm sorry" written on the paper.

"Stop being sorry just let me help you."

I got up and headed towards the door.

"Aria wait," he ordered, grabbing my waist.

I drew in a sharp breath. He looked at me skeptically before lifting up my shirt a little ways. I pushed at his hands but it was too late; he already saw the scratches, burns, cuts, and bruises. He then looked up at me and slowly took off my scarf. I pushed at him but he held me still. Once it was off he backed away from me took the lamp that was sitting nicely on the table and threw it against the wall.

I flinched back and away from him, was he angry with me? I waited for him to come over and attack me. He walked slowly over to me and I backed myself against the wall.

"I'm sorry, I'm not going to hurt you." He promised.

He grabbed my hand and led me back to the couch.

"Who did this?" he asked.

I shook my head and pleaded with my eyes for him to let it go.

"Arrabella!"

I took the notepad.

'Please don't do this.' I wrote.

"Just tell me who did this," he repeated.

'Why?' I wrote.

"So that they can go to jail," he growled.

'No, why do you care?' I clarified.

"I care about you."

'Why?' I wrote.

"I told you I feel protective of you and you make me happy," he admitted, smiling a full and complete Tyson smile.

I gave him a small smile back.

"So please, who did this to you?" he repeated.

I stared at him for a long moment.

'My dad.' I wrote slowly.

He sucked in a breath.

"What about your mom?"

My mom, a person I never like to think about.

I shook my head.

"Where is she?"

Rotting in hell I hope.

My mother left me when I was eight. Eight was a big year for me: my mother left, my father's abuse got worse, and I stopped talking.

Wow, what should a normal eight-year-old be doing? I don't know. Maybe learn to ride a bike? Have their first sleepover? I was never taught to ride a bike and I have never had a sleepover.

"Aria?" Ty asked, snapping me out of my thoughts.

"You need to get away from your dad."

NO! This was what I was afraid of.

I shook my head.

"Why do you still want to live with him?"

I don't want to. I have to! I got off the couch and walked towards the door once again.

"I'm not going to let you go back to your house and get abused."

I turned to him.

"I know you're scared Aria, but you have to get away from him."

Where was I supposed to go?

"You're staying with me." He added like he read my mind.

I stared at him in shock.

"Is your dad home right now?"

I shook my head.

"Great, let's go get some of your things." He smiled.

I shook my head and stared at him like he was crazy.

"Don't give me that look Aria." He snorted and then led me outside.

He drove me to my house; he must have seen me run to it one time, otherwise I have no idea how he actually knew where I live.

'Wait here.' I wrote.

"I want to help you with your things," he replied.

'There is not a lot. I can do it.' I wrote.

"Okay go fast."

I nodded.

I ran in and grabbed some shirts, jeans, shorts, tank tops, undergarments, tennis shoes,

and scarves, which I stuffed into a duffel bag.

I also put in a hairbrush, toothbrush, toothpaste, shampoo, conditioner, hair ties,

and tampons.

I then grabbed my diary, shoved it to the bottom of the bag, and ran downstairs.

I got into the car and threw it in the backseat, finally taking a deep breath.

"Aria, Aria, it's okay. Look at me."

I looked over at him.

"This is for the best. I'm proud of you."

I stiffly nodded.

Proud— a word that has never been directed towards me.

He is proud of me?

I like this feeling right now. I want to hug him but he's driving.

Would he want me to hug him?

He pulled up to his house again and we got out. He grabbed my duffel bag and then helped me out. We went upstairs. He opened the door to a bedroom with navy blue walls. There was a blue comforter on the bed and black dressers.

This must be his room. I turned around and raised my eyebrows at him.

"This is my room," he whispered. *Did he blush?*

I walked over and pinched his cheeks.

"Stop it," he teased.

I smiled up at him and then hugged him. He hugged me back instantly.

"So um do you want to unpack your things?"

I shrugged and went over to my bag.

"You can use these drawers," he added, pulling out some clothes and putting them in the closet.

I unpacked my clothes and stuffed my diary in my backpack. I kept my bathroom stuff in my bag.

I then sat down against the wall. I wonder what my dad will do when he finds out. He will be getting home from work in five minutes.

In five minutes, dinner won't be on the table and he will look in my room and see my most of my stuff was missing.

"Aria?" Ty asked.

"Are you okay?" he asked, sitting next to me.

I shook my head. I have to get home before my dad does. I got up and walked out of the room. If I get home before he does I might be able to throw something together.

"Aria, Aria where are you going?" Ty asked, standing in front of the door.

I looked for a notepad and found the one I was using earlier.

'Can you drive me home?' I wrote.

"Aria you are safe here. He won't find you," Ty said confidently.

'What about school?' I wrote.

"Don't worry about it," he begged.

Don't worry about it? I sighed and then went to try to find Carter.

"Carter won't take you either," he called.

I groaned.

"Come on." He sighed, grabbing my hand.

I walked with him as he led me into the kitchen. He pulled out a stool from the counter and gestured for me to sit. I sat and then placed my arms on the counter and rested my head in them.

"It's going to be okay. I will protect you." Ty stated.

A few moments later I heard a plate being set in front of me. I raised my head to see that he was now sitting next to me. We each had a plate of food in front of us.

He made me dinner?

There was a small pile of spaghetti in front of me with a roll and green beans. I looked over at him and saw he was watching me; his food was untouched. I put my hands in my lap and waited for him to tell me what to do.

"Aren't you hungry?"

I slowly nodded.

"Then eat," he encouraged.

I pointed at him and then his plate.

"I should eat?"

I nodded.

"I'll make you a deal. If you eat, I will too." He smiled.

I nodded and then picked up my fork. I ate it all and for once I was full.

"Do you want more?" he asked, standing up to get some.

I shook my head and then grabbed a pad of paper.

'Thank you.' I wrote.

"You don't have to thank me for giving you food." He laughed.

I nodded and smiled back.

After that I followed him to the living room where we watched *Twilight*.

'The book is better. ' I wrote for Ty to read. He laughed and said the book is always better.

It's inevitable though. The book is like your own personal movie in your head and then Hollywood makes it into what should be going on in your head, but really they just ruin it for creative kids everywhere.

"You ready for bed?" he asked.

I yawned and nodded.

The movie took my mind off of what's probably going on at my house right now. We walked into Ty's room and he started laying a blanket down on the floor. I stopped him because I am capable of doing it myself. I then lay down on it.

"Aria you aren't sleeping on the floor." He laughed.

I sat up and grabbed my notebook.

"I was setting it out for me," he added.

'No this is your room.' I wrote.

"I'm not letting you sleep on the ground. You can have my bed." He shrugged.

I shook my head in protest and lay back down.

"Aria," he snorted.

I then felt two strong arms go underneath me and then the ground disappeared.

I opened my eyes right as Ty was laying me on his bed.

'No Ty!' I scribbled down and forcefully shoved the notepad in his face.

"Ty?"

'It's what I call you in my head.' I wrote, blushing.

"I like it." He grinned.

I sighed and then thought of the only other possibility.

'If you won't let me sleep on the ground then will you sleep up here with me?' I wrote.

He grinned widely and then pulled himself together.

"Gosh Aria you should have just said that's what you wanted in the first place."

I slapped his arm as he climbed into the large bed.

I had changed into my sweats before the movie and so had Ty. I had also taken a shower. Ty said he takes his shower in the morning because it makes more sense, but really it doesn't because then it's like going to bed dirty.

"Good night," he whispered, turning off the light.

Great, first, I move in with a boy I met a week ago and now we are sharing a bed; this is going to be one hell of a night.

Chapter 8

Dear Diary,

I squirmed out of Ty's arms to write to you. At one point in the night he must have wrapped them around me because we started out on opposite ends of the bed.

It felt nice and for once I felt safe.

Ty looks peaceful right now and innocent.

I better go before he wakes up.

~Aria

I crept back to the bed and lay down once again.

Almost immediately Ty's arms found me and once again I was in my warm bubble.

It was about four in the morning so we still have about two hours to sleep.

With that in mind I slowly drifted back to sleep.

* * *

I woke up to the alarm clock and Ty moving around to try and turn it off.

I moved so I was on my back and I could look over at him.

"Good morning." He smiled.

I yawned and sat up.

"Did you sleep okay?" I nodded and tried to hold in my laugh.

"Don't do that." I looked at him questioningly.

"Don't stop yourself from laughing." I grabbed my notepad from the nightstand and pointed to the word sorry.

"Yeah, I know," he replied, getting up to grab some jeans and a brown t-shirt.

"I'm going to get in the shower," he said, walking into the bathroom.

"Don't go anywhere," he added, shutting the door.

I shook my head and then took out my clothes for the day and put them on. I then used the mirror in his room to comb my hair. Ty walked out of the bathroom, looking incredibly good, and smiled when he saw me.

"Are you ready?" I nodded, grabbing my backpack. We headed downstairs where we stopped in the kitchen. He pulled out a cereal labeled "Lucky Charms" and poured some into a bowl.

"What kind of cereal do you like?"

Are we going to eat again? I was honestly still full from last night, but Lucky Charms sound really good right now. I remember my mom and I sitting at the kitchen table on Saturday mornings eating them together. I think that stopped happening when I turned six.

'I'm not hungry,' I wrote.

"Will you eat at least a few bites of something?"

'Fine.' I wrote.

He smiled and then poured some more into his bowl. He then put two spoons into his bowl. I raised my eyebrows at him.

"Why waste another bowl?" I laughed at that. He smiled at me knowing I didn't hide it or cough to cover it. I just laughed, and it felt pretty good. He then sat down next to me. I had a few bites and remembered just how much I love Lucky Charms.

After we finished, Ty drove me to school. We got some pretty weird looks when I stepped out of his car. We walked into English together and sat down in our usual seats.

I can't say I'm not a little scared right now. In fact, I kind of expect my father to come barging into the classroom. When English was over, Ty and I walked out to break.

"Aria please calm down. Your dad's not going to come." He soothed, sounding sure at the same time.

I took a deep breath and nodded.

"So about your arm," he started to say.

I grabbed my notepad and pointed to the word *Dad*.

"Your dad broke it again," he almost screamed.

'What did you think happened?' I wrote.

"I don't know. You fell off a swing again," he said it like he was teasing me but I think it was all that was keeping him from destroying another lamp, or whatever he decided to throw this time.

'Why didn't I think of that?' I wrote and smiled to try and lighten the mood.

"Never defend him. You can tell me anything." I nodded and then hugged him. He finally relaxed and then break was over so we headed inside. Wait a minute. Ty isn't in my next class with me. *What if my dad comes in and takes me?*

"Aria nothing is going to happen to you. I will meet you here after class okay?" He once again soothed me.

I nodded and then walked into the class. I looked back after I walked to my seat and waved at Ty. I was a nervous wreck the whole class period. The bell finally rang after three lifetimes and I sprinted out of the room. Ty was waiting outside like he promised. I smiled and ran up to him. We then walked to chemistry together.

We watched a movie and I was about to fall asleep when luckily the bell rang. Ty and I headed to lunch. Ty must have been starving because he grabbed a lot of food. We then sat down by my tree and he handed me the pizza on his tray. I looked at him, confused.

"What? Did you think this was all for me?" he mocked.

I smiled but then nodded.

"Do you like pizza?" I nodded again even though I couldn't even remember the last time I had pizza. The day went by pretty fast after that.

"Let's go." Ty smiled, leading me to his car.

I got in and he drove us to his house. We walked in and he grabbed my backpack and set it in his room. He then came back downstairs and headed to the kitchen. I followed him and then sat down on the stool.

"Are you hungry?"

I shook my head.

"No?"

I nodded.

"I think you are."

I rolled my eyes and then grabbed my notepad.

'You eat too much.' I wrote.

"Are you calling me fat?" He laughed.

I smiled and then sighed.

'When are you going to take me home?' I wrote.

"That is not your home." He dismissed.

'He will come for me.' I wrote.

"And I will deal with it," he confidently replied.

'Why did you get yourself into this?' I asked.

"I'm in this for you."

'Why?' I asked.

"Do you want to go back there?"

I shook my head. *Ugh! It's more complicated than that!*

"Listen Aria I like you okay, and I just want to keep you safe," he added.

He likes me? He barely knows me. I nodded.

'You're not bad yourself.' I wrote, grinning like an idiot.

"Not bad?" He snorted.

I shrugged.

We then walked upstairs. Ty was carrying a bag of chips in his arms, and we headed into his bedroom and sat on his bed.

"So do you want to try talking?"

I shook my head.

"Practice makes perfect, come on," he encouraged.

'I don't want to.' I wrote.

"So you can talk?" 'Physically, it's complicated Ty.' I wrote.

"Try me."

'I JUST CAN'T!' I wrote, throwing the paper at him.

"No Aria, you can."

I sighed and wrote 'You don't get it.'

"So explain it to me."

I closed my eyes and thought back to the last time I had talked, besides the incident a few days ago when my dad told me too. I wiped the tear that had fallen and then opened my eyes.

'He wouldn't let me.' I wrote.

"Your dad wouldn't let you?"

I nodded.

"But he can't keep you from talking at school." 'Ty that's not the point.' I wrote.

"What is the point?"

'He abused me. I've been traumatized since I was little. My mom picked my brother over me and left.' I wrote, tears were streaming down my face now.

"Aria," was all he said. He grabbed me and pulled me onto his lap.

"It's okay, I'm here." He soothed.

"No one will ever hurt you again." I hugged him and breathed in his scent it smelled like home.

"I want you to beat him Aria. Prove to him that you are better than him and he can't win." He sighed.

'I want to win too.' I wrote.

"Good you don't have to talk today or tomorrow or next week, but we are going to work on this." I grinned and then hugged him again. He hugged me back and then lay me down on his bed.

"Can I see how your bruises are doing?" he asked.

I nodded.

He lifted up my shirt just a little past my belly button and ran his hands softly over them. It didn't hurt at all; it actually felt like Ty's hands were healing them.

"Where else?" I pointed to my neck. He sat me up and then ran his hands over my neck.

"Is that it?" I shook my head.

I pointed to my shoulders, rib cage, and thighs. He sucked in a breath.

"It will take time for them to heal, but if they look discolored or odd tell me and the doctor can check them out." I nodded.

"And your arm will hopefully heal soon." He sighed, looking at my cast.

I nodded again.

"Okay, so write done something positive about yourself," he encouraged.

I looked to see if he was being serious. I then laughed out loud.

"Aria," he chuckled.

I peeked up at him.

"I'm being serious." 'You do it too.' I wrote.

"Fine we will both do it," he replied, rolling his eyes.

'Smart,' I wrote down.

"Okay what did you write?" I showed him my paper.

"Okay good, this is mine." He showed me and I rolled my eyes when I read 'Sexy as hell' written on his paper.

'How sexy is hell?' I wrote.

"Pretty damn sexy." He laughed.

"Write something you want to say to me." 'This is stupid.' I wrote.

"It's not stupid. I want you to feel comfortable with me but judging by that, you already are starting to." He chuckled.

I slapped his arm and pointed to the door because someone was knocking. He ninja rolled off the bed and answered it. It was Carter. I got off the bed and waved to him.

"Hey Aria um dinner is here. We ordered Chinese and your parents won't be home this weekend. They are staying a little longer," he said.

"Okay thanks for the update," he replied but he seemed frustrated.

We walked downstairs and ate Chinese; it was the first time I've ever had it and it was pretty good.

"That's all you're going to eat?" Ty complained.

'I'm full.' I wrote.

"One more bite," he teased.

I smacked his arm.

"Please," he pouted.

I shook my head smiling.

"Pretty please." I laughed a little.

"Pretty please with cherry on top." That time I laughed.

Carter came into the kitchen, looking shocked and happy at the same time.

"You've got a great laugh." He complimented, grabbing a soda and leaving.

"Pllleeaaassseeeeee," Ty drew out.

I rolled my eyes, eating one more piece of orange chicken.

"Thanks," he sang, giving me a cheeky grin.

After we were done eating, we went back upstairs.

"Do you want to take a shower?"

I nodded, grabbing my things and heading into the bathroom. After about a ten-minute shower I walked out to find Ty eating the chips he brought up earlier. *Seriously this boy should weigh like five hundred pounds. He was actually really fit; he most likely had an eight pack, not to mention his really toned arms.*

Ugh what am I thinking?

'PIG!' I wrote in big letters.

"Hey I'm a growing boy." He smirked.

I squinted at him.

He laughed and then pulled me onto his lap so I was straddling him. I pushed at his chest but he pulled me in closer. He then sniffed my hair?

"Did you use my shampoo?" I grabbed his pillow and smacked him in the head.

"Hey now, I didn't say I minded." That earned him another whack with the pillow. He then pushed me off of him and lay me down, hovering on top of me.

"Don't start something you can't finish," he said in a husky voice.

He then rolled off of me and sat back down with a smirk on his face.

I rolled my eyes; this is going to be a long night.

Chapter 9

Dear Diary,
I got out of Ty's grip once again to write to you.
UGH!
For once I can't put his feeling to words...maybe it's because having someone here for me is a foreign feeling.
I really thought Ty would have given up on me by now but he hasn't. In fact, we keep building a stronger bond every day and every day I feel more and more comfortable with him.
Every day I want to talk to him even more.
~Aria

I climbed back into bed and looked over at the clock.

It was only 2:00 am.

I sighed in content; I still have four more hours of sleep.

The next couple of days went by about the same. Every day Ty and I went to school together and then came home and he had these things for me to do. Friday finally came! It's weird because my dad hasn't even tried to get a hold of me since I left.

"Come on please." Ty pouted.

'I can't think of one.' I admitted.

He asked me to draw my favorite memory.

I then drew language class with him and I sitting in it.

'Meeting you.' I wrote under the picture.

He looked confused for a second and then really happy.

"Aw I'm flattered," he said in honesty but he was mocking me at the same time.

I rolled my eyes.

"What's your favorite number?"

'13' I wrote.

"Isn't that an unlucky number?" he teased.

I stuck my tongue out at him.

"Favorite season?"

'Fall' I wrote.

"When's your birthday?"

I thought about it for a moment. Oh yeah, I remember.

'June 2nd,' I wrote.

"Where is your diary?"

'What?' I asked.

"I want to read it." He laughed.

'NO!' I wrote.

"Where is it?"

'At my dad's,' I lied.

He didn't even catch the lie; he just sat there half stunned half about to pee himself over happiness.

'Care to share why you look like you're about to pee yourself?' I wrote.

He chuckled.

"You didn't call it home," he explained.

I shrugged that place wasn't home.

"But seriously where is it?" he asked, jumping off the bed.

'TY STOP!' I wrote, standing in front of him and holding it up.

"Aw did you write about me?" he teased.

I blushed and avoided eye contact.

"YOU DID!" He laughed.

I punched him.

"Come on Aria, I'm just teasing," he mocked.

I pointed at the bed.

"No. I really want to read it now."

'Too bad it's at my dad's.' I wrote.

"Too bad it's not." He snorted.

I groaned and pushed him.

"Fine." He pouted.

I yawned and looked over at the clock. It was almost midnight!

"Wow we lost track of time." He chuckled.

I nodded and set my notebook on the side table. Ty turned out the lights and climbed into bed. I climbed in after him and sighed in content.

"Did you just sigh?"

I nodded even though he probably couldn't see me. The bed shifted and I reached out my hand that came in contact with his face. I giggled and then squinted. My eyes were already adjusting and I could now tell that he had propped himself up on his elbow. I turned my head more to look at him.

"You're beautiful," he said, stroking my cheek.

Could he even see me right now? My stomach dropped a little: a little in happiness but also a little in fright.

"Well good night." He sighed and lay back down.

Well that was weird. I rolled over to my stomach and closed my eyes. I can finally go to the place where I can talk.

* * *

"NO DADDY," I screamed while he looked at Ty murderously.

"Shut up!" He screamed.

"TY!" I shouted.

He disappeared in the forest.

My dad started to come towards me.

"TY!" I screamed. Where is he?

A wolf came out of the forest. Wait a wolf?

"No," I sobbed.

My dad was suddenly gone.

My mom was standing, motioning for me to come closer. Is she crazy? There is a giant wolf about ten feet from her!

"LEAVE ME ALONE!" I screamed.

"Come on Aria." Ty called. Wait where is he?

"TY!" I screamed.

I felt shaking. Was there an earthquake?

"ARIA!" a voice screamed.

"NO, TY HELP!" I pleaded as tears streamed down my face. Ugh, I don't cry. Stop it Aria!

"WAKE UP!"

Wake up?

"Ty," I sobbed.

"I'm right here. Come on open your eyes," he pleaded.

I squeezed my eyes shut and let the blackness take over.

"Come on. Try," I groaned, opening my eyes. I saw Ty's concerned face. We were in his room. I wiped my face to realize I had actually been crying. Wait if I was actually crying does that mean I was actually screaming? I froze at that thought. My throat started closing up.

"HUH!" I gasped for air.

"Aria?"

"Huh!" I tried again.

He ripped me from the bed and ran downstairs.

"HELP!" he demanded.

A light in the doctor's room went on and the nurse came out.

"She can't breathe!" he shouted.

He lay me on the bed while the nurse put a mask on me. It made it easier to breathe; it also made me really tired. I mean seriously what time is it?

* * *

"She is mentally traumatized," a female voice concluded.

"Traumatized?" Ty asked. TY! Where is he?

"When she talks, it triggers something in her brain that makes her go into a panic attack."

"How do I fix it?" he questioned.

"She needs to realize that it's okay to talk and nothing will happen when she does," the female voice answered.

Oh shit they were talking about me. So I was actually screaming? Ty is going to make me talk.

Well maybe this will actually help. Maybe I will get my voice back.

"Aria?" he asked.

I groaned.

"Open your eyes baby."

Baby?

"Aria."

"Arrabella."

I opened them and realized I was back in Ty's room and the nurse was gone. I went to sit up but he pushed me down.

"Nope today we are staying in bed." He smiled.

I rested my head on his shoulder and nodded.

"Do you know what happened last night?"

I nodded.

"You screamed for me in your sleep." I nodded.

"You know that?"

'It's safe to talk in my dreams.' I wrote.

"You know it's safe to talk now too?" I shrugged.

"What happens when you talk?" 'Can't breathe.' I wrote.

"Why not?"

I lifted my head off him and sat up. He watched me carefully as I angled myself towards him.

'You don't have to do this.' I wrote.

"Do what?"

'THIS! I know it's okay to talk Ty. You don't need to play therapist.' I scribbled down.

"I'm not playing anything," he growled.

I froze. That sounded like the growl from my dream, but who was it that growled? I backed away and tried to get off the bed but my legs felt weird.

"You can't walk Aria," Ty said.

I looked at him confused.

"The gas mask."

I nodded but tried to anyways. Ty grabbed my hips and pulled me away from the edge of the bed. *Well this is just perfect. I'm trapped!*

"Aria please, why can't you talk?" I looked down and started biting on my thumb.

"Arrabella what happens when you talk?" 'I can't breathe!' I wrote.

"That's not true. You make yourself think that."

'That's not true Ty.' I wrote.

"It is. You have a panic attack."

'Sorry I can't control it.' I wrote.

He scooted closer to me and I flinched back.

"I can prove it to you, say something." He encouraged.

'I'm tired.' I wrote.

"Fine, sleep." He sighed, helping me lie down.

I closed my eyes and Ty turned out the lights and lay next to me.

* * *

"Come on you can do it." Ty encouraged.

I laughed at his eagerness.

"It's just like laughing," he bribed.

I nodded.

"What should I say?"

He laughed.

"I like you Aria."

"I like you Ty."

* * *

"What?" A voice from the outside said.

I squeezed my eyes and let myself fade into the blackness. I then opened my eyes to see Ty looking at me in awe. I looked at him questioningly.

"Hold on nurse!" Ty shouted.

Yeah right, like the nurse has nothing better to do than come and observe me. The nurse came in, and I rolled my eyes.

"Aria you just said Ty," he announced.

I blushed. *He heard me again? Why didn't I say the rest of the sentence? Oh my goodness what if it's not safe to talk in my dreams anymore?*

Why do I keep talking out loud? I started coughing.

"You're fine, it's fine." Ty soothed, holding me.

I took some deep breaths and snuggled into him.

"Thank you, you can leave," Ty ordered and I assume she left.

"See you talked and it was okay."

I took a deep breath again, Ty's scent is amazing, and then pulled away to meet his eyes.

"I'm proud of you."

I grinned and his face mirrored mine. Maybe it is okay to talk.

Chapter 10

Dear Diary,

I'm working up the courage to talk to Ty. Today is Sunday
and he hasn't really pushed me to talk since yesterday.
We have watched movies for most of the day.
I'm supposed to be in the bathroom right now, but you know
me always thinking about you.
~Aria

I walked back into the living room where Ty was taking the Hunger Games DVD out of the player.

He smiled at me and without warning pushed me on the couch and started tickling me, being careful not to touch my bruises. I can't believe he remembers where they are!

I laughed and pushed at his hands.

"Nope I like it when you laugh." He laughed in evilness.

I glared at him. He stopped and I let out a breath in relief. He smirked and then moved his hands closer again. I squirmed under him and then pushed at him so I was straddling his stomach. I then took my hands and started tickling him. I got to this one spot on his neck where he cringed and pleaded for me to stop. I laughed and then jumped off him and the couch.

"Don't start something you can't finish," he challenged.

I giggled and then ran to the stairs. It was too late because he was already caught up to me.

"Do you give up?" he asked.

I nodded. He let me go and I punched him in the arm.

"Oh yeah?" He challenged, pinning me to the wall.

I laughed until my arm started hurting.

"What's wrong?" he instantly asked.

I sucked in a breath and then held my cast-covered arm.

"Oh shit," he muttered, scooping me up in his arms and taking me to the couch.

"Are you okay? I'm so sorry. I forgot, how could I be so stupid?" He went on.

I scanned the room for my notepad but I must have left it upstairs.

"Are you mad? How much does it hurt? Does it still hurt?"

I put my hand on his arm to stop him but he kept going. I need something more! I cleared my throat but nothing came out.

TALK! I screamed in my head. I tried but nothing came out. Ty was now going on about how he needs to be more careful.

"Ty," I whispered. I didn't think he heard it.

His head snapped up.

"Ty, stop." I silently commanded.

I froze and my stomach flipped.

"Aria," he beamed.

I started to breathe heavily.

"Shh, breathe."

I nodded but I couldn't. I groaned and felt my throat closing up. Ty swung me into him and ran to the nurse. I fought with her as she put the mask on me, I can do this! She held my hands and forced it on me and once again I drifted away.

"She talked!" Ty exclaimed I could tell he was beaming.

"At least we know she wants to," the nurse, Sherry, added.

"Of course she wants to. My baby talked," he repeated.

I groaned.

"Aria?"

I opened my eyes and saw him. He reached down and hugged me. I was back in his room. I smiled at him.

"You did it babe."

I grabbed my notepad.

'Babe?' I wrote.

"It's a nickname."

I rolled my eyes.

"I love your voice."

I faked a glare.

I sat up.

'Help please.' I wrote.

"Come on Ar say it."

"Help," I whispered.

He grinned and then picked me up.

"Where to?" I pointed to my notepad.

"You don't need it."

I sighed and cleared my throat.

"Downstairs." I couldn't get my voice above a whisper but at least I can whisper without the memories coming back. He sat me at the bar and then he headed to the fridge.

"Do you want some chicken nuggets?" I nodded.

"Aria," he sang.

I smiled, shaking my head.

"Come on you have to get used to it." I sighed.

"Yes," I whispered. Ty grinned and then put the nuggets in the oven.

Carter walked in smiling.

"Do I smell chicken nuggets?" he asked.

I raised my eyebrows at him. They have been in the oven for a minute how could he have smelled them?

"Make your own dip shit." Ty laughed, sitting next to me.

"Hey Aria!" he greeted.

I smiled and waved and then ducked my head into Ty. Ty chuckled and I pushed my face deeper into him. After we had lunch we went back upstairs and sat on Ty's bed.

"Aria?"

I looked up at him.

"What's your middle name?" he asked, smiling.

I shook my head.

"Can I guess?"

I shrugged.

"J, right?"

I nodded. This is so embarrassing!

"Jessica?" He asked.

I shook my head.

"Hey if we are going to play you have to say yes or no." "No," I whispered.

"Jaylee?" He smiled.

"No."

"Um Joyce?"

"No." I laughed.

"Joy?" he shot out.

"No."

"Jackie?"

"Nope." I smiled.

"Jason?"

"No." I laughed.

"Hey it could be a middle name for a girl."

I felt my face heat up.

"Wait, is it a boy middle name?"

"Maybe," I teased.

"Jackson?"

"No." I sighed.

"Jacob?"

"No."

"John, Jude, Jack, Jeremiah, James?"

"Yes." I smiled.

"Which one?"

"James," I replied, blushing.

"Arrabella James Middleton?"

I sighed.

"That's not even embarrassing." He chuckled.

'Yes, it is,' I wrote on my pad of paper. I don't think I'm ready for sentences yet.

"Oh sure." He snorted.

'What's yours?' I wrote.

"My full name?"

I nodded.

"Guess," he teased.

'At least tell me your last name.' I wrote.

"Benson."

'First initial of middle name?' I wrote.

"D."

'Danny?' I wrote.

"No." He smirked.

I rolled my eyes.

'David?' I wrote.

"Nope."

'Denis?' I wrote.

"No." He repeated.

'Drew?' I wrote.

"No." He smiled.

'Dalton?' I wrote.

"Bingo and we have winner," he teased.

'Tyson Dalton Benson.'

"Yep, that's my name." He laughed.

'When am I going back?' I slowly wrote.

"Back, you mean to your old house?" he growled.

I looked down and nodded.

"Why are you still thinking about going back?" 'It's not like I can stay here forever.' I wrote.

"Why not?" he asked, mad and hurt at the same time.

I looked up and gave him in an "are you serious" look.

"You can live here."

'I know Ty but eventually I have to face it.' I wrote.

"You will never face him, not alone."

'Stop.' I wrote.

"You stop, Aria I don't even know what this is about." He sighed.

I looked down again and sighed.

"Look at me."

I shook my head, keeping it down.

"Aria."

"Arrabella."

"Arrabella James."

He then put his hand under my chin and held my head up. I pushed him away but kept my head up.

"What is it?"

I looked back at him and was at a loss for words.

What could I say? I mean I like Ty a lot but I don't want him trapped in my problems. He just told me to live here with him but what about after high school? Won't he go to college or something?

'This is my problem.' I wrote.

"Well I'm making it mine." He shrugged.

'Why?' I wrote.

"I care about you."

'Why?' I rewrote.

"Because I see something in you that not even you see in yourself."

'Thanks Ty.' I wrote.

"Anytime." He grinned.

* * *

I woke up and heard talking from outside the door.

I looked over at the clock and saw that it is only 11:30.

"Hey man that's what I heard," I heard a voice say.

"Then whose left?" another one said, and I know that was Carter.

"Um, I don't know Aiden found his mate yesterday," The first voice declared.

Mate?

"Yeah I heard that so that leaves me and you man." Carter laughed.

"Yeah who would have thought Tyson would have found his mate before us?" the first voice asked.

"Yeah but hey she's going to be great." Carter defended.

"Yeah I hear she's really doing well. I wonder when Tyson will tell her," the voice

wondered.

"Same here. I hear he's going to tell her soon too, well man I'm going to bed." Carter yawned.

"Yea night man," the other voice called.

I thought about Tyson with another girl and it made my heart clench. Why is Carter always here anyways? I mean does he live here too? Just then Ty grabbed me and pulled me into him. I snuggled into him and he mumbled something in his sleep. I then let my eyes close and I slowly drifted away.

Chapter 11

Dear Diary,

I'm on a mission today. It's about mates.

I'll report back when I find out more.

~Aria

Ty stepped out of the bathroom and smiled.

"Do you have any idea how beautiful you are?" he asked.

I blushed, looking away.

"I'm serious." I followed him down to the kitchen where we ate breakfast and then drove to school together.

"Are you in deep thought or something?" he asked, snapping me out of the internal debate going on in my head.

I nodded. He looked over and then shrugged.

"Fair enough." During school I couldn't keep my mind off of the whole mate thing!

I mean seriously why is Ty wasting his time with me when there's another girl in the picture who is probably normal. I finally came to the conclusion that it had to be Claire. I mean who else could it be?

"Aria please you're killing me." We were currently watching some movie that he had put in. Well I'm not watching, I'm thinking. We have been home from school for about two hours now. We are in Ty's room and he is about to give himself a heart attack. I took my notebook and started to write.

'What is a mate?' I wrote.

He read it and then looked shocked.

"Where is this coming from?" 'I heard Carter talking about it.' I wrote.

"What do you think it is?"

'I don't know Ty, but he said you have one.' I wrote.

"When was this?" 'Last night.' I wrote.

"Is that what you've been thinking about all day?" 'Yes, who is your mate?' I wrote.

He looked shocked and then amused.

"Who do think it is?"

'Claire." I wrote.

He laughed at that. I hit him with the notebook.

"Listen we will stay home from school tomorrow. I've got a lot of explaining to do," he said. I could tell he was enjoying himself.

'Wipe that smile off your face.' I wrote, which made him smile even more.

"Why? I like smiling," he mocked.

I raised my eyebrows at him and then got off the bed.

"Where are you going?"

I grabbed my notepad.

'Away from you.' I smirked.

He frowned and put his hand over his heart.

"Who would ever want to be away from me?"

'Me.' I wrote, smiling.

"You know it's been a while."

I gave him a questioning look.

"Since you've talked."

I shrugged. It hasn't been that long.

"Yes, it has."

I rolled my eyes and then left the room. Carter was in the hallway about to walk down

the stairs.

"I'm going to get you." I heard Ty shout from behind me.

I ran over to Carter and stood behind him. He looked back at me confused, until Ty ran out.

"Great hiding spot." Ty laughed.

"Oh sure Aria, use me as a shield," Carter teased.

"Step away from the girl," Ty mocked.

"Only if the girl wants to go with you." Carter played along.

"Aria, tell him." I shook my head.

"The girl will stay," Carter chuckled.

"Not unless I hear her say it."

Carter turned to me, raising his eyebrows.

I giggled.

"She says she doesn't want to go with you." He smiled.

"No she didn't." Ty pouted.

I nodded.

"Arrabella," he sang.

"Come with me."

"No stay with me," Carter mock begged.

"Well who do you choose?" Ty smirked.

I narrowed my eyes at him and then hugged Carter's waist.

"Carter," I replied.

Carter laughed and I buried my head into him so Ty wouldn't see my face. I heard a low growl, which made Carter laugh harder. I let go of him however because after hugging Carter, I wanted to be back in Ty's arms. I ran over to him and hugged him.

"Just kidding," I whispered.

"You better be."

I nodded.

"Whom do you choose?" he teased.

"You." I smiled.

Carter rolled his eyes at us and then walked downstairs.

"You should talk more. Your voice is adorable," Carter called after reaching the bottom.

I wanted to shout to him to shut up, but my voice wasn't above a whisper yet. So I rolled my eyes and followed Tyson into the game room.

After I beat him in Mario Cart three times in a row he decided that we should play some tank game, which he creamed me in.

"Come on shoot."

I shot, but it hit him instead and he died. I laughed and then aimed at the enemy.

"You shot me!" He yelled in horror. I shot the rest of the tanks charging towards me and then looked over at him.

"Arrabella James," he scolded.

I shrugged.

"You cannot shoot your partner in tanks and just simply get away with it," he teased.

I shot up out of the beanbag and ran towards the door. After sprinting down the hallway I found the stairs and ran down them. Carter and some other guy I didn't know were talking in the kitchen.

"What did you do this time?" Carter teased.

I smiled and ducked down behind the bar.

"I know she's in here," Ty sang.

"We don't know what you are talking about," Carter replied.

I crawled over to the side.

"Aria you might as well surrender," Ty sang.

I stayed put and tried to make my breathing quiet. All of a sudden, a grinning Ty was in front of me. I squealed in shock as he picked me up and carried me out behind the bar and up the stairs. I squirmed a little bit, but then stopped because the last thing I needed was for him to drop me. I held on to him a little tighter at that thought.

"I'm not going to drop you," he said confidently, making it up the last step. He set me down on his bed. I yawned and he smiled.

"Why don't you take a shower?" I nodded and then he grabbed my arm.

"Not until you say you're sorry for shooting me."

I rolled my eyes and grabbed my notebook.

'What if I'm not sorry.' I wrote.

"Then I hope you enjoy going to bed unwashed," he mocked.

'Fine I'm so very sorry Tyson.' I wrote.

"You have to say it." I got off the bed and grabbed my sweatpants and tank top.

"Sorry." I smiled before walking into the bathroom.

After my shower I walked out of the bathroom to find Ty watching some football game. I crawled into bed with him and watched for a while.

After about twenty minutes I was fighting to keep my eyes open, but I couldn't. So I gave in and closed them.

About a minute later sleep took over my body.

* * *

I yawned and looked over at the clock. It read 6:30!

I twisted out of Ty's hold and shook him a little.

"Arrabella." He groaned, pulling me back into him.

I squirmed out of his grip again; he sighed and opened his eyes. I pointed at the clock. He looked over at the clock and then back at me.

"We aren't going today, remember?" He chuckled.

Oh right today he was going to tell me who his mate was! I nodded and sheepishly smiled. He rolled his eyes and pulled me into him again. I pulled away again.

"Arrabella." He sleepily complained.

I smacked him. He popped one eye open and I laughed at how ridicules he looked.

'I can't sleep now.' I wrote.

"Why?" He sighed.

'I'm curious about the whole mate thing.' I wrote and gave him a duh look.

"Please sleep." He yawned.

I shook my head.

"Five more minutes." I glared at him. *Sure five more minutes times fifty!* I shook my head.

"Come on Aria," he pleaded.

I sighed. He smirked and then pulled me into him. I tried to get out of his grasp but he tightened it. I kept trying until I got tired.

"Ty," I complained.

He loosened his grip.

"Don't move."

I groaned and then snuggled closer to him and tried to fall back to sleep, which wasn't really hard, with Ty holding me.

* * *

I woke up again and pulled out of Ty's grip and started jumping on the bed.

"Arrabella James," he warned.

I laughed.

"Are you jumping on the bed?"

He then opened his eyes and then got up and pulled me down. I laughed and pushed him

away.

'Tell me.' I wrote.

"What?" he teased.

I smacked his chest.

"Violence," he said dramatically.

I nodded.

"I will tell you but if you have any questions you have to ask me, out loud." I nodded. He gave me a flat look.

"Deal." I whispered.

"A mate is a girl you like a lot," he started to say. "It's like a soul mate. When you see her it's like nothing else matters but her." He talked with so much passion that I envied whoever this mate of his was.

"Who?" I asked.

"Who do you think?"

"Claire," I replied.

"Nope. My girl is gorgeous."

Wow she's better looking than Claire. Was she a super model or something?

"Hey Aria." He chuckled.

I looked up at him.

"You are my mate." He grinned.

Chapter 12

Dear Diary,
I am writing this in Ty's bathroom.
I am his mate. Now all I have to do is figure out what that
means.
Wish me luck…
~Aria

"Are you okay?" Ty asked as I walked out of the bathroom.

'I don't get it.' I wrote.

"Ar, use your voice."

I shook my head.

"What don't you get?"

'Why am I your mate?'

"Because we were made for each other."

He must be crazy! Is this like all those sappy movies when someone finds true love?

"Why don't you believe me?" he growled.

'We don't belong together.' I wrote.

"WE DO!" he yelled, throwing the remote. There he goes getting pissed again! I got off the couch and ran out of the room.

"Aria wait!" he called. I could hear the regret in his voice.

I kept running until I found Carter. I ran into him.

"What's wrong?" he asked.

"Ty," I mumbled into his chest.

"Ty what?" he asked.

"Aria I didn't mean it," Ty called.

I ran out of Carter's hold and then out the front door.

I can't just stay with Tyson. I mean seriously he's crazy. Plus my dad started throwing things like Ty and then he started to direct the abuse towards me.

The only problem is I have no idea where I am.

"Aria," Ty said, and I screamed because he was right behind me.

"I lost it for a split second. I'm trying to control my anger around you." He sighed.

He stepped close, but I stepped back.

"Don't," I whispered.

He looked broken. I wanted to hug him, make him smile again.

"I wasn't mad at you Aria. I'm mad because you don't see yourself clearly."

I was about to talk when I couldn't find my voice. I wanted to shout at him for being so violent but I couldn't because of the pain. I started gasping for air as I felt my throat closing.

"Aria?"

I didn't look up. I just tried to fight it! In about a span of a second Ty had scooped me up in his arms and then I was lying on the nurse's table. She was grabbing the mask. I moved my head away and pushed at her hands.

She was too strong however and I felt myself slipping into the darkness, once again.

* * *

"Arrabella?" I heard Ty ask.

I opened my eyes and found myself back in his bedroom.

I groaned and sat up. I moved to the edge of the bed and thought about army crawling my way out of the room.

"You wouldn't even make it out past the bathroom," Ty said confidently.

I flipped him off.

"Do you want to tell me why you can't shout back at me? Because I know you want to."

"I do," I snapped, but it was still soft.

"Shout at me Aria."

"Shut up."

"Why?" He smirked.

"Shut up," I said, a little louder.

"Is it bothering you that I can yell and you can't yell back?"

I know what he was trying to do and it sure as hell was working. I glared at him.

"I mean seriously if I were you I would just want to scream at me until my lungs gave out," he added.

"Ty stop talking!" I shouted. He was a little shocked and so was I.

"Don't think about it."

I looked over at him.

"See Aria, nothing happens when you talk. You're fine see?"

I nodded. I was fine.

I guess all those times when my dad punished me just stayed with me. Now I'm with Ty and he can't hurt me anymore.

"My dad."

"What?"

"Why I can't shout back: it's because of my dad," I repeated.

"Did he do something?"

"You'll get mad."

He pulled me into him and kissed my head.

"I won't," he promised.

I sighed.

"Peanut butter," I whispered.

"You're allergic to it."

"Whenever I talked he would shove peanut butter down my throat."

I heard him growl.

I remember it vividly. I was seven when he did it the first time. I was shouting at him about how I was his daughter and he shouldn't be treating me this way. He got so mad that he took a jar of peanut butter and held me down while he shoved spoonfuls into my mouth.

It made my throat swell up so I couldn't breathe; this happened every time I talked for the next year until every time I talked it felt like my throat was closing.

So I stopped talking all together unless my dad asked me to.

"Your throat would close so you couldn't breathe." Ty connected the dots, snapping me out of my thoughts.

I nodded.

"How are you still alive?" he asked in anger.

"We went through a lot of EpiPens."

"I'm so sorry this happened to you." He soothed, holding me closer.

"Listen to me. You never have to feel that way again. You are staying here, and you should never be afraid to talk."

I nodded.

"I still don't get the mate thing," I admitted, taking a deep breath. Talking is okay, I reminded myself.

"I will explain it to you further. I just can't yet."

"Okay." I shrugged.

"So no more writing?"

"Talking."

"So you have a brother?"

I looked at him confused. *He remembers that?* I wrote him that on the first few days we met.

"It's okay if you don't want to talk about it."

"He's dead," I whispered.

"What happened?" Ty asked.

"My mom was pregnant with him," I started.

"Okay."

"My dad asked my mom to choose between me or Trevor. He was still in her uterus."

"She chose you?"

"No, she chose my brother." I sighed.

"So then how did he die?" Ty questioned.

"My dad punched her in the stomach repeatedly, and she started having contractions. It made my mom go into labor and he was stillborn."

"Then she went to rehab?"

"Yes, she started drinking a lot after Trevor," I whispered.

"I'm sorry Ar." Ty soothed, pulling me into him. I snuggled closer to him. I can't help but be happy for Trevor. Maybe he was too good to be brought into this messed up world. I wish I could have met him though.

"You're so special Aria and even if your mom picked Trevor, I would pick you any day."

"Thanks Ty," I mumbled against his chest.

"Now you need to eat." He grinned.

"Ty don't." I squealed when he picked me up and carried me out of the room.

"Ty I'm serious."

He ignored me, starting to walk down the stairs.

"Please don't drop me."

"Aria you weigh nothing." He snorted.

"Yeah but you aren't that strong," I teased. That made him stop.

"Are you serious?"

"Yep." I smiled.

He then ran down the stairs and sat me on his lap. He then took his shirt off.

"Want to take that back?" he asked, flexing his muscles.

I shook my head.

"No?" He challenged.

"No Ty, I think Carter is more muscular." I grinned.

"CARTER!" Ty called.

"What?" Carter asked.

"Arm wrestle."

He looked at me and then shrugged. I slipped off of Ty's lap and rolled my eyes.

Ty won all three rounds.

"That doesn't prove appearance wise." I smiled, wiping the smug smile off his face, and Carter spit out the water he was drinking and started rolling on the floor in a fit of laughter.

"Come here."

I went over to him, and he pulled me onto his lap.

He then tickled the side of my stomach where I am most ticklish and have no bruises.

"OKAY!" I shouted.

"Say, Ty you are the sexiest and strongest man alive."

"Tyson you are the sexiest and strongest man alive," I repeated.

"So I've been told many times." He smiled, lifting me off his lap to go to the fridge.

It's true in my eyes. Ty is the hottest guy I've ever laid eyes on, not the mention his abs and arms are like those in a movie.

"Hey Ty?" I asked.

"Yeah?" he asked, setting a plate of turkey and mashed potatoes in front of me.

"That one day in school," I started.

"Way to narrow it down," he teased.

"Anyways, you said I sure do yell at you a lot in my head, what did you mean by that?" I asked.

"You always get this look on your face when you're mad and it was certain times when I could tell you were screaming at me." He chuckled.

"Oh." I laughed.

"Now eat."

"I'm not that hungry." I sighed.

"You sure were more obedient when you couldn't talk," he teased.

"No, I wasn't."

"You were more violent though." He laughed.

"How else was I supposed to tell you to shut up?"

"You could have just kissed me."

"Ew." I laughed. I felt my throat closing.

"HUH!" I gasped.

"Ar, breathe."

I nodded. I got my breathing back to normal and smiled at him.

"I'm good."

"You sure know how to scare me." He chuckled.

"Speaking of scaring me, the nurse looked at your arm while you were out and she thinks that she can take that cast off." He smiled.

"Really?" I grinned.

We walked into the small room and she said my arm was fine. It's weird though and gross. It's all white and deflated.

"Here." Ty soothed, softly kissing my arm.

"Thanks, Ty that sure did the trick." I laughed.

"Come on kisses make it better." I shook my head at his nonsense however I guess that's how most kids are raised. They get hurt and their parents kiss them where they got hurt to make it better.

This is the first time anyone has ever kissed me to make it better. I like it. It's probably Ty though; I think his kisses could make anything better.

Chapter 13

Dear Diary,

I told Ty about Trevor yesterday. It was nice to tell someone about it.

I wonder what my dad is doing right now. I wonder if I ever cross his mind.

Ty and I are good. He still has to explain to me more about mates but I think I'm starting to get it. Just kidding I don't really understand.

~Aria

I can't really sleep that well for some reason. I keep having these weird dreams.

Ty is asleep, and he has his arm around my waist.

I snuggled into him, but I really have to pee!

I moved out of his grip and then walked over to the bathroom.

I walked out and climbed back into bed.

"Ar," Ty mumbled.

"Yeah?"

"Are you okay?"

"Yeah, I just can't sleep." I admitted.

"Do you want a drink of water?"

I don't know how water was going to help!

"Yeah I'll be right back." I sighed.

I walked downstairs to find Carter sitting at the bar eating a bowl of cereal. I looked over at the clock; it was one in the morning.

"Really Carter?" I laughed.

He looked over at me and smiled.

"I got hungry." He shrugged.

I grabbed a water bottle and sat next to him.

"Do you live here?" I asked.

"Yep."

"What about your parents?"

"They are with Tyson's parents a lot." He sighed.

"Where is that?"

"You ask a lot of questions." He laughed.

"Answer them."

"They are away on um business."

"What do they do?"

"Arrabella." He groaned.

"Carter." I groaned back.

"Cute," he teased, ruffling my hair and putting his bowl in the sink.

"Ask Tyson," he added before walking out.

"Bye!" I called.

I then drank some of the water and then walked back upstairs. I got into bed and snuggled into Ty.

"Have fun?"

"Yep." I laughed.

"You took a while."

"Were you timing me?"

"No I just missed you." He sighed, pulling me closer to him.

I fell back asleep and didn't have another dream that night.

* * *

"So does everyone have a mate?" I asked Ty.

"No only certain people."

"Like a club?" I questioned.

"Kind of."

"Are you in a cult?"

"Arrabella." He snorted.

"Well you act like the leader and order everyone around."

"I'm not in a cult."

"Fine and stop calling me Arrabella."

"Why?" he asked.

"I don't like it," I replied.

"Why?" He smirked.

"What do your parents do?" I asked, hoping to change the subject, and I was actually curious.

"Where did that come from?"

"Why does Carter live here?" I asked.

"Aria, slow down." He smiled.

"Tyson." I groaned.

"My parents and Carter's parents work together. They are very high up in our family business." He explained.

"What business?" I asked.

"A very important one, anyways a lot people live in this house which is why it is so big."

"I never see a lot of people."

"That is because the um, children of the higher power parents live on this side of the house."

"Oh, I guess that make sense."

"You don't get it, do you?" He laughed.

"Shut up." I said, pushing at his chest.

He grabbed my hand and pulled me closer to him.

I looked up and into his brown eyes; they were holding me captive and I was vaguely aware of both of our heads getting closer.

Ty let go of my hand, his hand cupping my face guiding me to his.

I closed my eyes and then felt his lips on mine. An explosion of sparks and butterflies erupted inside me. Our lips moved in harmony, and he pulled me onto his lap so I was straddling him.

I pulled away after a moment to breathe, but Ty didn't stop; he started kissing down my neck. He got to this one spot on my neck that made my back arch and my body press closer to him.

He smiled against my skin and then he looked up at me; his eyes were slightly darker. I slid off his lap and he grabbed me and sat me next to him.

"Ty?"

"Yeah?" he replied, turning his head towards me.

"This mate bond thing, I can feel it too right?"

"Yes." He laughed.

"Good, I thought I was going crazy." I laughed.

"You're not crazy, just violent." He smirked.

"Whatever, I couldn't hurt you even if I tried." I scoffed.

"Trust me Ar, you have a lot of power in your hands and you are probably the only person who could ever hurt me."

"Are we going to school tomorrow?"

"Well it's a short week." He laughed.

"It is?"

"Yeah we only go Monday and Tuesday." He laughed.

I nodded and then rolled off the bed.

"Where are you going?"

"Shower." I smiled.

He laughed and then turned on the TV. I grabbed my sweatpants and tank top and then headed into the bathroom. After my shower I found Ty half asleep.

"Tired?" I laughed, lying down next to him.

"Yeah, aren't you? I mean you didn't sleep well last night."

"I guess I am." I yawned.

He chuckled and then turned the lights off.

I slept all night and I only had good dreams...of Tyson.

* * *

"Arrabella likes it," Carter insisted.

"No Carter, I don't."

He put ketchup on his eggs!

"It's disgusting man," Ty agreed.

"You're disgusting," he retorted.

I laughed.

"Ar, stand up for me." Ty pouted.

"Carter, apologize." I demanded.

"No," he stubbornly replied.

"Carter."

"Sorry," he mumbled.

"What was that?" Ty smirked.

"SORRY!" he shouted.

I burst out laughing again. They were like little kids!

"Carter I'm going to ride with you," a boy I didn't know said to Carter.

"Aria, this is Aiden." Carter introduced.

"Hi," I whispered, ducking my head into Ty.

"Ready to go?" Ty chuckled, kissing my head.

I nodded and then waved to Carter and Aiden. We arrived at school and sat in our usual spots in English.

"I'm serious!" Ty laughed.

I smiled and shook my head.

"You don't believe me?"

No, I don't believe that he and Carter had read Twilight!

"Carter wouldn't put it down. In fact I wouldn't stop talking once and he threw the book at my head."

I imagined Carter doing this and started laughing, which made every person in class stare at me. I looked down and Ty growled and gave death glares to all the students, making them snap their heads forward.

"Ty." I scolded.

"It's not polite to stare."

"You stare at me all the time."

He laughed.

"You're beautiful." He shrugged.

I snorted and then faced forward. Ty reached his hand under my chin and pulled my head so that I had to stare him dead in the eye.

"Do you believe that?"

"What? That I'm beautiful? No I don't believe that." I laughed.

"Well believe it, you are," he growled.

"Whatever Ty."

"Say it."

"No, stop it," I complained, pulling my head away from him.

He balled up his fists like he did when he was angry, usually resulting in him throwing something.

Why is he so mad anyway? I'm not beautiful and it's fine. Am I pretty? I wouldn't even say that. I would go with average.

So why the hell is he so mad that I don't believe him? I mean it's not even the truth. It's an opinion, his opinion!

The bell rang and I stood up.

"Why don't you believe it?"

"Why are you so mad at me?"

He stopped and pulled me to the side.

"Aria, I'm not mad at you."

"Yes, you are."

He sighed.

"I promise I'm not. It's just you don't see yourself clearly at all." He groaned.

"Yes, I do."

"Really?" He snorted.

"Really."

He fake glared at me.

"Then say it."

"Say what?"

"I Arrabella James Middleton am beautiful."

"You're strange." I laughed, walking away.

I sat down against my tree. Ty sat next to me.

"Say it," he chanted.

"Tyson." I groaned.

"Arrabella."

"FINE!" I shouted.

That earned me a few stares.

"I'm pretty." I sighed.

"Great, now say what I told you to say." He smirked.

"No." I shrugged.

"No?"

"Why is the word no not in your vocabulary?"

He raised his eyebrows at me.

"Were these remarks going through your head every time I talked?" He chuckled.

"Yeah pretty much," I teased. Even though it was true. I always answered his questions in my head.

"Come on Ar, for me?" he begged.

"I Arrabella James Middleton am beautiful," I mumbled.

He grinned.

"Was that so hard?"

"Yeah it actually was," I mocked.

Ty is probably the only person on this planet who honestly believes I'm beautiful.

Chapter 14

Dear Diary,

No more school!

Well for a week that is.

Ty and I kissed! I don't know what that means, but it felt magical.

He calls me beautiful. He has called me that at least fifteen times today.

The funny thing is I'm actually starting to believe it.

~Aria

"Really Ty, the woods?" I asked.

He told me he had to show me something, but why does it have to be in the woods?

"Yes." He laughed.

I sighed. He then took my hand in his, and we entered the forest.

"You aren't going to kill me, are you?" I teased.

"Oh yeah Ar, you got me." He smirked.

We walked deeper into the woods when Ty stopped.

"What?" I asked.

"I have to tell you something," he whispered.

"So then why are we in the woods?"

"Just promise to listen and stay until I'm finished, okay?"

"Sure, I promise."

He nodded and then took a deep breath.

"The reason why I have a mate is because I am a werewolf."

I laughed.

"Ty seriously, why are you such a jerk?" I mocked.

"Aria, listen," he groaned.

"Fine," I smirked.

"I am the alpha of my pack and that means I'm in charge. Carter is my beta. He is second in command. When a werewolf finds his mate, he has to be around her or he will go crazy."

"When I saw you that first day I instantly knew that we were mates. You see I have my wolf in my head that yells at me, like right now he's sad because he thinks you are mad."

"Ty this isn't funny."

"It's not supposed to be."

"Stop." I said, walking away from him.

"You promised you would stay!" He called.

I stopped. I did promise that. I sighed and then walked back.

"So you're telling me you like me because a wolf in your head tells you to?"

"No not at all," he growled.

"Really Ty, that's what you just said," I spat.

"You're my soul mate. We were made for each other."

"You're a wolf?"

"Yes."

"Prove it." I smirked.

He shrugged and took his shirt off. I snorted. In the blink of an eye, a six-foot tall wolf was standing in front of me instead of Ty. It was as black as night, but had Ty's eyes.

I ran.

Yes bolted, what else was I supposed to do?

I could see the house and I ran in. I wiped my tears and went into Ty's room. I grabbed my backpack and ran down the stairs.

"Whoa, Arrabella what's wrong?" Carter asked.

"Nothing, please drive me home."

"I don't know Aria." He sighed.

"PLEASE!" I pleaded.

"Carter, get out," Ty said, walking into the living room. Carter glanced at me and left.

"Aria you told me to show you."

"You were lying to me this entire time!" I shouted.

"No, I wasn't." He groaned.

"Yes, you were Ty. I told you everything and you kept this from me. You know what? I don't even want to be your stupid mate!" I shouted.

I watched relief, sadness, and then anger flash over his face.

"Don't say that."

"Go find someone else to lie to," I replied.

"I'm not lying to you nor have I. I knew you would freak out."

I watched as he came closer. I took a step back. I regretted it when sadness filled his eyes.

"I don't want to be near you right now," I whispered.

He nodded.

I went back upstairs but I didn't go to Ty's room. I went into the room where Ty and I play video games. I didn't want to play; I just wanted to lie in one of the bean bags.

I plopped down on the black one and shut my eyes. Ty is a wolf, a freaking animal. That means Carter is one too, and everyone in this house! I've been living in a house full of them.

Though I feel safe here, I feel unsafe at the same time.

I really like Ty but he has anger problems, and I know he would never hurt me, but he has the power to physically or mentally.

"Aria?" A voice asked.

I opened my eyes to find Carter standing in the doorway.

"Hey."

"Are you okay?"

"You're a wolf?"

"Yes." He chuckled.

"Is that why you let Ty boss you around?"

He laughed and then sat down across from me.

"He is the alpha."

I nodded.

"You know we've all been wolves the entire time. You shouldn't be scared or worried. You are safe here."

"I know." I sighed.

"So why are you still scared?"

"If Ty is a wolf then he's really strong, and I knew he was strong before, but he gets really angry sometimes," I whispered.

I gasped.

"What's wrong?"

I held up my finger to tell him one minute.

I tried to get my breathing under control. Talking about this made me remember how strong my dad was and how weak I was.

I tried to steady my breathing.

"Aria?" Carter asked.

Ty came bursting through the doors.

"SHERRY!" he yelled.

He came over and sat near me.

Not by me, just near. Sherry came in with the mask. I pushed her away, but Ty came over and held my arms behind my back.

She put the mask on.me and I started drifting away.

I woke up in Ty's room. I looked over and saw him sitting on the bed, but away from me.

"Why did you do that?"

"You couldn't breathe."

"I could have controlled it."

"Arrabella, your face was turning blue," he groaned.

"Tyson, I'm not a child. You can't make that decision for me."

"Aria, you couldn't breathe. I can't see you like that and not do anything." He sighed.

I rolled my eyes. *Really Ty great plan;* he's making me weak! Now I'm pretty much trapped in his room with him because I can't walk.

"I don't want to be in here."

"Where do you want to be?"

"I don't care, just not here."

He got off the bed and eagerly reached for me.

"No," I said, pushing his hands away.

"Ar, you can't walk."

Dammit, I don't want to feel the sparks between us.

"Fine," I muttered reaching for him. He smirked and then picked me up and carried me to the room across the hall.

It had purple walls and a queen-sized bed.

He set me down on the bed.

"I'll be right back."

I nodded and then I leaned back against the pillows and shut my eyes.

"Here." I heard Ty say.

He had a bowl of soup in his hands.

"Can you put it on the nightstand? I'm not that hungry."

"You haven't eaten in a while." He worriedly added, setting the bowl on the nightstand.

"I'll eat it later," I promised.

He nodded.

"I'll be across the hall. If you need me yell."

"Okay, thanks Tyson."

"Yeah," he added, walking out of the room.

I knew he was upset but I thought we both needed some time away from each other.

I want to be with Ty. I know that. *Ty may only want to be with me because his wolf tells him to?* I mean how crazy does that sound? If Ty weren't a wolf he would probably be with Claire. He would have ignored me like the others.

Maybe it is fate.

I mean I miss him and he is right across the hall. When did things get so complicated?

Chapter 15

Dear Diary,

Ty is a wolf. His wolf tells him we are mates, soul mates.

I think I'm going to sleep in a different room tonight, in this room across the hall with the purple walls.

I just don't know what to think anymore.

I will tell you when I decide how I feel about all this...

~Aria

I put my diary back in my backpack and pulled out *Twilight*. The book seems real now. I picture Ty as Jacob, however the vampire is winning.

"Hey Ar," I heard Ty call.

I looked up and then set my book down.

"Are you, or do you, can you just come to bed?" he stuttered.

"I think I want to sleep in here tonight," I whispered.

"Is it because you can't walk?" he asked hopefully.

"No," I carefully answered. I watched pain fill his features.

"Is it because you're mad at me or because you are scared of me?"

"I don't know Tyson."

"You don't know?"

"How I feel," I clarified.

"Are you scared of me right now?"

"Yes," I carefully answered.

"Why? Ar you know I would never hurt you."

"You're scary when you're mad or when you don't get what you want," I whispered. I knew he heard me. It actually explains a lot. When my voice was barely audible to myself Ty could always hear me, because he's a wolf so he has spectacular hearing.

"I never want you to be scared of me, but I don't think you are Aria."

"What?"

"You're a strong person. You came here away from your dad. You find out I'm a werewolf and here I stand in the same room as you. You talked to me when you wouldn't to anyone else. I was the first person to make you laugh and smile in a long time, or even to hug."

"Ty," I started to say.

"That is why I am completely and unconditionally in love you with you. It has nothing to do with my wolf."

I gasped. *Ty is in love with me?*

LOVE!

Love?

Love.

Ty loves me. Do I love Ty?

"Say something," he pleaded.

"Ty I-I," I stammered.

"Don't say it back until you feel it. I just want to let you know I'm not going anywhere and I will always be here for you. Tonight it may be across the hall, but know you can come to me anytime and I will be waiting."

"Good night Ar," he added before leaving .

I breathed in and out a few more times. *Pull yourself together Arrabella!*

I sighed. I like Ty a lot, but love? It is a foreign thing to me. I don't know what it is like to be loved or what it's like to love. I mean I guess I love Trevor but I never experienced it because he was gone before I even got to say hi.

My dad never said I love you. My mom did, but it wasn't like how Ty just said it and not just because he means it in a different way.

When Ty said it, it felt, magical. Like no matter what, I'm safe. Safe.

I really wanted to go to Ty's room. I didn't like being across the hall. However, he was right earlier: I still can't walk, but maybe some space will be good for us. I could handle space. I just have to think of something else.

No Ty thoughts starting now. . .

* * *

I woke up cold, but I didn't feel alone. I opened my eyes and looked at the clock that read five in the morning. I looked over and sighed when Ty wasn't there, but that was my fault.

Then why do I feel Ty's presence? It wasn't until I looked down when I saw Ty asleep on the floor!

He looked so peaceful; I threw a pillow at his face and laughed.

"Arrabella?" he asked, sitting up.

"Why are you in here?"

"I missed you and I wanted to make sure you didn't leave or anything." He sheepishly admitted.

"I still can't walk Ty," I said, rolling my eyes.

I watched as concern and some pain flashed through his eyes.

"It didn't wear off yet?"

"Nope." I shrugged, yawning.

"You should go back to sleep."

"What's wrong?"

"Hmm?"

"What's wrong?" I repeated.

"If you could walk, would you leave?"

"No," I replied.

"Okay." He shrugged, lying back down on the floor.

"Why would you think that?" I asked. *Oh because I just said that.*

"It was sarcasm Ty. Even if my legs worked I wouldn't leave." I laughed.

"Okay Aria, I just worry." He chuckled.

"I know you do." I sighed.

"Night Arrabella," he sang.

"Hey Ty?"

"Yeah."

"You can sleep up here, if you want to."

"Do you want me to?"

"Yes."

"Great." He chuckled.

"You would have ended up here anyways." I accused.

"Goodnight Arrabella." He chuckled.

"Night Tyson," I mocked, closing my eyes and easily falling back to sleep.

* * *

I woke up and was happily surprised when I could move my legs.

I sat up and yawned. I then looked over at Ty who was still asleep next to me, or so I thought.

I went to get off the bed when Ty grabbed my arm.

"Where are you going?" he asked, his eyes still shut.

"Uh, the bathroom."

"Hurry," he grumbled, releasing me.

"I will take all the time I need," I sang, walking across the hall into his room and into the bathroom.

When I was finished I walked back into the bedroom and lay back down with Ty.

"I missed you," he mumbled into the pillow, grabbing me.

"I was gone for like three minutes."

"That's one hundred and eighty seconds."

"Not long at all," I mumbled against his chest.

"Hey Ar."

"Hmm."

"I love you," he whispered, kissing my head.

"Goodnight Ty," I whispered and then let myself once again fall asleep in Tyson's arms.

Chapter 16

Dear Diary,

Ty told me he loves me.

Love.

I don't know how I feel about all this yet my thoughts are all jumbled up. I have never known what it's like to be loved or how to love someone back. I think I love Ty, however I just don't know how I feel about the whole wolf thing…

I'll get back to you on all of this.

~Aria

I woke up tangled in Ty's body.

With all the heat radiating between us, I'm surprised I didn't even break a sweat.

Tyson's still asleep. I love watching him sleep. This was the only time he was vulnerable. He wasn't acting tough or anything— he's just innocent like a child.

When he sleeps sometimes his lips move up and down; it's so cute like he's dreaming or something. His face is totally relaxed as well, like he doesn't have a care in a world. His body language is completely different however.

He holds onto me like I'm his life preserver. If I make the slightest move his face changes for a second like he's making sure I'm still here. Then he wraps his arms around me tighter. I don't know if he knows he's doing that or not.

I wonder if he has ever watched me sleep. No, he probably falls asleep the same time I do, besides my face is usually pressed into him so he wouldn't even have the chance to.

It's kind of creepy after a while. Just watching someone sleep like a creep. That rhymed.

"Arrabella?" Ty asked, making me jump. It's funny I was staring right at him yet I didn't even realize he had opened his eyes.

"Yeah?" I asked, refocusing on his face.

"What are you thinking about?" he asked. His brown eyes boring into mine. Ty's eyes reminded me of a puppy.

"My thoughts are all over the place," I admitted.

He nodded and I wiggled out of his grasp.

"Do you know when you sleep you move your lips up and down?"

"Yeah, I have since I was a baby, at least that's what my mom tells me." He chuckled.

"Where are your parents?"

"They work for the pack before I became alpha and before Carter became beta his parents were betas and mine alphas. They are always away because they are out helping other packs," he explained.

I remember him mentioning his parents were alphas and Carter's were betas. I guess I just will never really understand all of it.

"Oh yeah, you mentioned that before."

"Did you know you talk in your sleep and you scrunch up your nose like a bunny at times?" he asked.

"Yes, I did know that, and did you just compare me to a bunny?" I laughed.

"Yeah I think I did." He chuckled.

"Did I talk in my sleep last night?" He a blushed a little and then slowly nodded. Seeing him blush made me blush!

"TY! What did I say?" I shouted.

"You will never know," he teased.

"Tell me," I demanded, pushing at his chest.

"Ow," he mocked.

"Ty."

"I'm not going to tell you Ar. It's private," he teased.

"How is it private when I'm the one who said it?" He shrugged.

This is getting nowhere.

"Fine don't tell me," I sighed, getting off the bed.

I walked out of the room and went downstairs.

"CARTER!" I shouted when I saw him sitting at the bar.

He looked up from his cereal bowl and smiled.

"Hey crazy." I rolled my eyes and that's when I noticed the boy was topless. *What is it with these guys and their muscles?* I mean he looks photoshopped. Of course, Ty looks better. Way better.

"I'm not crazy." I pouted, sitting next to him.

"Where's Tyson?"

"I'm not talking to him."

"Because he wouldn't tell you what you said in your sleep?"

My jaw dropped to my feet.

"How did you know that?"

"Wolf hearing."

Oh damn I forgot about wolf hearing. That's awkward Carter probably hears everything we say to each other.

The whole pack can probably hear us!

"Wait did you hear what I said in my sleep last night?" He stopped short.

"YOU DID!" I shouted.

"Well kind of." He chuckled.

"Spill."

"I can't."

"Carter, tell me."

Just then Tyson walked into the room. He chuckled at my frustration.

I hopped off the stool and ran upstairs. When I made it to the hallway Ty was in front of me.

Damn he's fast.

I crossed my arms over my chest.

"You aren't going to talk to me?". I nodded.

"You're very stubborn you know?" I shrugged.

"Anything you want to say to me?" I shook my head.

He lifted me up and carried me to his bedroom.

I was about to scream at him but I restrained myself. I won't give him the satisfaction of hearing me talk.

"You scare me when you don't talk," he whispered when he set me down on his bed.

I sighed.

"Okay Ar, I'll tell you. Just say something," he groaned.

"Tell me." I smirked.

He rolled his eyes and then sat down next to me.

"Okay, okay."

"Is it that bad?" I laughed.

"You said I love you Tyson," he confessed, scratching the back of his neck.

I sat there for a moment. In all the confusion of the past few days this was the one thing I'm sure about: I love Ty.

"I do love you Ty," I whispered.

His head snapped in my direction and he gave my goofy smile.

"Sorry I missed that." He grinned.

"I'm not repeating it."

"Guess what?" He beamed.

"What?"

"I love you too." He grinned, pecking my lips.

"You shouldn't be scared Ty."

"Scared?"

"I'm not ever going to stop talking again. In fact, you will now probably never get me to shut up."

He chuckled.

"I wouldn't want it any other way." He smiled.

"Well good because I owe it to you."

"You did it yourself babe." He winked. I laughed. *Babe? I don't really know what Ty and I are. I guess we're mates. A mate is like a lifelong partner so does that mean Ty and I are dating?*

"Do you have a question?" Ty asked, snapping me out of my thoughts.

"Mates are lifelong partners, right?"

"Yes exactly." He grinned. I think he was really happy that I was finally getting it.

"So if we were going to put a title on our relationship…"

"Arrabella?"

"Tyson don't call me that."

"Aria James will you be my girlfriend?"

I started coughing. *Girlfriend?*

I nodded, smiling.

"Yes?" He beamed. I nodded again while once again coughing. This is too much to handle.

"Are you okay? SHERRY!" He shouted.

"NO!" I said coughing. I'm pretty much choking on my own spit right now.

"Alpha?" Sherry asked, entering the room.

I tried to stop coughing, so I held my breath.

"Are you holding your breath?" Ty asked. I let it out and another cough came out.

"I'm fine," I choked out.

"Alpha?" Sherry asked again as if she was asking for permission. She just probably wants to gas me again!

I took a deep breath and finally got myself under control.

"I was choking on my spit Ty." I said, slapping him in the chest.

"Oh sorry, Sherry you are excused." He chuckled.

"It's not funny and you can't freak out like that every time I start coughing."

"I know Ar. I just worry about you."

"That's because you're a good boyfriend." I smiled.

He grinned back, pulling me onto his lap. I leaned my head against his chest while he stroked my back. Ty's touch felt magical; just being in his arms made me feel safe.

"You know we have to talk about what happened in the woods babe," he sighed.

"I know."

He nodded and then dropped the subject. We spent the next hour just sitting and taking in being in each other's presence.

The next morning Ty and I talked about what happened. I told Ty I just needed some time to adjust to the whole werewolf thing. Most of all because of Ty's temper; it reminded me of my father's.

Well on the subject of my father, I really wonder what happened to him. I mean he hasn't tried to come see me at school or try and contact me in any way. I know he doesn't want to come for a visit. I just thought he would want me back to take his anger out on and feed him; I mean he can't even make himself cereal.

Ty acts weird when I bring up my dad. He says I shouldn't even be thinking about him. How can I not think about the man of my nightmares? Ty won't even let me go by the house, see if he's there or anything.

In fact, when I brought up visiting the house Ty threw a table! A table! He just picked it up like it weighed nothing and threw it against the wall.

I know he's keeping something from me and I'm going to get to the bottom of it.

Chapter 17

Dear Diary,

Hey, it's been a long week. School has been okay and we get out in one week. Ty says we have tests on the last two days. The bigger issue is when I bring up my dad. Ty acts like I'm bringing up the end of the world. I don't want to see my father or anything. I just want to know what Ty is keeping from me.

It's been one week since I found out Ty is a wolf. One week since Ty said I love you, but most of all one week since I became Ty's girlfriend, even though we are way more than boyfriend and girlfriend.

Anyway, Diary I'm on another mission… a mission to find out what Ty is keeping from me.

I will report back soon.

~Aria

I woke up to Ty hugging the death out of me! It was Sunday morning and tomorrow we start our last week of school! Ty and I haven't really talked about what will happen after high school; I am kind of hoping he will bring that one up. I sighed in Ty's arms and then wiggled around, no use. I tried to pull my arms out from under his arms, no use again.

"Ty." I groaned.

"Tyson."

"TY!"

"Mhhm?" he mumbled, snuggling his head further into me.

"Ty I have to use the bathroom."

He grunted.

"I'm serious."

I wiggled again and he held on tighter. I didn't even think that was possible two seconds ago but guess what? It was possible.

"Ty." I coughed, knowing it might work. He loosened his arms slightly. I coughed again.

"Arrabella." He protested.

"I have to pee." I groaned.

He sighed and then released me.

I ran into the bathroom.

Ty and I are back in his room. I don't think Ty knows the meaning of space, and I don't think I really want space.

I walked out of the bathroom and looked at the clock. It was only six in the morning. I yawned and then climbed back into bed.

Ty didn't waste a second and grabbed me into his arms again. He took a deep breath and nuzzled back into me.

I feel like he's caging me. I can't protest too much because I love that Ty needs me as much as I need him. I guess we really are the perfect match.

I relaxed once again and fell back asleep instantly.

* * *

"Why won't you tell me?" I groaned. This has been going on for twenty minutes! I mean seriously this is my dad we are talking about; you'd think World War Three was about to break out.

"You don't need to check up on anything," he groaned back.

"You have no right to tell me what I need."

"Arrabella stop thinking about him."

"Oh so now you want to tell me what I can and can't think?" I shouted.

"He hit you; he abused you every day. Why do you want to go back there?" Ty yelled.

I stepped away from him. That felt like a slap in the face.

"I don't want to go back there. Why aren't you listening to me?" I screamed.

"I am listening Arrabella, you said it in your sleep last night," he shot back.

"I don't want to go back there I want to know what you are hiding from me!"

"I'm not hiding anything!"

"Then why are you yelling?"

"This isn't yelling!"

"Fine," I growled, stalking out of the room.

I heard something shatter and I ran down the stairs. I ran past Carter and I think Jason, then I went right out the front door. I started walking on the sidewalk. If Ty wouldn't take me to see what is going on with my dad then I will just walk past the house and see for my damn self.

I walked forward and made it about two sidewalk squares before I heard my name being called I knew for a fact it wasn't Tyson.

I turned around and saw Carter jogging towards me.

"Aria, wait."

"I've already stopped."

"Where are you going?" He laughed.

"I can't tell you." I replied, turning around and walking away.

"Hey, why not?" he questioned, easily catching up with me.

"You would go tell Tyson."

Carter stood in front of me, making me stop.

"Are you going to your dad's house?" he asked, but he already knew the answer.

"Bye Carter." I waved, stepping around him.

He didn't follow me. In fact he was probably telling Tyson right now. I sighed. I'm going to find out even if I have to fight with Ty all day.

"Arrabella!" I heard my name being called. I knew then it was Tyson.

I didn't stop walking. In fact I sped up a little, stupid I know, like I could outrun a werewolf.

Ty was in front of me.

"Go away," I muttered, pushing at his chest.

He grabbed my hands.

"You aren't going to his house."

"Tyson stop," I growled, pulling my hands out of his grip.

"You can come back inside or we can stand out here all day." "I'm going to my dad's," I snapped, stepping around him.

"If he saw you, do you know what would happen?" I kept walking. *That slug isn't going to see me.*

"If you just tell me what you've been keeping from me this will all be over."

"Aria," he sighed.

I turned around and waited.

"Your father, he died of alcohol poisoning last week." "You're lying."

"The cops think that drugs were involved as well."

"Why didn't you tell me?"

"You were doing so well I thought your mom would be notified from rehab and then she could set up a funeral."

"My mom's release date was five years ago. She's never coming back," I whispered.

"Aria, please you were doing so good. I didn't want you to stress about this." I started walking away. Who does he think he is? He was my dad. I know he was cruel and doesn't even deserve a funeral but seriously what else is Ty keeping from me?

"Aria," Ty demanded, stepping in front of me again.

"Move," I said through clenched teeth.

"Let's go back inside."

"If my dad's dead why does it matter if I walk by the house?"

"It doesn't, but you're upset."

"So what?"

"So come on." He said, taking my hand and turning me around. I sat down on the sidewalk and looked up at the sky.

I heard Tyson sigh.

"I can't do this," he muttered.

"Do what?"

"Don't move.". I rolled my eyes and lay down on the sidewalk.

"Got tired of standing?" Carter asked as he once again approached me. What is this, some version of good cop/bad cop, or in our case good wolf and bad wolf?

"I'm looking at the clouds," I replied, holding back a smile.

"Why?"

"My mom told me that people are like clouds. Other people can see them as they want but only the person knows who they truly are."

"Sounds like a smart person."

"No, she just had her moments," I replied, standing up.

"Come on Aria," he added, walking towards the house.

"Where did Ty go?"

"He just needs some time to settle down."

"I don't want to go in."

"Why?"

"Ty lied to me."

"You don't have to see him." Carter shrugged.

"I don't want to." I really don't care that much. I just want to see if Ty's making Carter get me into the house. I mean seriously he probably ordered him to do it.

"Did Ty order you to get me into the house?"

"Something like that." Carter chuckled.

That's what he meant by he didn't want to force me, so he's making Carter seem like the bad guy, that idiot.

"Come on help a brother out."

"I don't want to get you in trouble but I'm not going in." I shrugged.

He looked uneasy and I think he was about to do something he didn't want to.

"I'm sorry Aria, you have to," he whispered.

"No." I protested.

Then he threw me over his shoulder and carried me inside. I didn't fight it because I knew Carter already felt bad.

He set me down and I looked up at him.

"You were only doing your job," I said, walking upstairs. I walked into the room across from Ty's. I liked the purple walls. I shut the door and locked it.

I then sat on my bed.

Dead.

How can my dad be dead? I mean it seems so weird.

I can't say I'm going to miss him, but I can't say I'm not sad. I mean my father deserved a lot of things but death?

I know I should be happy his sorry ass is rotting in hell; however, I feel conflicted. No matter how many times he hurt me he was my dad.

There was a knock on my door.

"What?"

"Aria, open up."

"I don't want to see you."

"Aria," he pleaded.

"No."

"Arrabella." I said nothing back I just sat there staring at the door.

"Arrabella?"

"Arrabella James Middleton," he tried.

Then it was silent. Then I heard him again; he was unlocking the door. The door opened and he set the key on the dresser and walked over to me.

"Do you want to tell me what's really going on?"

"You said he died a week ago right?" I

"Yes last Sunday."

"Ten years ago on that day was the day my mother left for rehab."

"Then it got me thinking, what else are you keeping from me? Why can't I see the house? But what really gets me is how you think you can control me. Then what really tops it all off is how you could order Carter to make sure I got inside so that you wouldn't have to seem like the bad guy."

"First Ar, I didn't tell you because you were doing so good, then I got Carter to go get you because I didn't want to hurt you. I know you don't like it when I get mad so I walked away."

"I know Ty but you can't make those decisions for me."

"I know, I'm sorry. I just want to protect you and sometimes I go overboard."

"So why can't I see the house?"

"The house burned down Aria. Your dad set it on fire."

"What?" I asked. Did I just hear him correctly?

"I'm really sorry Aria."

"Yeah," I said because I really didn't know what to say.

"Are you okay?"

"It just doesn't seem real." I sighed.

"I know baby," he replied, pulling me onto his lap.

"I don't even know how I got to his point," I sighed.

"What point is that?"

"Where I have someone as amazing as you to talk to, actually talk." I smiled, looking up at him.

"I love you Aria." He grinned.

"I love you too Ty." I beamed.

We sat like that for a while and I felt myself slowly drifting away.

Chapter 18

Dear Diary,

My father is dead.

He burned our house down.

I don't know how to feel, numb?

I know I love Tyson Benson.

I know things are getting better.

Mission accomplished.

~Aria

I woke up in Ty's arms. We were at the bottom of his bed curled up in a ball. I silently chuckled and then looked at the clock. It was already four in the afternoon.

I untangled myself from Ty and then crept out the door. I walked downstairs to find Carter watching some weird movie and of course eating pizza.

He looked over and smiled when he saw me.

"Hey Carter." I smiled.

"Hey Aria."

"I just wanted to make sure we're cool.".

He looked relieved as he nodded his head.

"We're cool as ice." He smiled, his fist pounding my knuckles.

I laughed.

"Okay good, sorry you were put in that position."

"Oh trust me it will happen again."

"Looking forward to it."

"Looking forward to what?" I heard Ty ask from behind me.

I turned around.

"Sleeping beauty awakens!" I announced, running over to him and hugging him.

"Are you going to answer my question?" He chuckled, hugging me back.

"The next time you're being a dick," Carter called from the couch.

I laughed.

"Oh you find that funny?" Ty asked.

I nodded against his chest. He then lifted me up so I was eye level with him.

"Please don't drop me."

"Please have you seen these guns?" He smirked.

"Yes, so again I say please don't drop me." I smirked back.

I'm pretty sure the spitting sound was Carter spitting out his pizza. I could hear him choking and laughing at the same time.

"Is that so?"

"Indeed." I smiled sweetly.

He then lifted me up over his head and placed me on his shoulders.

"TY!" I squealed.

"Tell me you love me."

"I love you!"

"Who's the strongest person alive?"

"Um Taylor Lautner?"

"Arrabella, I am four times stronger than that chump." He pouted.

"He is not a chump Tyson."

"I guess you want to stay up there."

"What if I fall backwards and die?" I asked. He froze for a second, and then he was holding my hands.

"Tyson Dalton Benson is the strongest wolf person there is."

"Aww thanks," he teased, squatting so I could get off.

"Never again."

"Yes ma'am." He chuckled.

I looked over at Carter who was picking up the pizza on the floor. So he did spit out his pizza!

I giggled.

Carter looked over and fake glared at me.

"Sure laugh about it. I could have died," he said dramatically.

"Yeah but you didn't." I smirked.

He snorted and continued eating his pizza. I rolled my eyes at him and then turned back towards Ty. He was still obviously proud of being called the strongest wolf person alive so I rolled my eyes at him as well.

"What was that for?" He pouted.

"You can't honestly believe what I just said." I shrugged, trying to play it cool. Of course I know Ty is like the strongest person alive!

"Yes I can because you said it." He smirked.

"Only because you made me."

"No, you actually believe it." He grinned.

"No, I actually don't." I smirked.

"Arrabella."

"Tyson."

"Who do you think is the strongest person alive then?" He challenged.

I tapped my chin, pretending to think about it.

"I don't know I haven't met everyone in the world."

He rolled his eyes and then mumbled something about me being ridiculous under his breath.

"I think you're the ridiculous one," I replied, walking over to Carter and sitting down next to him.

"Ew, Carter what are you watching?" I asked, shielding my eyes.

"Oh come on, that scares you?"

"Let's see, a man going around slitting people's throats? No shit that scares me!"

Ty sat down next to me and pulled me onto his lap.

"I'll protect you." He chuckled, nuzzling into me.

"Thanks babe." I laughed, hiding my face in his chest.

It didn't really help. I could hear the screams. Carter and Ty were both enjoying the film, what idiots.

"Is the scary part over?" I asked, lifting my head.

"YES!" Carter shouted over Ty's 'no.'

I peeked at the scream and regretted it. Of course, I looked at it right as a guy's head gets shot off.

"Please turn it off," I groaned.

"No way," Carter protested.

"Tyyy." I pouted.

"Put something else on," Ty told Carter.

Carter muttered something under his breath, and I think I caught the word pushover.

"Just wait until you find your mate," Ty said defensively.

"I feel bad for whoever that person is," Jason added, grabbing chips from the pantry and walking up the stairs.

"Shut up dickwad," Carter shouted at him.

Dickwad? Is that even a word?

"Aww Carter, I want you to get a mate so that you become all soft," I added.

"I will never be soft." He grunted, taking out the DVD.

"Yes, you will." I nodded.

"Yeah you will man. I mean you are already soft when it comes to Aria," Ty commented in approval. Apparently, everyone was supposed to protect me and stuff because I'm the alpha's mate, weird right?

"That's because she's so tiny and fragile," he pointed out.

"Hey don't underestimate her lest she punches you in the arm." Ty warned.

"Come at me," Carter challenged.

I shrugged and then walked over to him, but as soon as I brought my hand up, planning on socking him in the stomach, he threw me over his shoulder.

"Ty catch her!" he called. *Wait, catch?*

Before I knew it, I was being tossed in the air like a football, landing in Ty's arms.

"Are you kidding me? I could have died!" I shouted dramatically.

"I would never let that happen," Ty reassured, kissing my cheek and putting me down.

He led me upstairs and then looked over his shoulder for a second.

"Oh, and Carter, ever touch my girl like that again and I will cut your balls off." I shook my head and laughed. Werewolves will be the death of me.

Chapter 19

Dear Diary,

We have tests today. I'm not looking forward to it.

Ty is starting to ease up as well. I can tell he's really trying to control his anger around me.

The only thing that will get me through these tests is Ty.

I am so happy that these are my last two days of high school.

~Aria

Ty and I were sitting in English waiting for our final exam.

He was bugging me about a guy who was apparently eyeing me up before school. Ty may be working on his anger but he needed to start easing up on his overprotective jealous side.

I mean he's usually fine when male pack members talk to me, but I guess he knows they aren't a threat to me and won't try anything.

Even when Carter and I were just playing around yesterday I could tell he was trying hard not to rip his throat out. Instead he gave a threat in jest, even though I don't think it was a joke to Carter.

"Thinking about Jack?" he asked. *Jack? Is that the guy's name?*

"I'm actually thinking about how stupid you are." I smirked.

He growled low.

"Arrabella, I did not like the way he was looking at you." "Sorry I can't control how people look at me Tyson." I snapped.

He sighed.

"I know, it's the fact that you are so oblivious."

"Oh, look if it isn't the mute freak." I heard a snobby voice say.

I looked up to see Claire. *What the hell is she doing in here? She's not even in this class.*

"Claire, leave," Tyson growled.

"Oh right. You only talk to Tyson." She smirked.

"NOW!" he yelled.

She flinched back and then ran out the door.

Ty turned to me but before he could say anything the teacher walked in. I took my test and probably failed. I mean with Ty distracting me all semester I didn't really learn anything; at least it was multiple choice.

We left right after the test.

"Are you okay?" he asked.

"I'm fine." I sighed.

"You don't look fine."

"Well I am Ty." I groaned.

He took another step and stopped me, standing in front of me. We were now in front of my history room.

He took my jaw in his hand and yanked my head up. I looked in his eyes, trying to stay strong so that he would drop this.

"Okay I will be here after the test."

"Alright." I smiled, turning around and walking in.

After history was chemistry, and I kept Ty busy by asking him random questions.

It was like a game show, but he kept up well.

He is now walking me to math where I will take my last exam for today.

"Poptart or Toaster Strudel?" I shot out before he could say anything.

"Arrabella just take this math test. We can talk when we get home, and Poptarts." He chuckled at the last part. I nodded and walked into math.

I waved at Carter who was in his seat and then sat down.

I took the test and was done with twenty minutes to spare. I looked over at Carter who was also done. He caught my eye and gave me a thumbs up. I rolled my eyes and then stood up to hand in the exam.

"You are free to go when you finish." My teacher announced.

Carter stood up and followed me out of the room.

"Tyson is still finishing his history exam. Do you want me to wait outside with you?"

"Do I actually have a choice?" I asked sarcastically.

"Nope, you're stuck with me." He grinned.

I smacked his arm.

"Ow, okay Tyson's right. You're tough." He surrendered.

We walked outside where I saw Claire texting away on her phone. She looked up when she saw Carter and I leave the school.

She walked over to us and I groaned inside.

"Oh so you also talk to Carter. Or is it just boys you little slut?" She smirked.

"Back off Claire," Carter warned.

"What? Can the little bitch not speak for herself?" She chuckled darkly.

"Oh, I can speak for myself you skank!" I yelled right before Carter cut in.

Carter looked just as stunned as Claire.

"Oh, so you were pretending this entire time?" she asked.

"No, I wasn't actually and you thinking that Tyson would ever want you is funny to me actually," I spit out; I don't know what's happening. I barely even knew the words coming out of my mouth! Ty should be with someone as pretty as her.

"What would make you think he would want garbage like you?"

"What would make you think he wants a bleach blonde fake tanned Barbie like yourself?" I demanded.

"It's called tanning, and I know I'm perfect."

"Yeah just like Barbie: plastic with no brain."

"Maybe you should go back to not talking!"

"Why would that matter? Ty wanted me even when I couldn't talk. What does that say about you that a mute is more interesting than yourself?" I smirked.

She opened her mouth and then shut it.

"You're an ugly whore and I would rather be blue then ever even resemble you." She sneered.

"For you to insult me I'd actually have to value your opinion, nice try though," I shot back.

I walked around her, not because I was finished but because I was having trouble breathing.

"Aria where are you going? That was awesome!" Carter beamed.

"Carter, huh, I need, huh…" I panted.

"Aria? Can you breathe? Are you okay? What do I do?" He panicked.

"Arrabella breathe," Ty demanded, appearing out of thin air.

"Where, huh, did you, huh, come from?" I asked.

"School is over, just breathe," he repeated.

"I'm, huh, fine huh."

"Deep breaths."

I nodded and then hugged him.

He chuckled.

"So you told Claire?" He smirked as I looked up at him.

"Oh yeah, huh, you heard that, huh?" I asked, becoming slightly embarrassed.

"I'm so glad you stood up for yourself." He grinned.

"Yeah, hey I'm fine. Can we leave?"

"Sure babe." He smiled.

"Bye Carter, huh, see you at the house." I waved.

"See you later guys." He waved.

We arrived back at the house, and Ty took me up to his room.

"So what's wrong?" he asked.

"Nothing?"

"You seemed weird all day and then you yelled at Claire, which was awesome but is everything okay?"

"Ty calm down. I didn't believe anything I said to her," I sighed.

"What?"

"I said I didn't believe…" I started to say.

"I heard what you said Aria. What didn't you believe?"

"I don't know. Words just started coming out and I couldn't stop them. I feel awful for calling her those names. It's just I couldn't get the time that you guys kissed out of my head."

"Arrabella she came over, sat on my lap, and kissed me. I pushed her off just in time to see you walking into school. I swear kissing her is like kissing a plastic doll," he confessed, lightly chuckling at his reference.

"Yeah well Barbie is pretty," I mumbled.

He looked at me like I was crazy and then I realized he heard me; *I should probably stop mumbling and just keep these things in my head.*

"Yeah pretty, that's nothing compared to your gorgeous, stunning, perfect, outstanding, remarkable beauty."

"Thanks Ty, but you have to think that you're my mate."

"I don't have to think it because we're mates babe. I believe it." He smiled.

"Thanks Ty." I smiled, leaning over and hugging him.

"So what was bothering you?"

"Nothing is bothering me." I laughed.

"I know there is and you always laugh to cover it up."

"That's not even true!"

"Then you shout."

"Ty stop," I groaned, smacking his arm.

"Then you hit me." He smirked.

"I think we're done here." I sighed, walking out of his room.

"We are not done here," he replied, grabbing my hips and pulling me back into the room.

I shoved at him and looked up into his brown eyes; the little dork was trying to show me who's boss. I almost laughed but contained it.

I leaned forward and pressed my lips against his. I felt his lips against mine for a split second and then he kissed me back eagerly. I smiled against his lips as he sat down and brought me onto his lap so I was straddling him.

I slowly moved my hips up and down and I could tell he was getting turned on so I cranked it up a notch and moved my hands to his hair.

Now I haven't kissed many guys however it's not rocket science. Ty moaned against my lips and licked my bottom lip like I was waiting for him to do. I kept my mouth shut however.

I could tell he was getting slightly aggravated and I suppressed a smile. I started moving my hips again and now I know he is getting hard. I squeezed my lips shut even tighter as he tried to force my mouth open. He then moved his hands from my hips to my butt and that's when I pulled away.

I looked into his darker eyes and smirked at him.

"I guess I showed you who's really running the show around here," I added, jumping off his lap and out of the room.

I knew it would take him a second to calm himself down and process what happened, so I took advantage and ran straight into the game room.

Carter was in the bean bag playing some games with guns and he looked over when I came racing in.

"Hiding again?" he asked in amusement.

"Yes, you never saw me," I added, sliding behind the TV and sitting down.

"Arrabella get out here," Ty demanded, entering the game room.

I put my head in my legs to stop myself from laughing.

"She's not in here," I heard Carter say even though it was no use.

"Arrabella I'm going to count to three."

"One," he started. I rolled my eyes. *I'm so scared Tyson.*

"Two."

"Three."

I then saw the TV moving away from me. Then Tyson was in front of me.

"Great hiding spot."

"CARTER HELP!" I screamed, covering my eyes.

"You're on your own kid!" Carter called.

I looked up at Tyson and sweetly smiled.

"I love you." I tried.

"I love you too."

"I love you more than Bella loves Edward."

"I love you more than Romeo loved Juliet."

"I'm sorry baby."

He sat down next to me.

"Aria, did it really bother you that I freaked out over Jack staring at you?" He sighed.

"I just wish you would understand that I don't even notice other guys because I only care about you."

"I know that. I just get mad when they look at you like that." He growled.

"I know just glare at them, scare the shit out of them. I don't care. Just don't freak out on me." I laughed.

"Alright deal," he replied, flashing me a billion-dollar smile.

"You know you shouldn't start what you can't finish." He smirked, pulling me back onto his lap.

I nodded.

"Care to finish?" he whispered.

I didn't reply. Instead I once again pressed my lips to his. This time I let his tongue enter my mouth the first time he tried.

I can't believe I have someone as amazing as Tyson to call mine.

Chapter 20

Dear Diary,

Ty is a great kisser, no an outstanding kisser.

However, he freaks out when any guy looks at me. I know he only does because he loves me but I showed him who was boss yesterday.

Anyway, I also told Claire off yesterday and it felt pretty damn good.

Today is my last day of high school and my last day of tests! Wish me luck.

~Aria

I put my pencil down and sighed in relief; my tests are over! I looked over at Carter who was still taking the test.

I walked over to the teacher's desk to drop my exam off and then left. I know that Carter is probably supposed to watch me right now but I think I can handle waiting for Ty to finish his test all by myself.

"Hey," I heard an unfamiliar voice say.

I turned around and saw Jack standing there. *Well shit.*

"Um hi."

"So you do talk?"

I laughed and nodded. He's cute I guess. He's nothing compared to Ty though. His brown eyes don't sparkle like Ty's and his lips don't look kissable at all.

In fact, the thought of kissing Jack made my stomach churn.

"So what are your plans after high school?"

"I don't really know. I haven't given it much thought," I replied.

"There you are," Carter called, walking up to me.

"Here I am."

"What's going on here?" he asked, glaring at Jack.

Oh, great Carter's just as bad as Ty.

"Nothing. We were just talking." I shrugged.

"Yeah man, I thought you dating Tyson, Arrabella?" Jack asked.

"I am."

"What's going on?" Ty asked, half jogging over to us.

"What happened? Are you okay?" he asked, looking me over.

"Ty I'm fine. Carter's overreacting." I sighed.

"Overreacting about what? What did you do?" he shouted at Jack.

"Nothing man, she was out here alone so I started talking to her."

"Well don't do it again." He took my hand and walked me to his car.

"Ty, calm down. You're acting crazy."

"Get in the car."

I sighed and then waved to Jack so he knew I was fine.

We drove in silence on the way home, and I ran out of the car when we arrived.

"AR!" Ty called after me.

"What did we just talk about yesterday Tyson?" I shouted.

"You shouldn't have been outside alone. I told Carter to go with you," he growled.

"He was finishing the test!" I shrieked.

"What did he want?"

"Are you serious? We were just talking Tyson."

"Carter looked like he was about to kill him so what did he say to you?"

"I don't know. Why don't you ask him?" I snapped.

Just then Carter came through the door.

"What did he say to her?" Ty demanded.

"Nothing I was trying to intimidate him."

"You should have been outside with her so she didn't have to talk with some stranger!" he shouted.

"Chill Tyson."

"You are unbelievable!" I screamed, marching upstairs. I stalked into the game room and locked the door.

"Aria let me in." Ty sighed.

"I don't want to see you!" I called back, lying in a bean bag.

I heard him grumble something and I rolled my eyes at him even though he couldn't see me.

"Aria, it's me. Open the door." Carter tried.

"I don't want to see either of you."

"What about me?" Another voice tried.

"I don't even know you," I replied confused. *Jason maybe?*

"Aria, come on," Ty pleaded.

"Just give me some space Tyson."

He didn't reply. I sighed and let my head fall back.

Why does Ty have to complicate things? I mean I like that he's protective, but not being able to hold a conversation with another guy is ridiculous. In fact, I should be able to do whatever I want. Ty's my boyfriend, not my father.

I heard the door opening. *Shit he must have gotten a key.* I put my hands over my face so I didn't have to see whoever came in, and they couldn't see my face either.

"Don't hide your face from me Arrabella," I heard Ty demand.

"I told you I didn't want to see you."

"Have you been crying?" he almost shouted.

"No."

"Then remove your hands."

"No." I shrugged.

I heard him suck in a breath and then I felt his hands on mine. Instead of forcing them away from my face, he kissed my hands.

I laughed and removed my hands just to shove him.

"I knew that would work." He chuckled.

I looked at him and slightly frowned. Why is it that I can't stay mad at him? That every time I see him, the anger in me vanishes and I can't even put up a good fight. It has to be those brown eyes of his.

"What is it baby?"

"This is why I didn't want to see you." I sighed.

"Why?"

"It makes me forget why I'm angry." I sighed.

"I intend to make that work to my advantage in the future." He smirked.

"Ty, what's the real reason why you won't let me talk to guys?"

He looked over at me, and his face softened.

"I'm going to try and explain this the best I can. Just hear me out and then you can ask questions." I nodded in agreement.

"So remember how I told you I am an alpha? Do you remember what that means?"

"Yeah the highest rank."

"Exactly. Well when an alpha finds his mate he finds the person that completes him. This is true for any werewolf however for an alpha everything is different because we are the most powerful. We find the one person who can say no to us and challenge us and just drive us crazy. However, it's the best kind of crazy in the world. The thing is I'm used to people always doing things on my terms when I tell them to do it. You do exactly what I don't want you to do and I have no say over it; it's extremely frustrating because I care about your life more than my own. Then the whole protective thing is because I don't want anything to happen to you. I want to keep you safe and believe me if I could I would glue you to my side so I never have to be away from you."

"I know Ty, but can't you control it a little?"

"I'm trying Ar. It's easier when you talk to pack members because most of them already have mates and the mate thing is new to me like it is to you and I'm still trying to figure it out." I giggled at that.

"All I know is that I love you like crazy." He smiled.

"I love you too." I grinned.

"Good because I will glue you to me." He mock threatened.

I laughed and slapped his arm.

"Hey Ty, is that why you hold me close at night?" I asked.

"Yeah when you shift even the slightest it freaks me out." "Doesn't that get annoying?" I asked.

"Not at all." He shrugged.

"Sometimes it's like you're sniffing my hair."

"That's because your scent is amazing." He chuckled. *I knew it! Now I know I'm not crazy.*

"What?" He asked. I probably have a crazy look on my face.

"You do it every night when you pull me into your side," I replied.

"I didn't know you were paying attention." He laughed.

I shrugged.

"Are you still angry with me?"

"I'm not angry with you. I'm angry at your possessive alpha traits."

"I'm working on it babe." He winked.

"That's all I ask," I replied dramatically.

"Good, now consider us stuck like glue." He chuckled.

Yes, I have been stuck to Ty ever since my eyes landed on his, just like glue.

Chapter 21

Dear Diary,

Today I will bring up what happens next. Maybe.

I really hope Ty brings it up.

Well wish me luck, again.

~Aria

I woke up and smiled because I am free from school! My smile grew even wider when I realized I was in the arms of my stunning mate.

I turned my head so I could see his face. I like sleeping Ty. He's like an innocent puppy. His face is fully relaxed yet alert. The only thing I don't like is that I can't see his brown eyes when he's sleeping.

I studied him a little longer until the urge to pee was overwhelming. I maneuvered out of his grip but just when I thought I was free Ty pulled me right back into him.

"Where are you going?" he mumbled.

"The bathroom." I sighed.

"No." He whined like a child, gripping me tighter.

"Tyson my bladder is going to explode."

"It won't," he whispered.

"Do you have to do this every morning?"

"Do you have to pee every morning?"

"Yes." I shrugged.

"No," he protested.

"Tyson, I will be back in like three minutes," I groaned.

He grumbled but removed his arms.

"Why thanks," I sarcastically replied, getting out of bed.

After I used the bathroom and washed my hands I looked over at the clock. It was only six in the morning and I intend to go back to sleep!

Well I want to harass Ty a little first of course.

I walked over to the bed and stood up on it.

"Don't you dare." Tyson warned, popping one eye open.

I raised my eyebrows at him.

"Ar, it's too early." He groaned.

I took off, bouncing all over the place.

"Don't make me get up," he warned.

I kept jumping and before I knew it Ty was taking off the blankets and standing up. Now my plan was to run but I stayed in place seeing Ty in just his sweatpants threw me off.

He was now standing up on the bed and was in front of me.

He grabbed my hips to steady me. I poked him in the ribs, or eight pack in his case, and he cocked his eyebrow at me.

"Let me go," I added.

"Never," he replied, turning me around and pulling me down.

"Fine. I guess a few more hours of sleep won't hurt." I yawned.

"Great idea," Ty replied, rolling his eyes.

"I could go sleep in the other room." I threatened.

He growled low, lying back down and pulling me into him and as usual taking a deep breath as he snuggled his face into my hair.

I laughed and snuggled into him. *How did I get so lucky?*

* * *

"Ew Carter," I protested, once again reaching for the remote, which he once again held away from me.

Ty was upstairs on the phone and he left me with this beast! I think it's kind of serious though because Carter was watching me carefully out of the corner of his eye.

"I think I'm going to find Ty," I announced, standing up.

"Nope you have to stay with me kid."

"I don't like you," I mocked. He put a hand over his heart, pretending to be hurt.

"Aria I thought we were best friends," he gasped.

"You thought wrong." I smirked.

"Carter, stop harassing Aria." I heard Ty call. I looked over and saw him jogging down the stairs.

I ran over to him and hugged him.

"Carter's a bully," I mumbled into his chest.

"I know babe." He sighed.

"What's wrong?" I asked, looking up at him.

"I have to meet my parents in Denver," he growled low.

"Why?" I asked.

"Pack stuff."

I looked at him questioningly and then shrugged it off. Ty didn't really talk about his parents so I didn't push him; however, I was curious.

"Which means I have to leave you with Carter for the day."

Carter laughed, and I almost died on the spot.

"NO!" I groaned.

"Hey come on," Carter added.

"Ty, please. I'll die," I begged.

"Aria stop being a drama queen," Carter chimed in.

"Carter, you aren't even in this conversation."

He put his hands up in surrender and went back to his stupid movie.

"I'm sorry Ar. It's too dangerous for you to be there." "Dangerous?"

"For a human, baby."

"How long?" I asked.

"I'll be back before you wake up tomorrow." He promised.

"Okay." I sighed.

"I love you." He smiled, but it wasn't a Ty smile; it was sad smile.

"I love you too," I replied, offering him a small smile.

He looked a little torn like he was going against his will. He pulled me in for a hug and then gave me a small peck on the lips. I watched as he walked over to the door.

"I'll see you tomorrow beautiful."

"Okay Ty, bye!" I called. He whispered a few things to Carter that I couldn't hear and then left.

I plopped down next to Carter. This was the first time I will be away from him.

"Come on don't be sad," Carter pleaded.

"I'm not," I sighed.

"Come on give me a smile."

"Carter," I groaned.

"Hey do you want to go play some video games?"

"Sure." I shrugged. Maybe that will help take my mind off Ty.

* * *

"You cheated!" Carter said.

"Is it even possible to cheat in this game?"

"It must be because you did." He shrugged.

"Don't be such a baby." I laughed.

"I'm not being a baby."

"Yeah you kind of are."

"Am not. Are you hungry?"

"Not any more hungry than when you asked me five minutes ago," I teased.

"Great let's eat."

"I swear I'm going to get fat," I sighed, standing up and walking out of the room with him.

"Fat?" He laughed.

"You guys eat every five seconds," I added.

"Oh please Aria. You're like the size of a fourteen-year-old." He chuckled.

"I am not," I protested.

He glanced back at me and rolled his eyes.

"You are too."

I followed him into the kitchen where he warmed up some soup. He then handed me a bowl and a spoon.

"Why thanks." I smiled.

"The pleasure is mine," he mocked.

I rolled my eyes and started to eat it.

"Hey man have you seen Catalina?" Jason asked.

"Nope I've been in the game room with Aria." He shrugged.

Jason looked stressed. This Catalina girl must be his mate. He is mirroring the worried look Ty does when he's worried about me. *Ty—man I miss that dork.*

"Jason, you should check the garage. I think I heard someone wander off in that direction earlier." He suggested. Jason nodded and headed to I'm guessing where the garage is.

"Who's Catalina?" I asked.

"Jason's mate."

"Do you ever wonder when you will find yours?"

"Yeah sometimes, but I'll find her when the time is right." He shrugged.

"Do you want to find her?"

"Yes, but I'm also scared." He chuckled.

"Why?" I asked.

"I don't know. I mean people change when they find their mates, in a good way of course, but I don't know if I'm ready to find the girl of my dreams yet. I'm scared I won't live up to what she's been expecting, scared of rejection."

"Rejection?"

"When we find our mate, we can get rejected."

"Like not being with them?" I asked in shock.

"Yeah, I guess. I don't how though because from what I see you pretty much go crazy over this person."

"How do you reject them?" I wondered.

"Well you can simply say I reject you, but for humans who don't know what's going on all they have to say is 'I don't want to be with you' or if they know 'I don't want to be your mate. ' I mean the wolf in this relationship probably wouldn't stop trying but I don't know I'm more of an on-my-own kind of guy." He smirked.

That is why Ty freaked out when I yelled at him after he told me he was a wolf.

"If my mate's a werewolf I'll mark her then and there." "Mark her?"

"Yeah it means biting her neck so everyone knows she's mine." He smiled.

"Doesn't that hurt?"

"No." He chuckled.

"I think it will be funny when you find your mate."

"Why is that?" He chuckled.

"Because you will be in love," I replied dramatically.

He rolled his eyes and then I heard a girl's voice.

"Because Jason that's not fair!" she added.

I looked over and saw Jason and a girl, probably Catalina, walk into the living room.

"It is fair baby," he sighed.

She sighed in frustration.

I looked over at Carter who was watching them in amusement.

"Hey Carter don't you think he's being unfair?" The girl asked, looking over at us.

Carter put his hands up in surrender.

"Don't bring him into this." Jason groaned.

"Oh hey. Are you Ty's mate?" The girl asked, walking over to me.

I nodded and offered her a small smile.

"I'm Catalina." She smiled back.

"I'm Aria." Carter gave me a reassuring smile and I took a deep breath.

"Well we are all really happy Ty found his mate," she went on.

"Are you a werewolf too?"

"Yeah." She laughed.

"Cool." Catalina was nice and chatty. She' was gorgeous with her light blue eyes and long wavy blonde hair. She talked with me for a while until Carter told her I should be getting to bed.

I went up to Ty's room and took a shower. I decided to wear Ty's shirt because I knew it will be hard going to bed without him. Otherwise I think I did pretty well today.

I combed my hair and brushed my teeth. Then I slipped into bed. I was about to reach over to turn off the lamp when Carter came in.

"Hey Aria?"

"Yeah?"

"Ty wants you to know he loves you and will be back in a few hours." He smiled.

"Okay." I nodded.

"Alright, night kid." He smirked.

"Night loser."

I then turned off the light and lay down. I tossed and turned for forty-five minutes I sighed. *This is useless.* I thought about Ty for a while and was surprised when I realized I was crying.

Well damn. Now I can't breathe through my nose. I groaned and got out of bed to blow my nose and calm myself down.

After ten minutes of getting myself to stop crying I went back to bed. It took a while but I slowly fell asleep.

I woke up to someone shuffling in the room. I sat up and squinted.

"Sorry baby did I wake you?" A voice asked.

"Ty." I smiled, getting up.

He chuckled and pulled me into a hug.

"You're wearing my shirt?" he whispered into my ear. I nodded and held onto him tighter.

"Hey," he soothed, pulling away. I think he's looking at my face, but I can't tell because it's too dark.

"Were you crying?" he asked, running his thumbs under my eyes.

"Yeah, a little," I admitted.

This made him pull me back into a hug.

"I love you," he soothed, kissing the top of my head.

"I love you too Ty." I laughed.

"Come on let's get to bed." I nodded and then climbed back into bed, and this time it felt right because I was instantly in Ty's arms.

Chapter 22

Dear Diary,

So I didn't bring it up yesterday, but it wasn't my fault because he was gone all day!

Today I will ask him about it, I think. I mean who knows maybe Ty wants to go to college.

As usual Diary, wish me luck.

~Aria

Ty and I are currently in the game room, playing a competitive round of tanks. I for one don't get the whole thing because we are on the same team however you want to get the most tanks.

"Ah got it!" Ty cheered.

"Those invisible tanks are dumb." I pouted.

"Aw, don't be sad babe." He winked, turning the TV off.

"Ready for lunch?" he asked. He looked at me like he already knew I would say I wasn't hungry. Carter must have told him that I didn't eat much yesterday.

I don't see what the big deal was; I just don't get that hungry.

"I'm not really hungry but sure." I shrugged, getting up from the bean bag.

"You're never hungry."

"You only think that because you're hungry all the time."

"Aria, you're too skinny," he sighed.

"I'm sorry you think that," I sighed.

"Did your dad ever call you fat?"

"My dad called me a lot of things Ty, but never fat," I replied honestly.

"Do you think you're fat?"

"If this is because Carter told you I said that yesterday, I was joking. I said that if I ate like him I'd become fat," I groaned.

"Okay I'm just checking because you never want to eat."

"My body just isn't used to a lot of food." I shrugged. He growled low at that and then pulled himself together.

"I'll change that." He smirked. I then followed him into the kitchen.

After lunch we went into the living room and I am trying to figure out how to ask him about his future plans. I guess I could just blurt it out but Ty takes everything I say so seriously.

"What are you thinking about babe?" he asked, turning the volume on the TV down.

"Nothing." I shrugged. *Wow I'm a coward.*

He rolled his eyes and pulled me onto his lap so I was facing him. Our faces were almost touching. I know how to get out of this but I don't want to have to worry about it anymore. Ty does look really kissable right now—the way his brown eyes are boring into mine waiting for me to say something.

I felt myself inching closer and then our lips met. I smiled against his lips and just when I thought he was going to ask for entrance he pulled away.

"You aren't getting out of it babe." He smirked.

I sighed and ran a hand through my hair. I hate when Ty takes control and part of me wants to prove to him that I can get out of it.

My body acted before my brain and I moved my hands to his hair and started rubbing my hips up and down him.

He closed his eyes and took a deep breath. He grabbed my hands in one of his and with the other hand he held my hips still.

I was too scared to ask him. I blurted out the first thing that came to my mind.

"Why haven't you marked me?" I blurted out.

He stopped short and chuckled.

"Carter told you about that?"

"Yeah he said that's the first thing he's going to do when he finds his mate."

"Well wouldn't you have wondered what the hell I was doing if on the first day you started school I came up to you and bit your neck?" He smirked.

"Yeah," I sighed.

"Listen babe everyday my wolf screams at me to mark you. I just wanted to wait until you were ready."

"I'm ready." I shrugged.

"It's going to hurt babe," he sighed.

"Carter said it doesn't." I pouted.

"It does for the first ten seconds."

"I think I can handle ten seconds of pain Ty."

"I don't want you to cry."

"I promise I won't."

He grinned at me and then carried me upstairs. I felt his bed underneath me and then he was kissing me all over my lips, my jaw, everywhere.

He started sucking on a spot on my neck, which made my back arch, and our bodies became even closer together.

I felt his teeth on my neck and then pain. I whimpered a bit and then I felt this jolt of stinging run through my body. I squeezed my eyes shut. SHIT! *This hurts. Carter is such a–.* I felt warmth flow through my body, a feeling I've never experienced before: want. I want Tyson.

I looked up at him, his eyes meeting mine. I felt a pull towards him that I can't quite describe.

"I love you," I whispered.

He smiled and then pecked my lips.

"Sleep Ar." He chuckled.

He then rolled over so he was lying down next to me and then sleep hit me.

* * *

I woke up and what happened before I had fallen asleep hit me. I bolted up and ran into the bathroom.

I moved my hair away from my neck to see a huge mark. Okay I'm overreacting a bit, but it's big.

Then Ty was behind me. He smiled and then kissed me where my mark was. I had to grab the sink to keep myself from melting onto the floor.

I could tell Ty liked the fact he had this effect on me. I smiled as well because I was happy and because I got out of asking Ty about college.

"Hey Aria, just thought I'd let you know," Carter started to say as he entered Ty's room.

"Whoa." He smirked, holding up his hand which Ty grabbed and they did a weird high five thing.

"You guys are weird." *Wow I really need to stop blurting out the first thing that pops into my head.*

"I came in here because I just wanted to let you guys know I'm about to put in a movie." He smirked.

"No," I cut off before he finished.

"Just thought I'd ask," he replied, grinning.

"Aww, Carter are you lonely?" I mock pouted.

"Nope not at all." He shrugged, taking a swig of his soda.

"By the way getting marked does hurt," I said, glaring at him.

One look at my face and the soda was out of his mouth and all over the floor.

"CARTER!" I shrieked, backing away.

"You're kind of threatening." He nodded in approval.

"I know."

"In a cute puppy kind of way." He smirked. Ty growled low but contained himself. *Leave it to Ty to get possessive when I talk to Carter. Of all people he should be the guy Ty is least worried about!*

"Do you always have to have something in your mouth when you find something funny?" I added.

"I'm talented." He shrugged.

"Well go be talented at watching a movie by yourself."

He chuckled and then left.

"Aww I think you hurt his feelings," Ty whispered, attacking me with a hug.

"Yeah, he'll get over it," I whispered back, turning around to face him.

Before I knew it, I was being swung around Ty's body. My legs wrapped around him and he was carrying me towards the bed. I smiled against his lips as he gently laid me down and hovered over me.

I broke away after a while to breathe which made him start trailing kisses down my neck until he reached my mark. I held back a moan and took a handful of his shirt in my hand.

This felt like nothing I could ever put to words. Possibly bliss or something better than bliss, better than life, better than anything I could ever imagine.

"You're beautiful," Ty whispered, pecking my lips and helping me sit up.

"You're not so bad yourself." I smirked.

He reached for me and pulled me onto his lap.

"Not so bad?" *What was I going to ask Ty again? Oh yeah college. Wait there was something else from a while ago. This is going to bother me.*

I snapped out of my thoughts when Ty planted his lips on mine. I smiled against his lips and then pulled away.

"I have a question."

"Ask away." He chuckled. *Oh vampires. There it is! Just in time to save me.*

"Are vampires real?" I blurted out.

He looked at me in a 'are you serious' kind of way and burst out laughing.

"TY!" I groaned.

"You were just so serious when you asked" He laughed.

"It's not funny," I sang.

"No, it's hilarious." He laughed.

I rolled my eyes and then got off the bed and ran out the door. I ran downstairs to see Carter watching his movie in anticipation.

"Vampires," he scoffed when he saw me.

"They're real?" I shouted.

"Don't be dumb. They are myths." He waved me off.

"Yeah and I always thought that about werewolves."

"Shape shifters are a completely different thing. It's in our blood, not because you get bitten or whatever."

"In your blood?"

"Yeah like my dad's a wolf."

"What about your mom?"

"Nope." He shrugged.

"What about Ty's mom?"

"Yeah both his parents are."

"Where are his parents again?"

He looked over at me and rolled his eyes.

"You ask too many questions," he groaned.

"Do you want your mate to be a wolf?" I whispered.

He looked at me like 'what kind of question is that' until his face softened, seeing what I was getting at.

"I actually don't."

"Why?"

"I want to protect her and I want her to be easy to surprise. Like human mates are so much better because you get to show them everything and it's a bonus because they're slow and not nearly as strong." He chuckled at the last part.

"You're stupid. I hope you have a wolf mate." I smirked.

His eyes looked beyond me for a brief moment and then he was the one smirking.

"Also humans are better mates because they are nearly deaf," he added.

"What?" I started to say, but I was suddenly being lifted into the air.

"Tyson!" I screamed, laughing.

He set me down and put his arms around me.

"It's true babe. You're deaf." Ty laughed, kissing my cheek.

I smacked him in the chest and then smirked up at him.

"Oh yeah?" he asked.

"What are going to do about it?" I egged him on.

"I'm going to do this!" He shouted, grabbing me and tickling my sides.

"TY!" I roared in laughter.

"Give up yet?" He laughed.

"I can't breathe." I gasped.

He instantly stopped and spun me around to face him.

"I win." I smirked, racing upstairs.

I ran into the bedroom and crawled under the bed.

"I know you're in here," Ty sang.

I held back a laugh and scooted further away from the edge of the bed and closer to the wall.

"Under the bed? Really Ar?" he asked. He crawled under and grabbed my hand and led me out.

Once he got me out instead of helping me up he pinned me down and hovered over me.

"What am I going to do with you?"

"Love me," I suggested.

"Oh, I'll love the hell out of you." He grinned, moving his head down so his lips met mine.

I love kissing Ty, I really do, but I can't put this off any longer. It's pretty much gnawing at my soul; okay that might be a slight exaggeration.

"What's wrong babe?" Ty asked after pulling away from the kiss.

"Um can we talk?" I asked.

"Of course." He chuckled, taking my hand in his and leading me to the bed.

He sat down on his bed and then I did the same. I took a deep breath. *This isn't anything hard, just college. I mean it's not the question it's the answer. If Ty goes to college then what does that mean for us?*

"Ar?" Ty asked.

"What?" I asked.

"I said what is it you wanted to talk about?" He chuckled.

"Oh um, I was just wondering," I started to say.

"Yeah?"

"So we're done with high school and all," I started.

"Are you wondering what happens now?" He chuckled.

"Yes." I sighed in relief.

"I'm not going anywhere Ar." He smiled.

"Good." I beamed.

"Neither are you, unless...did you want to go to college?" He smirked.

"Ty, I hate school."

"I thought so." He chuckled.

He leaned in and planted his lips on mine for the fifth time today; I could kiss Ty all day every day.

Chapter 23

Dear Diary,

Ty isn't going anywhere. His job is this pack, which I still haven't completely met yet.

My thoughts have been wandering towards my mother lately. Before Trevor and before rehab she actually wasn't too horrible of a person.

~Aria

"I just want to drive by Tyson," I sighed.

"It's not going to be pretty Aria," he groaned.

"I never said it was Ty, but I need this." He looked at me for a moment, muttering something under his breath.

"I love you." I smiled hugely, skipping out the door.

I asked Ty to take me past my old house, or what was left of it. I wanted to see what survived the fire.

We entered my old neighborhood and I took a deep breath. It was worse than I imagined. Basically, what was left of the house was wood. There was just ash and dirt everywhere. You could tell by the wood that remained standing that it was a house at one point, but the outside finally resembled what was happening on the inside.

"Stop." I told Tyson.

He stopped the car, and I stared at it for a minute.

I reached for the door handle and got out of the car. Ty didn't stop me. He just watched me carefully. I walked up to the mess and stared a little closer.

I turned around and got back in the car.

"Aria," Ty started to say.

"Just get me out of here," I whispered. With that he took my hand in his and drove back home.

I walked out of the car and went inside the house.

"What's wrong?" Carter asked when he saw me. When I didn't answer he looked over my shoulder where I'm assuming Ty was standing. Carter nodded at something Ty must have done and he gave me a small smile.

"I'm going to go finish my movie," he said. With that he walked over to the couch and sat down.

"Aria?" Ty asked.

"I-I'm just going to go lie down," I whispered, walking upstairs.

I walked into Ty's room and looked at the bed for a moment. Then I crawled in and closed my eyes.

I felt the bed move slightly and I turned my head to see Ty lying next to me.

I put my head in his shoulder and tears began flowing from my eyes.

"It's okay baby." Ty soothed, stroking my hair.

I tried to regain control of myself. That house was the source of abuse. All the memories and pain I felt happened in it. All that just burned down with it. Most of all any memories or pictures or things from my childhood had vanished. Gone, like it never existed. I wish I could burn the memories in my mind, but I can't; they will stay with me forever.

Any hope of my mother ever returning burned down with it. If I ever saw my mom today just walking down the street I may go right up to her and slap her across the face. She left her innocent daughter with a monster. She chose her son over me and then left me to suffer. I suffered all right, but worst of all I suffered in silence.

"Please stop crying baby," Ty pleaded.

I tried to take a deep breath but it wasn't working.

"Please Ar."

I looked up at his face and saw a tear slide down his cheek. I reached up and used my thumb to wipe it away.

He smiled sadly and used his thumbs to do the same.

"It hurts me so much to see you in this much pain," he sighed.

"Thank you," I whispered.

"What?" he asked, confused.

"For letting me see the house, thank you."

"I love you." He smiled.

"I love you too," I sniffled, sitting up.

"Are you okay?"

"I will be." I nodded.

* * *

"That's not true." I laughed, setting my juice down.

"I think it is." Ty shrugged.

Carter entered the room and smiled when he saw me laughing.

"I'm glad to see your smiling face this morning." Carter grinned.

"I'm not happy to see yours," I mocked.

He playfully glared at me and then turned to Ty.

"Tyson you still going to that thing today?" he whispered swiftly to him. I don't know if they know I heard that but I'm getting pretty good at picking up what they are saying.

"I don't know if I should leave her," he whispered back.

I played with my bacon, pretending to be oblivious of the current conversation they were having.

"She seems fine," Carter encouraged.

"Hey babe?" Ty asked.

"You can go Ty." I sighed, pushing my plate to Carter so he could finish my bacon.

"You heard that?" He smirked.

"Indeed." I smirked back.

"Are you sure you're okay?"

"I'm fine babe."

"You could come with me."

"I don't really feel like going anywhere."

"Understood, and sorry to say this but Carter's in charge." He smiled.

I looked over at Carter and slapped my hand to my forehead.

"On second thought please stay," I begged.

"I'll be back in five hours tops, " he promised.

"Okay where exactly are you going?" I asked.

"I'm going to the Midnight Packs territory. They need help after being attacked," he said, kissing my head.

"Attacked? Ty that's not safe. I protested.

"It is love. I've done this before." He chuckled.

"Okay fine." I pouted.

"Hey Carter and you can go out in the city, get you out of the house just for a little bit at least."

"Okay." I shrugged.

"Okay I'll see you later baby." He smiled, pulling me into him.

I leaned up and pecked his lips. He smiled against my lips and then deepened the kiss. I heard Carter making gagging noises, which I laughed at and then pulled away.

"I love you." He smiled.

"I love you too." I grinned.

He left and I sat back down on the stool.

"You heard him. Go get dressed," Carter mocked.

"I don't feel like it," I started to say.

"Nope, go."

"Fine." I sulked, dragging myself upstairs.

I pulled on some skinny jeans and a white tank top with a pink and purple flower on it. I then pulled on some gray boots. I combed through my hair, brushed my teeth, and added some mascara to my eyes. I then walked back downstairs. Carter had changed too. He was now in jeans and a black tight shirt.

"Let's go." He smiled, leading me out to his car.

"Ew, you're driving."

"I'm a good driver," he protested.

"Sure you are," I muttered, getting into the passenger side.

"Do you want to drive?" He laughed, pulling out of the driveway.

"I would love to, but I don't have a license." I laughed.

"What? How old are you?" he asked.

"Eighteen."

"We've got to get you a license Aria." He laughed.

"Where are we going?" I asked.

"First we are going to McDonald's because I am hungry." "Carter we just ate," I groaned.

"We're going," he replied sternly.

"I miss Ty." I pouted.

"Why would you need Ty when you have me?" He snorted.

"Because I love him." I shrugged.

"I'm hurt that you don't like spending time with me."

"Just watch the road." I laughed.

We reached McDonald's, and Carter nearly sprinted in.

I sat down at a table and waited for Carter to bring the food. I had no idea what the idiot was going to bring me but whatever it was I'm sure I won't eat more than a quarter of it.

"Arrabella?" I heard someone ask.

I turned around to see Isaac. He was the reason my father made us move the last time, the reason I got beaten up almost every night.

I looked at him, tears forming in my eyes and stood up to get away from him; this hurt too much.

He grabbed my arm and tried to pull me in for a hug.

"Carter!" I screamed. Isaac seemed shocked at the scream that just came from my mouth. Carter appeared instantly.

"Let go of her!" Carter growled.

"Arrabella," Isaac demanded. I hid my face behind Carter.

"Back off man!" Carter threatened.

"I should be saying that to you. What have you done to her?" Isaac protested.

It was too much for me to take. My breath caught in my throat and it started closing up.

Isaac. He was my best friend when I was little. When I stopped talking he took it the worst. He would yell at me and try to get me to talk. When I was thirteen he kissed me and my father saw. That was the first move. Then this move was because Isaac found us and threatened to call the cops one night on my father.

"Arrabella breathe," Carter pleaded.

I was being thrown into the car and my throat was barely holding on.

The last thing I remember was screaming before everything went black.

Chapter 24

Dear Diary,

Isaac is back.

Ty wouldn't like him.

It's dark wherever I am right now, but oddly warm.

~Aria

"So how do you know her?" I heard Ty ask someone.

"I've known her since preschool," Isaac said.

Why is Isaac here? Wait, where am I?

"Aria, baby?" Ty asked.

"Mhm," I moaned.

"Open your eyes baby." He soothed.

I opened them and saw his face. I was in his room with him, Carter, and Isaac.

"Leave," I weakly told Isaac, looking him straight in the eye.

"When did you start talking again?" he asked.

"LEAVE!" I shouted.

"Carter," Ty growled.

Carter led Isaac out, and Ty sat next to me.

"What time is it?" I asked him.

"Three."

"I was out for four hours?"

"Yes." He chuckled.

"My legs don't work." I pouted.

"I know baby." He soothed.

"Why is Isaac here?"

"I don't know. You kicked him out." Ty chuckled.

"Right."

"Should I bring him back in?"

"Yeah."

"Help me sit up first."

"Okay." He smiled, pulling me up to a sitting position so I was leaning against one of the pillows.

Isaac and Carter walked back in, and Isaac looked relieved.

"Why are you here?" I asked him.

He came closer to the bed and sighed.

"I heard about your dad, so I figured this is the town you are in now."

"Why do you care?"

"You know that I've always cared about you."

"If that were true, you wouldn't have let me go through what I did!"

"You wouldn't talk to me."

"I couldn't!"

"You are now."

"Isaac, you knew what was going on. You knew about Trevor and my mom, you still kissed me and made me pay for it every night!" I yelled, letting a few tears roll down my face.

"What?" Ty growled.

"Ella, you know that I didn't know you were getting abused," he replied.

"Don't call me that," I warned.

"Fine. Just explain why you wouldn't talk to me."

"I couldn't Isaac. You think I didn't want to? Every day I wanted to."

"Then why didn't you?"

"You reminded me of her," I added, avoiding his questions.

"I know and I know now what he did to you, and I swear I didn't know back then how bad it was."

"Leave," I replied dryly, turning my head away from him.

"Ella," he started to say.

"Stop calling me that!" I warned.

"Come on."

"Ty make him go," I cried.

Ty's head snapped from me to Isaac and he nearly threw the latter out of the room. Carter followed after him. Ty then sat next to me and I leaned my head into his shoulder.

"Don't be upset baby," he begged.

"I'm not," I sniffled.

"What exactly happened between you two?"

"I don't want to talk about it," I replied, leaning my head back.

"Ar, I need to know so I know what to do with him."

"What?"

"Keep him around or not."

"I don't care." I shrugged.

"I think you do."

I tried to move but my legs still didn't work.

"You can't move babe. Don't strain yourself."

"Isaac was my best friend until I turned eight. I stopped talking, and he went crazy. I lost all my other friends, but he was adamant to get me to talk again. I would avoid him at school and take different routes home just so I didn't run into him. His mom and mine were good friends and so we knew each other for a long time. Then when we turned twelve he got so mad at me one day that he hit me. I wanted to shout at him so bad that I was already getting abused at home. He started trying to take control of me like he owned me or something. Then when we turned thirteen he kissed me and my father saw. We moved after that. My dad was so mad that Isaac still talked to me that I got beaten just because of it. Then Isaac found out where we moved and tried to apologize and get back into my life. That's why we moved here. Then he saw the story of the house burning down, came to this town, and ran into Carter and me at McDonald's."

"He hit you?" Ty growled.

"Ty stop," I pleaded, wrapping my arms around him to stop him from shaking.

"Aria, I need to get away from you."

"Calm down."

"I can't right now baby. I need you to let go of me."

"I missed you."

"I missed you too princess. Let go now."

I let my arms drop, and Ty stalked out of the room.

I heard him yelling at Isaac. How could he hit me when I was already being abused at home? I heard him ask Isaac why he was so obsessed with me. I also heard a stream of curse words directed towards him. I then heard some things break, a weird banging sound, and then silence. Isaac must have said something that made Ty stop.

I could hear their voices but I couldn't make out what was being said. I heard Carter say my name and Isaac add something. Ty must be keeping them from coming back in here.

I tried moving my legs again but it wasn't working. *Great. I guess it's just my thoughts and I.*

Isaac looked about the same. He's pretty tall now though standing around five feet eleven inches, I would guess. Ty's way taller than him and more built.

Isaac still had his sandy blonde hair and light brown eyes. Isaac's eyes are nothing compared to Ty's. Nobody's eyes are anything compared to Ty's.

"Hey Aria." Ty smiled. I smiled hugely when my eyes met his chocolate brown ones.

"What happened out there?" I asked.

"Nothing um, do you want to rest?"

"Lie down with me," I demanded, reaching for him. He chuckled and walked over to me.

"I love you," he whispered into my hair, helping me lie down.

"I love you more." I smiled.

"That's impossible." He smirked, turning his head to look at me after he lay down next to me.

"I love you more than you can even imagine." He grinned.

"Don't underestimate my brain Ty." I laughed.

"I don't, ever." He smiled, kissing my head again.

"Don't leave when I fall asleep, okay?"

"Okay baby." He smiled.

I snuggled into him and shut my eyes, knowing I would wake up looking into his eyes.

* * *

I woke up and looked over to see Ty had fallen asleep. I groaned when I realized my legs didn't work. I looked at the clock and realized I had only napped for an hour. *I wonder what Isaac and Carter are doing.*

"Ty," I whispered, shaking him slightly.

"Mhm?"

"I have to use the bathroom, but I can't walk." I pouted.

He smirked.

"Stop being a pervert and help me."

Ty got out of bed and carried me into the bathroom.

"Why do you always have to pee when you wake up?" He chuckled.

"I don't know. Ask my bladder." I smiled.

"How do you want to do this?"

"Well first put the lid down on the toilet." I said. He used his foot to do so.

"Then set me down." I shrugged. He set me down on top of the closed toilet and waited.

"Leave so I can pee," I said.

"Are you sure you don't need help getting your pants off?" He smirked.

"OUT!"

He chuckled and then left.

After using the bathroom, which was way harder than I expected it to be with legs that didn't work, I called for Ty.

"Can you lift me onto the sink so I can wash my hands?"

"Sure."

After washing my hands Ty carried me back into the bedroom. Isaac and Carter were in the doorway.

"Come in." Ty sighed.

He then set me on the bed so I was once again leaning against the pillow and then he sat next to me and placed my hand in his.

"I'm sorry you didn't get your McDonald's Carter." I smirked.

"Yeah, you owe me." He smiled.

"Um Isaac has something to tell you Ar," Tyson added.

"What?" I asked, turning my attention to him.

"First I have a question. Why was Tyson carrying you out of the bathroom?" he asked.

"I had to go to the bathroom."

"Why was he in there with you?"

"He wasn't. I called him in when I was done."

"Why couldn't you just walk out?"

"Dear Lord Isaac. My legs don't work after I get the gas to help me breathe. I don't just get carried around," I shot back, annoyed.

"Oh, that makes sense, but that was a valid question."

"What do you need to tell me?"

Ever since I was eight I was wondering what it would be like to hear those words come out of a person's mouth until now when it was actually happening and I just feel numb.

"I know where your mom is. She wants to be back in your life," Isaac said loud and clear.

I let sadness turn to anger, and in that second, I knew I will never be the same after this conversation about my mom. Mom. A daughter's first hero right? No, my mom will never be my hero.

Chapter 25

Dear Diary,
Mom.
My mom is wondering how I'm doing. I don't even think she
should be allowed to call herself a mother.
~Aria

"How are you in contact with her?"

"She contacted my mom after she got out of rehab, but you guys were already gone."

"She knew where we were."

"No, she didn't."

"Yes, she did. She didn't come back."

"Ella your dad was the one who sent her to rehab."

"She chose to go there."

"That's what your dad wanted you to believe."

"You're lying."

"I'm not." I've known Isaac for like my entire life and there was no evidence of a lie written on his face.

"So what exactly are you saying happened?"

"Your dad sent your mom to rehab after Trevor. He made it look like she was a drunk who beat herself up to kill her baby. She went so crazy in rehab they detained her longer. When she got out she went back to your house to get you, but you guys had moved. When I found out where you were, when you saw me, your mom was with me. You just didn't get a chance to see her. Then you guys left again, and we've both been trying to find you ever since."

"Where is she right now?"

"At the apartment we're renting."

"Where is your mother?"

"I'm eighteen Ella, and she understands that it is important for me to find you."

"Why?"

"I wanted to apologize."

"Thanks for telling me all of this but my mom was a drunk. She could have called the cops and gotten him for kidnapping. Most importantly though I don't care, she's not my mother."

"Don't say that Ella."

"Leave and tell her she's wasting her time."

"Okay we will give you some time." He shrugged, leaving.

"Tyson has my number when you decide to come to your senses."

"Are you okay?" Ty asked.

"I'm fine Tyson."

"Are you lying?"

"No," I mumbled.

"I'll be downstairs." Carter awkwardly chimed in.

"Okay," Ty replied, his eyes never leaving mine.

"Stop," I demanded, turning away from his captive stare.

He grabbed my chin in his hand and moved my head so my eyes were once again under his hold.

I shut my eyes and smirked.

"Arrabella."

"I'm fine Tyson," I said, keeping my eyes closed.

"Then look me in the eye and say it."

I opened my eyes, allowing myself once again to fall under his gaze.

"If my legs worked right now," I started to say.

He leaned in and gave me a smack on the lips. I giggled in surprise and let him fall over me.

"Just tell me baby," he whispered.

"Tell you what?" I asked, dazed.

"What's bothering you."

"Nothing," I whispered, leaning my head towards his lips once again.

"Tell me."

"There's nothing to tell."

"Aria," he teased, moving his lips down to the spot on my neck where he had marked me.

He kissed it, and I was already gripping onto his shirt in pleasure.

"Tell me or no kisses." He smirked.

"Do you really want to play this game with me?"

"No." He sighed.

"Thought so." I grinned.

He then rolled off of me and helped me sit up.

"Since I have you captive I find it only in your interest to tell me." He smirked.

"Why is that?" I laughed.

"I may just tickle you." He warned.

"Ty seriously nothing is bothering me." I groaned.

"I think there is babe." He shrugged.

"Well it could be that Isaac is trying to get back in my life, or the fact that my mom thinks she has the right to come see me after she let her husband abuse me for all my childhood."

"I know love but maybe you could talk with her."

"I just can't right now Ty, maybe I'll be able to eventually but right now I need you on my side."

"I will always be on your side Aria. I just want you to try and heal from all of this so you can move on."

"I know Ty. That's why I love you."

"I love you too." He chuckled.

* * *

"How much did you give her?" Ty asked the nurse. My legs still didn't work, and I was starting to get worried.

"She was barely breathing alpha. I waited to take it off until she gained control of her breathing."

"When will she be able to walk again?"

"I'm not sure. She's pretty tiny. It must just take longer for it to wear off."

"Okay, thank you." He sighed.

"I'm sorry baby," he said when he walked back over to the bed. He knows how much it tortures me when I can't walk.

"It's okay Ty. It's not your fault."

"Ar, why is it that you don't want to see your mother?"

"I don't want to talk about it," I replied, shutting my eyes.

"I think you should."

"I'm not going to."

"That's not healthy."

"Shh," I shushed.

"Ar." He groaned.

"I'm fine."

"Look at me."

I opened my eyes to meet his brown ones.

"She picked Trevor," was all I said.

"Yes, but she's been searching for you."

I sighed. I want to tell Ty the real reason I really do, but I'm afraid of what he will do, what he will say.

"Is there something else?" he asked, scrunching his eyebrows together like he always does when I confuse him.

"You're cute when you do that." I laughed.

"I'm not cute Ar."

"I think you are." I shrugged.

He rolled his eyes and kissed my cheek.

"Try to move your legs."

"I can't feel them."

Ty didn't really push me on the subject of my mom after that.

I can't tell Ty that if I see my mom I'm afraid I'll lose my voice again. I'm afraid of getting the feeling in my gut when I see her. She wasn't well most of my childhood. She used to be a good mom. When I was five she started drinking. My dad started abusing her verbally, then physically. Over the next few years his abuse directed towards me. When she found out she was pregnant she was happy again. I saw a light in her eyes that was beautiful. She started singing and laughing more. Even my dad seemed to be happy; he was going to have a son.

I remember helping pick out the name with them. Then I remember the fighting starting again. How the bills piled up and for a few days we didn't even have electricity.

When my baby brother was seven months old in my mother's womb he was murdered. He had his life snatched up before he even realized what life was.

"Aria wake up baby. You're dreaming." I heard someone soothe. I believe it was Ty.

I think I was crying but I was too lazy to open my eyes or make any effort to let him know I heard him.

"What about Trevor baby?" he asked.

"No, mom," I mumbled.

"What about mom?"

"I promise." I sighed.

"What do you promise?"

I recited what I told her a million times, growing up.

"I won't fight. I won't shout. I won't talk at all." I sighed then I felt myself slipping back into darkness.

* * *

I woke up in Ty's embrace. I don't think what happened last night was real, at least I hope not.

"Baby?" Ty asked.

"Yeah babe?" I asked, turning my head to look at him.

"So your legs work?"

I jumped up when I realized they did.

"Thank goodness I have to pee!" I shouted, running to the bathroom. I heard him chuckle.

I returned and sat back on the bed.

"Do you remember our conversation from about two this morning?"

"I'm not sure."

"What did your mom use to tell you?"

"Shit," I muttered.

"I don't think that was quite it," he teased.

"I didn't think that was a real conversation," I admitted.

"Are you afraid that if you see her you won't be able to talk?"

I nodded.

"I can stay in the room with you."

I had to face this. I know I do. I sighed and then I nodded my head in agreement. It's time to put on my girl pants and deal with this.

"Let's do it." I smiled.

Ty called up Isaac. They will meet us here at the house. When the doorbell rang, I felt my throat start to close.

"Don't think about it," Ty whispered.

He opened the door and just like I imagined, I saw my mother's face, and my voice vanished.

Chapter 26

Dear Diary,
I'm afraid I lost my voice.
I love talking and now it's once again been taken away from
me.
I hope I find it soon...
~Aria

"Come in." Ty politely motioned.

My mom entered, and we sat down in the living room. I saw Isaac waiting in the car for her.

My mom looked the same but slightly older. She let her blonde hair grow out; it was to her rib cage now. Her green eyes mirrored mine and when she smiled. She had dimples like me.

We sat down in the living room and I just stared at her, not knowing what to do. Ty took my hand and squeezed it lightly, assuring me everything was okay.

"I'm Tyson, Arrabella's boyfriend." Ty smiled.

"Boyfriend," my mom repeated, looking over at me.

"You sure have grown up to be beautiful Ella."

I nodded and gave her my "what do you want" look.

"I know you aren't happy with me."

I swallowed the lump in my throat and finally found my voice.

"I have every reason to be angry with you," I spat. The anger flowing through me like wild fire.

She seemed taken aback by my boldness.

"Ty can you give us a minute?" I asked.

"Of course." He smiled. He left and went into the kitchen and out of sight. I knew he could still hear us, however.

"I picked Trevor because I thought I could come back and get you."

"But you never did."

"I was sent to rehab."

"You got out, and you let him take me!"

"We had a no contact order."

"You could have called the cops and got him for kidnapping!"

"Ella in rehab I signed my rights over to him," she whispered.

"You gave me away?" I yelled.

"I had to in order to get out sooner."

"Leave."

"Ella, listen I never stopped looking for you." She sobbed.

"You knew he abused me!"

"I didn't know what to do."

"Isaac hit me. He was so mean to me and now what? You guys are living together?" I asked.

"Isaac is everything I wanted Trevor to be. That boy cares about you Ella. He was young and stupid but he has never touched another girl since that."

"I've had a shitty life until Tyson. I probably would have burned in that house if it weren't for him making me live here. Ty helped me find my voice again."

"I think Tyson's a lovely young man."

"You and Isaac need to leave."

"Why?" she asked, sounding hurt.

"I don't want to have everything I worked for fall apart."

"It won't. I just want to be back in your life." I looked at my mother's face, the woman who brought me into this world. I don't know if I could reject her. I am after all her only child. I want my mother to be a grandma to my children one day. I sighed and looked at her, offering a small smile.

"I think that might be a possibility."

"All Isaac wants is to be your friend."

"I know."

"Can I bring him in here?"

"Sure." She got out of her chair and went to the door.

I closed my eyes for a minute. I remember the day she left. I remember a guy escorting her out. Maybe she didn't want to make a scene in front of me.

She could have called, I think.

"Hey Ella." I heard Isaac greet.

"Hey."

"Your mom wanted to give us some privacy so she's in the kitchen with Tyson."

"Okay." I nodded.

"He seems to really care about you."

"Yeah he does." I smiled.

"He looks at you and all his eyes hold is love."

"He's really special."

"You think he's the one?"

"I know he is."

"Listen Ella, I'm so sorry for everything."

"I accept your apology. I want to say thank you for helping heal my mother. She really loved that baby. She loved him from the second she found about his existence," I sniffled.

"She loves you too Ella."

"Thanks Isaac." I smiled.

After they left Ty and I watched *Pitch Perfect*.

"Hey Ty?" I asked while he took the movie out.

"Yeah babe?" he replied, sitting back down on the couch.

"I want to meet your parents."

"My parents?" He repeated.

"Yes."

"They're really pushy babe."

"Pushy?" I asked.

"My mom will want to be your best friend and my dad will want us to mate."

"I want to meet them."

"Okay princess." He smiled.

"Does that make you happy?" I mocked. He was smiling like a small child, and it was so adorable.

"We have a party to plan." He smirked.

"A party?" I asked.

"When they come home, the pack gets together on the front lawn."

"The entire pack?"

"Are you up for that?"

"Yes," I said boldly.

"You sure?"

"Positive." I smiled.

* * *

"I don't know if I can do this" I panicked.

"Baby, you're perfect. Everyone will love you." Ty smiled in encouragement.

"Or they could all hate you, and you could be forever shunned by werewolves," Carter added sarcastically.

I looked at him in fear, which made him laugh.

"I'm kidding Aria. Everyone is really excited to meet you." He smiled.

"You're an idiot Carter," I muttered.

Ty laughed and grabbed my hand. We walked downstairs, and I could hear all the people outside.

I was wearing a purple dress with a brown leather jacket over it and brown cowboy boots to match. Ty is wearing a white button-down shirt with dark jeans and black shoes. He looks amazingly gorgeous.

"Be yourself princess. You're beautiful by the way." He smiled.

"I got this," I encouraged myself.

We walked outside hand in hand, and everyone looked in our direction beaming.

I offered a smile and Ty led me through the crowd and over to an older couple, I'm guessing his parents.

"There they are!" The women beamed, racing up to us and pulling me into a hug.

I was prepared for this because Ty told me to expect this from his mother, so I hugged her back until she let go.

"I'm so happy to meet you!" She smiled.

"Me too. I'm Aria." I grinned.

"I'm Emmalee, Tyson's mother."

She was a very pretty woman. She had blonde hair and blue eyes. She was pretty tall as well.

"I'm Tyson's dad, Dalton."

"It's nice to meet you. I'm Aria."

"You're so pretty." Emmalee chimed in.

"Thank you," I replied shyly.

Ty's dad looks a lot like Ty but older. His eyes are also a darker brown and not as vibrant and pretty as Ty's.

After Emmalee planned a girl's day out and Dalton talked about mating, Ty told them we were going to say hi to the other pack members.

I liked seeing Ty blush when his dad brought up mating.

"Jada." Ty smiled. I looked up at him, wondering why he was so happy to see her.

"This is Carter's mom, Jada." He introduced.

"No way." I laughed.

"Way, I can't believe I take credit for that kid." She shook her head. She was a very petite woman but taller than me. She had brown hair and she had Carter's pale blue eyes.

"Don't worry, I've been keeping him in line," I assured.

"Good to hear." She laughed.

"I can hear you." Carter pouted, walking over to us.

"Aw, don't pout." I teased.

"Mom, she's making fun of me," he protested.

"Carter's always been a pouter. In fact when he was seven," she started to say.

"MOM!" Carter cut off.

"Let her tell the story," I shushed.

"When he was seven his father told him that the ice cream truck only played music when it was out of ice cream, and when he found out the truth he sat in the driveway and pouted for three hours straight."

I started laughing so hard my stomach hurt.

"Okay mom that's great." Carter groaned.

"Speaking of my husband." She smiled when a man came over and grabbed her hand.

"This is Carter's dad and my husband, Joey." She introduced.

"Nice to meet you." I greeted, getting myself under control.

"The ice cream truck scam was one of my greatest successes," he added. He didn't exactly look like Carter but you could tell he was his father.

After talking with Carter's parents for a while Ty introduced me to some of the other pack members.

I met some really nice people. I also got to meet a lot of the children who live in the same house, which was great because I love babies.

"I'm exhausted," I said, crashing on the bed.

"They all loved you." Ty smiled, taking off his shirt and slipping off his pants and shoes, leaving him in boxers.

He then slipped on some sweatpants and joined me in bed.

"You were totally checking me out," he mocked, turning the lights off.

"You were totally checking me out all night." I laughed.

"I can't help it." He chuckled.

"You look like your dad."

"Yeah, but I'm more handsome," he said, and I could tell he was smirking.

"I don't know." I mocked.

"Were you checking my dad out?" he teased.

"Definitely," I replied sarcastically, laughing.

"I love you." He chuckled.

"I'm not sure how I feel about you," I whispered.

"What was that?" he asked, pulling me to him.

"I love you so much and you're sexier than everybody, even Taylor Lautner." I almost screamed before he started tickling me.

"So I've been told." He chuckled, loosening his grip slightly.

"Good night weirdo." I yawned.

"Night babe, love you," he whispered into my hair where he was now burying his head in.

"Love you." I smiled before slipping into the darkness.

Chapter 27

Dear Diary,

I like Ty's mom. She's like a best friend. Today we went to get our nails done.

It was my first time getting my nails done and it tickled so much when they used this sponge on my feet. Emmalee was laughing at me the entire time.

It was really fun. She's like the mom every girl would want.

~Aria

"So Aria owes me." Carter finished after giving Ty and me a full speech as to why I had to go to McDonald's with him.

"Fine." Ty sighed.

Carter's face lighted up, and he half sprinted out the door.

"Meet you in the car!" he called.

"Bye babe, love you." I laughed, hugging him.

"Love you," Ty replied.

I went out in the driveway and got into the car.

"Why couldn't you go by yourself?" I asked.

"No one wants to go to McDonald's alone." He shrugged.

"You're weird."

We went inside to get Carter's food to go, because apparently the drive through took too long.

"Can you go get napkins?" he asked me.

"Sure," I replied, walking over to the table.

"Um hi," a girl shyly greeted.

"Hey," I replied.

"Is that guy you're with your boyfriend?" she asked.

"No, he's my boyfriend's best friend." I laughed. *Carter my boyfriend? How ridiculous is that?*

"If I knew getting napkins was," he started to remark sarcastically but stopped short and stared in awe at the girl next to me.

"Mine," he whispered so fast and quietly I doubted the girl heard him.

I put his actions together and gasped.

This girl is Carter's mate! This poor girl!

"Hi." He greeted.

"Hi," she replied shyly.

"I'm Carter." He smiled.

"I'm Audrey." She smiled back.

"Wow, we sure know the right time to come to this place."

Carter rolled his eyes but laughed. It's true. First Isaac and now Carter finds his mate, he's going to be so whipped.

"This is my best friend's girlfriend, who I am babysitting," he added.

"Yeah you're babysitting me?" I scoffed.

Audrey laughed, which made Carter beam at her.

"Well do you want to hang out with us?" I asked because clearly these two could stand and stare at each other all day right in the middle of McDonald's.

"Sure." She nodded.

"Do you want to follow us back?" I asked.

"Yeah." She nodded.

"Cool, let's roll," I replied.

Audrey followed us back to the house and I sprinted out of the car when we got back to warn Ty.

"Hey what's wrong?" Ty asked, standing up from the couch.

"Nothing, Carter found his mate! She's human and coming inside right now!" I nearly shouted.

"No way!" He beamed.

Carter and Audrey came through the door, making Ty smirk.

"Audrey this is Tyson, Aria's boyfriend she was telling you about." Carter introduced.

"Hi nice to meet you." She greeted.

"You too." He smiled down at the blonde brown eyed girl.

"Well if you excuse us I have to surprise my girlfriend now," Ty replied.

"What?"

"Shh," Ty shushed.

"I don't like being shushed," I protested while he led me to his car.

He chuckled as he held the door open for me.

We drove around for a while until a small building came into view.

"You my love are getting your license today." He smiled.

"What? How?" I grinned.

"You just have to go in there and pass a written and behind the wheel test." He shrugged.

"Okay." I smiled.

* * *

"I passed!" I smiled, showing him the paper.

"I told you." He grinned, leading me over to where I have to get my picture taken.

"Arrabella!" The lady called.

I went up to the desk, signed my name, and let her take my picture.

After waiting for a while they gave me a piece of paper that serve as my temporary license until the card got mailed to me.

"Thank you for doing this Ty," I said on the drive back to the house.

"Anything for you babe." He smirked.

"Carter is going to be so fun to tease." I smiled.

"I feel bad for the poor girl." He nodded.

"He should tell her about werewolves soon though," I added.

"You can't just spring it on someone Ar." He scoffed.

"If it were me I would."

This made him go into a laughing fit.

"You a wolf." He laughed.

"Jerk," I muttered, punching him in the arm.

"Okay, okay." He surrendered.

When we arrived back at the house Carter and Audrey were sitting on the couch. I heard a familiar movie playing but it wasn't until I stepped into the room and saw it that I recognized it.

"You guys are watching *Titanic*?" I nearly shouted.

Audrey nodded and smiled, and Carter gave me a warning glance.

"Carter's watching—" I couldn't finish the sentence because I started laughing. In fact, Ty came over to help hold me up.

"Bye Aria," Carter added.

"Bye dork." I laughed, walking past him.

"Oh, and I am now officially a licensed driver." I gloated.

"Way to go kid!" He smiled, holding his hand up for a high five, to which I happily obliged as I walked by.

I heard him whisper something to Audrey, which made her smile and blush. I rolled my eyes and headed upstairs with Ty.

"He's already turning soft." I smiled, sitting on the bed.

"Mates can do that." Ty chuckled.

"Aww is Ty a softie?" I asked in a mocking voice.

"No." He grumbled.

"Yeah right." I scoffed.

"I could go a long time without giving into you."

"Fine then let's make a deal."

"Let's hear it."

"I bet you that you can't go all of tomorrow without giving into me." I smirked.

"Deal." He smirked.

"This means you can't do anything you wouldn't have done before you met me."

"Like what?"

"Girl movies or anything I make you do." I smiled.

"Also, you can't call me any names like princess," I added. That one will get him.

"And if I win?"

"I'll be your slave for an entire day." I smiled.

"And if you win I'll be yours." He grinned.

"Exactly."

All I can say is tomorrow was going to be one hell of a day.

Chapter 28

Dear Diary,

Yesterday I became a licensed driver!

Also, Ty and I made a deal.

I'm so going to win. There is no way Ty can go an entire day without giving into me.

I'll keep you posted...

~Aria

I woke up and smirked when I realized today was the day I prove Ty wrong.

I got out of bed to go to the bathroom and then climbed back in and sat on Ty's tummy.

"Wake up."

Ty pulled me off of him and lay me back down next to him.

I was impressed because he hadn't even opened his eyes!

"Ty." I groaned.

"Shh," he shushed.

"How many times do I have to tell you I don't like being shushed?"

"Shh."

"Oh hell no."

"Shh," he shushed. This time letting out a small chuckle.

"I want to watch a movie," I whined.

"Okay babe just go–I mean no go back to sleep." I laughed at him. He almost lost the bet already!

I didn't say anything. I just lay there with my eyes open.

"It's just that I'm not tired."

"Arrabella James."

"I bet if I watched a movie I would become tired."

Ty flipped me around so I was face to face with him. I finally got to stare into those brown eyes of his.

"Ty," I squealed, pecking his lips.

"Do you really think you could win the bet this early in the morning?" he asked in amusement.

"I almost did," I grumbled.

"Almost," he whispered, bringing his lips to mine.

"Nope." I smirked, pulling away from him. He rolled his eyes and I rolled mine back, making me realize that I was actually still tired.

"Well night." I said, cuddling him.

"Night babe." He chuckled.

* * *

"So then I asked her to be my girlfriend, and she said yes!" Carter beamed.

"Is she coming over again today?" Ty asked.

We were currently sitting on the couch watching sports, much to my dislike, and Carter was telling us about his night with Audrey.

"You should tell her about wolves tonight," I added.

"No way," Carter replied.

"Fine make her mad when you tell her," I sighed.

"Why would she be mad?" he asked worriedly. I laughed at his worried face.

"Because you kept it from her, plus she's probably going to be scared at first." I shrugged.

"Help me."

"When are you going to tell her?"

"Not tonight but the next time I see her."

"So tomorrow?" I grinned.

"OH NO!" Ty screamed at the television.

"They can't hear you."

"Come on baby, interception!"

"I like the team in the blue and orange jerseys." I said.

Ty and Carter looked over at me like I had just told them Hannah Montana and Miley Cyrus were the same person.

"What?" Carter laughed.

"What team do you guys want to win? The purple and yellow ones?" I asked.

"Purple and gold," Carter corrected.

"I don't think those two colors go well together," I added.

"Are you kidding me?" Ty laughed.

"You can't just choose the Bears over the Vikings," Carter stated.

"I just did." I shrugged.

"I don't think I can look at you the same way ever again," Carter replied dramatically.

"Can we watch a movie now?" I complained.

"No." Ty chuckled.

"This is boring," I whined.

"No." I stood up and sat down on Ty's lap so I was straddling him. He smirked at me, knowing this was one of my tactics to win.

"Please," I pleaded.

"No," he protested.

"Please," I whispered, touching my lips to his.

He kissed me back but I kept my mouth shut.

He knew I would do this so he moved his hands down to my butt, making me pull away.

I got off his lap and sat on the other end of the couch.

"What is going on with you two?" Carter asked amused.

"A bet." I smiled.

"Well if it's to make Ty's wolf go crazy then you're winning." He chuckled.

Ty stood up and sat next to me, grabbing my hand. I laughed knowing that it was working so I stood up once again sat on the other side of the couch that Ty was just on.

"Arrabella." He warned.

"Tyson," I mocked.

He rolled his eyes and picked me up only to set me down on his lap again.

I snuggled into him, knowing I could get him later.

* * *

"Well then I'm not going to eat." I shrugged.

I knew this would get him! He had ordered a pizza and I told him I wanted to have Chinese instead, however Carter and Audrey ate all the Chinese last night, so I think victory is coming my way.

"Come on Ar." Ty groaned.

"No." I smirked.

"Please," he begged, pecking my lips.

"Nope," I replied, jumping off the stool and heading into the living room.

"Playing dirty?" Carter smirked, giving me a fist pump.

"Always." I smiled, sitting down next to Audrey.

We were all going to watch a movie together tonight.

"Have you ever seen *Twilight* Audrey?" I asked.

"I love *Twilight*," she squealed.

"Me too. We should watch it." I smirked.

"Sure." Carter shrugged, smiling at Audrey because this made her so happy.

"Seeing that *Twilight* has werewolves and vampires on a killing spree I don't think it's classified as a chick flick." Ty smirked.

"Fine." I shrugged, knowing in about ten minutes he would give in on the food.

"You're still going to lose anyways," Carter whispered to Tyson.

"Yeah like you could win. You're sitting here watching a movie that you told Aria you'd never be caught dead watching." Ty smirked.

"Because I know for a fact the book is better," he defended.

"No way you actually did read the book?" I shouted.

"You thought I was kidding?" Ty laughed.

"I was interested in the werewolf portion," he hinted.

"Sure," I scoffed.

I remember Ty telling me a while ago that Carter had read it and I thought he was joking!

Ty sat down next to me and he handed me a plate with pizza on it. I smirked and set it on the ground.

Ty rolled his eyes, and I held back a laugh.

After about ten minutes of Twilight Ty wouldn't stop sighing and groaning. I cannot believe that me not eating bugged him this much!

"Look at me Ar." Ty demanded.

I looked over at him and let a small laugh escape my lips. He pouted and then pulled me onto his lap.

"Please eat," he begged, pecking my lips.

"Nope," I whispered.

"Please for me."

"No." I shook my head.

He sighed and I slid off his lap.

"You win babe," he said in defeat. Carter started laughing, and I kissed Ty.

"I always do." I joked, picking up the pizza and eating it.

"No way," he said amused.

"Way," I replied, taking a bite of the pizza.

"Then the bet is still on!" he announced.

"No way you said I win!" I nearly shouted.

"That was to throw you off but you ate the pizza so you gave into me." He smirked.

"Carter, tell him," I demanded.

"I'm sorry, but I have to go with Tyson. He would have had to gotten the Chinese food for you to win."

"UGHHH!" I groaned.

"I love you." He smiled.

"I'm still going to win."

"Sure." He grinned.

* * *

An hour later and I have not spoken a word. I think Ty thinks that I'm just into the movie, but really it's time for silent treatment. I know it's a low blow but it's my last chance to win!

"No way! Aria who do you think is better looking? Jacob or me?" Carter demanded.

I shrugged in response.

"Silent treatment?" He laughed.

I nodded, smiling at him.

"Silent treatment?" Ty repeated, turning me to face him.

"Are you serious?" He panicked.

I nodded, using my best poker face.

"Oh hell," he muttered.

The movie went off, and I waved to Carter and Audrey and headed upstairs. I walked into Ty's room and slipped on some sweatpants.

"You're seriously not talking to me?" Ty sighed.

I nodded, grinning.

"I bet I can make you."

I shrugged.

He then walked over to me and pushed me against the wall. Instead of kissing me like I had thought, he started tickling me.

I pushed his hands away.

"If you want me to stop you better say it," he teased.

I laughed and pushed at his hands. I did the first thing that came to my head I started to breathe heavily. Ty immediately stopped.

"Are you okay?" I nodded, gasping for dramatic effect.

"NURSE!" He screamed.

I got myself under control right as the nurse ran in.

"Yes alpha?" she asked. I glared at the gas mask in her hands.

"We're fine. Are you fine?" he asked.

I nodded.

The nurse left and Ty looked at me and cocked his head to the side.

"Was that just a tactic to get me to stop?" he asked amused.

I shook my head and ran out of the room and into the purple room across the hall.

I sat on the bed and waited for Ty to enter. He did a second later and I smirked at him.

"Let me guess you're sleeping in here tonight?" He smirked back.

I nodded.

"I don't think so," he replied, picking me up and carrying me back into the bedroom. He set me down and I raced back into the other room.

"Arrabella!" He demanded, entering.

I cocked my head to the side and grinned.

"I can do this all night." He challenged, picking me up and carrying me back into the bedroom. He set me down and this time blocked the doorway.

I pushed at him and he smiled down at me. I turned around and sat on the bed. Ty looked at me skeptically and shut the door, joining me on the bed.

I lay down and sighed.

"Finding it hard not to talk?" he asked.

I didn't make any move to indicate I heard him. He then pulled me into him, which made me push at him and scoot away from him. I didn't look at his face though because one look into those eyes and I would melt and he would win.

I saw his hand coming over to my chin and I bolted out of the room. I ran downstairs just as Carter was shutting the door after Audrey had left.

I ran behind him as I heard Ty sprinting behind me.

"Hand her over." Ty chuckled.

I held onto Carter, hoping he would side with me.

"Hmm, Aria should I?" he mocked.

I shook my head and smiled.

"What would I get in return for handing the girl over?" Carter teased.

"Carter." Ty demanded.

Carter chuckled and grabbed my arm and handed me to Ty. I let my mouth drop in shock.

"Sorry kid." Carter laughed, walking away.

Ty then turned me to face him, forcing me to look into those brown eyes of his.

"What do I have to do to make you talk?" I smirked and wrote on a piece of paper 'Tell me that I win.'

"You win princess. I love you way too much to not give into that face of yours." He sighed.

"I love you." I laughed. He rolled his eyes but beamed at the sound of my voice.

"I am unbelievably in love with you as well." He chuckled, pulling me into his chest.

"Get ready starting tomorrow you are my slave." I smiled, running up the steps. *This idiot better be ready, my idiot.*

Chapter 29

Dear Diary,

I'm meeting with my mom today.

I just haven't told Ty yet because Isaac will also be there for a while.

No surprise here Diary but I need you to wish me more luck.

~Aria

I woke up and turned to see Ty still in a peaceful sleep. I smiled and pecked his lips. He smiled when I pulled away and then opened his eyes.

"What do you want?" He chuckled.

"Oh nothing." I sang, standing up.

I wasn't fast enough though because Ty grabbed my hand and yanked me back onto the bed.

"TY!" I laughed.

"You expect me to believe you don't want anything?"

"Well you're my slave today."

"I know babe." He laughed.

"So I command you to let me go." He chuckled but let me up.

"So you're actually going to have an easy day because I'm going to my mom's." I swiftly added, bouncing downstairs.

"Back up. What?" he asked, following me. I reached the kitchen and then turned back around to face him.

"I'm going to my mom's."

"First, it's not going to be an easy day. I'd rather you be bugging the hell out of me than for us to be apart, and second why did you think I'd be opposed to that?"

"I don't know. You're weird and possessive."

"I am not." He pouted.

"Wait for it. Isaac will be at the house."

"No."

"That's what I thought, so my mom and I are going out."

"Out?"

"Yes, to lunch." I smiled.

"Without Isaac?"

"Yes." I laughed.

"How are you getting there?" He groaned.

"Your car." I smiled.

"Come on. I'm your slave for the day. Can I drive you?"

"No." I said like he had before.

He fake glared at me and then attacked my lips. I laughed and pushed at his chest.

"I have to go get ready." After I put on a nice summer dress and some sandals I headed downstairs.

"That's what you're wearing?" Ty asked.

"Oh, does it look okay?" I asked, looking down.

"You look beautiful, but I don't want other guys," he started to say.

"Hush." I cut him off.

"You're going right to lunch, correct?" I looked up into his eyes and sighed, I can't lie to him.

"Ar?" He demanded.

"I'm going in to visit Isaac and then my mom and I will leave."

"Visit?" he sighed.

"I don't like that either," Carter chimed in, popping out of nowhere.

"What the hell, Carter," I groaned.

"I'm just saying that Isaac still likes you," Carter said defensively.

"That's not even true!" I shouted.

"Stop!" Ty demanded.

"Carter, I know you feel protective of her but she doesn't understand so please go back to training," Ty ordered.

Protective? Carter has no right to tell me where I can't go! Neither does Ty for that matter.

"Don't be mad." Ty sighed.

"Don't tell me what to do and don't you dare tell me I don't understand!" I shouted, walking past him and out the door.

"What do you want me to say Arrabella? Go ahead and see your mother who left you with that disgusting man, go see the guy who hit you? It kills me Aria. It kills me. I want you to have a relationship with your mother, and I want you to able to go hang out with your old friend but something in here," he said, pointing to his gut. "Is telling me this isn't a good idea."

"It's just my mom."

"Carter is a beta. He naturally feels protective of you, and even he is getting a bad vibe. I don't know if I can let you go."

"It's not up for debate," I replied, getting in the car and locking the door.

I had grabbed Ty's keys this morning because I knew this would happen. I knew Ty would do this.

He banged on the door and I didn't look him in the eye. I just started the car and drove off. This was one hell of an idea.

* * *

I pulled up to the house and thought about just turning around. I feel awful about my fight with Ty. I mean that was our first big one.

I walked up to the house and knocked on the door.

My mom answered and gave me a welcoming smile.

"Hey," I greeted.

"Isaac actually isn't in right now. Let's just go he'll be back when we get back." She smiled.

"Okay." I nodded.

I drove us to Olive Garden and we were seating waiting for our food to arrive.

"So when did you get your license?" My mom asked.

"Not that long ago. Ty helped me," I replied, looking down.

"What's the matter?" she asked.

"We had a fight," I sniffled.

"A fight?" she asked worriedly.

"Not a fist fight mom. He's never laid a hand on me."

"What about?"

"It doesn't matter."

"Alright," she sighed.

"Look I know you said Dad made you go but why didn't you try harder?" I whispered.

"I wrote you a letter every day when I was in there; they are in a chest at the house Isaac and I are renting. When we go back I want you to take them." She smiled.

"Why didn't you send them?" I asked.

"I had a no contact order with your father." She sighed.

I nodded.

We then talked about other things like summer and shopping.

I drove us back and walked in the house with her.

"Here take these on out," she told me, handing me a box of letters. I walked out and set them in the car.

I walked back in to see Isaac and my mother talking.

"Hey Ella." He smiled.

"Hi."

"You and Ty fighting?"

"Yeah but we will work it out."

"I want to tell you something Ella," he said, coming closer.

"Yeah?"

"I've always felt a pull towards you and I never knew what it was until now. I love you," he whispered.

"No, Ty loves me."

"Maybe he does but you and I are good together. We have been since preschool."

I looked over his shoulder to see my mother had disappeared.

"Ty's never hit me," I replied harshly.

"I didn't mean to."

"Bye Isaac," I replied, turning around.

"No, I won't lose you again!" I felt someone pull me back and away from Isaac. I turned to see Ty. I slinked away from both of them, ran out, and sat in the car.

Tyson was out about five seconds later. He started the car and drove. I'm assuming we are headed home.

I didn't say anything. I just stared out the window and focused on my breathing.

"Are you okay?" Ty asked, breaking the silence.

I nodded.

"Don't you dare give me the silent treatment." I nodded again.

"I wanted to let you go today. I could have stopped you, stood in front of the car. I let you drive off and I ran after you. I waited for you and then followed the car to the house. I was trying to give you your space and let you have this."

I nodded and let the tears slide down my cheek. The car stopped and I realized we were already back at the house.

"Come here baby." He soothed, unbuckling my seatbelt and pulling me onto his lap.

We sat like that for a while until my tears gave out and I slowly felt myself drifting away.

Chapter 30

Dear Diary,
Ty and I had a big fight last night.
I have nothing to say anymore. I feel like my chest has been
ripped out.
~Aria

I woke up in Ty's arms as usual. It wasn't until my heart ached that I remembered the events of the evening before.

"Hey beautiful." Ty smiled. I smiled at his brown eyes.

"That's not an Aria smile." He pouted.

"Don't be nice to me." I sighed, sitting up.

"What?"

"You should be mad at me."

"I told you. You made the decision to go." He shrugged.

"Why aren't you mad?"

"Do you know what it's like to watch the love of your life cry herself to sleep? I do. I don't want it to happen again."

"I'm sorry," I whispered.

"You shouldn't be." He smiled, kissing my head.

"Is that the chest my mom gave me?" I asked, noticing it in the corner of the room.

"Yeah it was in the car." Ty shrugged.

"Yeah." I sighed.

"So Isaac," he started to say.

"Isaac will just have to get over it."

"Okay." Ty chuckled.

"Um, I'll be right back," I replied, leaving the room. I walked downstairs and took a deep breath.

I sat on the stool next to Carter and thought about what to say for a minute. Luckily, he went first.

"You worried me yesterday," he said, turning to face me.

"I didn't know betas worried about the alpha's mate."

"They have the instinct and its worry for me as well because I actually care about you," he mocked.

I fake glared at him, making him chuckle.

"I'm sorry."

"Me too kid." He smiled.

"Just next time take my side okay?" I commented, getting off the stool.

"Don't worry I got your back," he teased.

"Bye dork!" I called, racing back upstairs.

I walked back into the bedroom where Ty was waiting for me with a small smile on his face.

"What?" I laughed.

"You're cute." He shrugged, pulling me in for a hug.

"Ugh bladder!" I shouted, running into the bathroom. I don't know why I always have to pee in the morning. Maybe it's because I go eight hours without going and then my bladder gets stunned or something. Yeah that has to be it. Look at me making conclusions. I should be a scientist or something.

I walked out of the bathroom and then took Ty's hand and led him downstairs.

"Carter!" I shouted because he wasn't in the living room like I assumed.

"What?" Carter asked, instantly showing up.

"You can't put it off any longer. We have to plan how you are going to tell Audrey." I smirked.

"Maybe it can wait," he mumbled.

"Carter it can't."

"I don't know if I can handle it." He sighed.

"You're going to tell her you're a werewolf and you're afraid you can't handle it?" I asked in disbelief, playing with Ty's fingers. He was currently watching Carter and my conversation, amusement flooding his vibrant brown eyes.

"It's hard Aria. After Tyson told you I thought you would never talk to us again."

"You're so dramatic." I smiled.

"Help."

"Aww, look who is begging for my help." I smirked.

"Don't push it."

"I think the way Ty told me was good." I shrugged.

"You do?" Ty asked in disbelief.

"Yeah Audrey can't be mad at you for lying since you guys have only been dating for a week plus after you show her your wolf I can talk to her."

"Really?" He beamed.

"Yeah." I shrugged.

"Yes, okay tonight then." He nodded.

"Sure." I laughed.

* * *

"Okay Audrey and I are going in the woods now," Carter hinted, taking her hand.

"Okay I'll be here." I smiled.

Carter nodded and Audrey waved at me. I waved back and shook my head at that boy. I mean he's so worked up over this. If Audrey feels about Carter the way I feel about Ty he has nothing to worry about.

"What's that smile for?" Ty asked, making me jump slightly.

"Oh sorry. Did I scare you?" Ty laughed.

"I was just in deep thought idiot." I giggled. He then lifted me out of my seat to sit back down and place me on his lap. I snuggled into him and sighed in content.

"Do you know what you are going to say to Audrey?"

"Yeah I have an idea." I laughed.

"Let's hear it."

"You can hear it later," I protested, knowing he and Carter would both hear the conversation.

"I guess that's my only choice. She's on her way back now and she's running," Ty added.

"Good luck. It's probably best I'm not around." He chuckled.

"Bye babe, love you."

"Love you!"

The door flew open and her brown eyes landed on me.

"Aria we have to get out of here!" She screamed.

"Come on." I laughed, motioning her to follow me.

She looked at me like I was crazy but followed me up the stairs. I led her to the game room and sat in the bean bag. She sat in the one across from me.

"We need to make a plan and run for it," she sniffled, letting a few tears escape.

"Why?" I asked.

"They're wolves!"

"Yeah they are, and we happen to be their mates."
I nodded.

"Mates they use to make wolf children with?" she nearly screamed.

"No, it's like a soul mate," I explained. I was trying to sound calm and like an expert. I really don't know what the hell I'm talking about! However right now it feels natural as if we were talking about the weather.

"Soul mate?"

"Yeah like love at first sight, which is why you two couldn't tear your eyes away from each other in McDonald's."

"I just don't like wolves or even dogs."

"I'm going to tell you my story, okay?"

She nodded and waited eagerly.

"Ever since I was eight I was abused by my father. He shoved peanut butter down my throat to prevent me from talking because I'm allergic to peanut butter. I stopped talking for ten years. I only just started again about six months ago when Ty found me. He helped me to talk again and not be so scared. I still sometimes have trouble and Ty's like the one person I can always count on. He loves me more than anyone could love a person. When I walk into the room and see him I get a feeling that I can't even explain. I'm telling you this because I freaked out after Ty told me about werewolves. The only thing that makes them different is their love for their mate. They are stronger and faster than most but they use that to protect their mate."

"Aria I'm so sorry that happened to you." She sobbed.

"Don't cry. It's in the past and that won't dictate my future." "So Carter's my soul mate?"

"Yes." I laughed.

"I guess I don't feel so stupid now."

"What?" I laughed.

"Well I thought I was crazy. The butterflies in my stomach when I see Carter, and I always think about him." I nodded and couldn't help the smile, knowing Carter was hearing this right now.

"Plus," she went on. "His blue eyes make me want to never look away from them. I've never seen anything so blue."

"I know the feeling." I nodded.

"It's just scary."

"Listen, Carter's going to bug the hell out of you but in the best way possible." I smiled.

"Has Ty ever hurt you?"

"No, no. Ty and I play around all the time. You'll see they use their strength to piss you off not hurt you." I laughed.

"I should've known. Ty's entire face lights up whenever he looks at you or even just when you talk."

"Really?" I blushed.

"Yeah." She laughed.

"Plus, Carter trusts you to keep this secret," I added.

"That's true." She smiled.

"But we have power over them as well."

"Like when you and Tyson had that bet?" She laughed.

"Yeah all you have to do is cry, not even that, and you have them in the palm of your hand." I laughed.

"This is going to be fun!"

"Totally." I nodded. "Do you feel better?"

"Yes, thank you Aria." She smiled, standing up. I stood up as well and it surprised me when she pulled me in for a hug.

"Do you want to go find the idiots?" I asked.

"Yeah." She blushed. I laughed and led her downstairs. Carter eagerly stood up off the couch. We made it to the bottom. Audrey looked a little scared, so I gave her a reassuring smile and she walked over and hugged Carter.

I beamed at the two and then ran to Ty.

He chuckled and kissed my head.

"Good work princess."

Dear Diary,
I finally understand what a mate is.
~Aria

Chapter 31

Dear Diary,
Audrey and Carter are so cute together! She's becoming more
comfortable with the whole wolf thing.
Also, I love Ty.
That's all I got for now.
~ Aria

"You were just acting like a Luna," Ty said proudly.

"I wasn't trying to." I shrugged, taking another spoonful of Lucky Charms and shoving it into my mouth.

Ty was telling me that I was acting like a "Luna," also known as alpha female, while talking to Audrey the other day.

"You're a natural." He beamed.

"You're a psycho." I accused.

"Say psycho again."

"PSYCHO!"

"It wasn't a challenge. You have an accent when you say that word." He laughed.

"I do not." I pouted.

"Don't pout angel, it's cute." He chuckled.

"Hey children." Carter smiled, walking into the kitchen.

"We're alphas, making you the child," I protested.

"Ty is alpha. You are only half." Carter corrected.

"What?" I asked.

"You aren't fully the alpha female until you and Ty completely mate." He smirked.

I blushed and smacked Carter.

"Ow, I was just saying," he said dramatically.

"So is Audrey coming over today?" Ty asked.

"Yep everything is in action." Carter smirked.

"What's in action?" I asked.

"You'll see." Carter smirked, leaving the kitchen.

"Spill."

"Nope." Ty grinned.

"Come on." I whined.

"It's a surprise." He chuckled.

"Ty."

"Aria."

I rolled my eyes. I'll just have to make him talk. I got off of the stool and headed upstairs. Knowing Ty would follow me. I sat on the bed. He walked in a second later smiling, knowing what I was about to do.

"Come here." I laughed.

He sat down and I straddled his lap.

I leaned in and basically attacked those lips of his. I could kiss Ty all day forever. It's a feeling that I never get tired of. It's like a thousand butterflies erupting in my stomach.

Just as things were heating up, I pulled away, got off his lap, and walked out of the room and back downstairs.

"Arrabella!" Ty called. I was already laughing and running into the kitchen. I went beyond the kitchen and found myself in an unfamiliar hallway. I went to the door straight ahead and opened it to find an office. I shrugged and sat down behind the bookcase. I heard the door open and I held my breath.

"I know you're in here babe!" I heard Ty call.

I let out my breath and waited.

I felt two hands grab me, making me scream.

"Found my office, did you?" Ty asked amused as he sat down in office chair and pulled me onto his lap.

"This is your office?" I asked surprised.

"Yep, look," he said, pointing to the screen saver on his computer. My mouth nearly dropped to the floor. It was a picture of me sleeping!

"You took a picture of me sleeping?" I shouted.

"Yeah, you're so damn cute." He chuckled, kissing my head.

"Why in hell did you upload it to your computer and make it your screen saver?" I asked, slapping my hand against my forehead.

"Because I like looking at it when I'm going through papers." He shrugged.

"When do you do that?"

"I did it the other day when you were out with Carter, mostly while you take a shower and then when I hear the water turn off I stop and go back upstairs."

"What do you have to do?"

"Just pack things." He shrugged.

There was a knock on the door, and Ty looked over and sighed.

"Yeah?" He called. Then Carter poked his head in.

"Audrey's here." He informed.

"Great." Ty smirked, lifting me off his lap and grabbing my hand.

We walked out and Audrey was in the living room waiting.

"We are taking you two on a date," Carter excitedly announced.

"We're going on a double date?" I asked.

"Yeah." Ty chuckled.

"You shall see when we get there," Carter replied dramatically.

"You're so dramatic." I grumbled, making Ty laugh and Carter roll his eyes.

I was bouncing in my seat, literally, making everyone in the car make fun of me. I just couldn't help it; surprises were never something I could handle. I mean I just like knowing!

"We're here." Ty laughed, shooting me a heart-stopping smile.

"YES!" I screamed, getting out of the car.

I looked around and saw tracks. They looked like racetracks.

"Are we go-karting?" I smiled.

"And we have a winner!" Carter announced.

"Yes! I'm such a good driver!" I grinned.

"Yeah right," Ty added in.

"I really am," I protested.

We got our karts and lined up. I had Ty to my right and Audrey to my left. Then Carter was next to Audrey. *I am so going to win!* Whoever made it over the white line first won.

"GO!" TY shouted. We took off and I was already laughing. I saw Ty shooting glances my way. I'm pretty sure he's a little worried since we were racing in death machines. I saw Carter giving Audrey the same glances, making me smile. I was in the lead until somehow Carter and Ty got way in front of Audrey and me! They were racing to the finish line, and from where Audrey and I were standing we couldn't tell who won! I saw Ty get out of his cart and gesture to his well you know, downtown, so I'm pretty sure he just told Carter to suck it.

Audrey and I made it back; I at least beat her, and got out of our carts.

"Did you win babe?" I asked, hugging his waist.

"I always win," he protested.

"Not against me."

"Not emotionally. "

"Fine you and I right now then." I challenged.

"You're on." He grinned.

We got back in our go-karts, Carter watching us amused and Audrey giving me a thumbs up in encouragement.

"GO!" Carter screamed.

I started off fast and whipped around the corner. Once around it I pressed harder and harder on the gas. I slowed down a little at the next turn. Ty however didn't and he raced past me. I sped up but it didn't work. Ty beat me.

I got out and punched him.

"Ow, be a good sport."

"I am." I sighed.

He lifted my chin up, making me smile at his brown eyes.

"You win no matter what princess."

"I know," I mocked, going on my tiptoes to peck his lips.

"I love you," he whispered.

"I love you too psycho."

"Hey Carter listen to how she says psycho," Ty called. Carter and Audrey were currently sitting on a bench, smiling at each other.

"I heard her, you from the south or something?" he mocked.

"Shut up," I muttered.

After that we got ice cream and went back home with Carter explaining how Audrey distracted him during the race otherwise he would have won.

I however don't care about that. I had a great time tonight and for the first time I felt like I have a family.

Dear Diary,

I learned something tonight. It was my first official date with Ty.

Anyways I realized that family doesn't necessarily mean the people you are blood related to. It's the people who come into our lives and never leave. I'm so happy Ty will be in my life forever.

~Aria

Chapter 32

Dear Diary,
You're almost out of pages.
I don't know what I'm going to do about this.
~Aria

"Arrabella quit it." Ty laughed. I had been repeatedly poking him in the side for the past five minutes.

"Admit it!" I shouted.

"Fine I went soft," he mumbled.

"Aww I know babe." I laughed.

Ty stiffened slightly, making me look over at him in question. I didn't have time to ask him what's wrong because the doorbell rang. I jumped up, making Ty grab me back down.

"I was going to get the door."

"It's your mom."

"Oh, well that's fine. I'll still get it." Ty released my arm, and I walked over to answer the door.

"Ella." My mom smiled.

I stepped outside and shut the door behind me.

"What are you doing here?"

"Can't I come see you?"

"You should call first, especially after what happened the last time you saw me."

"Isaac just snapped Ella. You have to understand the position he's in."

"Why are you defending him?"

"You didn't read the letters, did you?" my mom sighed.

"No. I can't say I have."

"Well call me when you have." She sighed, walking away. I groaned in frustration and stomped back inside.

"Are you okay?" Ty asked, standing up.

"I'm fine," I replied, walking past him and up the stairs.

I turned back around to see him, advancing toward me.

"Just don't follow me, okay?"

"Why?" He worried.

"I need to be alone for a while," I said, walking upstairs.

"Ar," he started to say.

"I'm fine, promise," I called. I walked into the bedroom and shut the door. I then went over and sat in front of the chest.

I opened it to find a stack of letters.

There was one from everyday my mother was in rehab, every damn day.

A tear escaped my eye from just knowing she wrote me every day. I then picked up the letter that just had "Arrabella" written on it and no date.

I opened it and started to read over what my mother had written.

Arrabella,

I will be giving you this chest of my letters tomorrow. What you choose to do with them is up to you. You may decide to burn them, read them, or just set them aside. I just want you to know that I did think about you every day. I still do.

I just wanted to be a good mother to you, I really did. I still want a relationship with you; I want to see you get married and be a grandmother to your children, the mother I wasn't for you.

The reason why Isaac and I have been searching for you is because we both love you dearly. I see so much in him that I would have loved Trevor to be; in a way Isaac healed part of the hole in my heart from the loss of your brother. Isaac is like a son to me.

You may wonder why I want you to be with him or why I'm living with him for that matter. It's because I've never seen a person love another person so much. I see the way Isaac's eyes light up when he hears your name and the way he was determined to find you.

I thought this was all going to go great until Tyson. Arrabella I have never seen a young man look at a girl with so much love and passion filling his eyes. The way you smile around him makes my heart swell. I can tell that boy is in love with you, and you are in love with him. I want you to know I approve of all your choices. Also, I'm proud of you. I know you were hurting too.

This is why I am sending Isaac on his way. I think he needs to find a girl who looks at him the way you look at Tyson.

It isn't going to be easy. Isaac really does care about you. I just want you to know I do love you Ella and I will always be here waiting. I just need you to tell me when you want a relationship with me.

I love you,

Mom

I let the tears hit the paper as I read those words. My mom really is a strong woman.

I heard a faint knock on the door as I wiped my tears and put the letter back.

"Baby, are you okay?" Ty asked, entering. I slammed the chest shut and got up and ran over to him. I hugged him as tight as I could. He stumbled back in surprise but then wrapped his arms around me and kissed my head.

"I love you," I sobbed.

"I love you too. What's wrong?"

"I just love you," I replied, burying my head into him.

"I know princess." He chuckled.

I looked up in his brown eyes and melted once again. I don't think I will ever understand how I got so lucky.

* * *

I woke up early the next morning and slipped out of Ty's hold. He grumbled a little but rolled over. I went over to the chest and sat down.

"Ar, what are you doing?" Ty asked sleepily.

"I'm fine babe. Go back to sleep."

"I can't without you." He pouted.

"Well try harder." I laughed.

He sat up, and I laughed at his bed head.

"It's not funny."

"Then why am I laughing?" I teased.

His eyes shifted from me to the chest and understanding dawned on his face.

"I'll lie down here, but I'll have you know I'm not comfortable." He sulked, lying back down.

"Night dork." I laughed.

I then opened the chest and pulled out the very first letter my mom wrote me on her very first day in rehab.

> *My Ella,*
> *I shouldn't be in here and away from you. I will be back soon though baby I promise.*
> *I promise to be a better mom. Remember what I told you. Don't fight with him don't even talk at all. Remember that diary I gave you; use that to write down your thoughts.*
> *I want to know everything about you Arrabella. I want to know your favorite color, your favorite food, favorite book, everything.*
> *I love you and I'm coming home soon,*
> *Mom*

I let a few tears escape. My mom wanted to know all these things about me.

I do remember her getting me the diary.

I wonder if she knows how much that helped me, in fact I still need it.

I sniffled and then went over and sat on Ty's back.

"Are you kidding me?" he mumbled.

I laughed but it even sounded sad to me. Ty somehow used his arms to get me off his back so he could sit up and face me.

"Are you okay?"

"Yeah, I need you to take me to my mom's."

"Okay let's go." He shrugged.

He pulled on a t-shirt and I pulled on some yoga pants and Ty's sweatshirt. The drive was short, but I was ready to talk to my mom.

"Do you want me to wait in the car?"

"Yes please." I nodded.

I got out and walked to the front door. I rang the doorbell and waited. My mom answered a moment later with a cup of coffee in her hands. I knew she would be awake because she always woke up early when I was little. I also knew Isaac would be asleep because he never wakes up before noon.

"Ella." My mom smiled. I walked in and sat in the chair.

"I read your letter," I sniffled.

"Oh Ella," my mom replied, a few tears escaping her eyes.

"My favorite color is purple. Lately I've been eating a lot of Chinese food. I love the book Twilight," I rambled on.

My mom grinned at me and I gave her a huge hug.

"I love you so much Ella."

"I love you too mom." I smiled.

I was wrong. My mom is my hero.

Chapter 33

Dear Diary,

I've patched things up with my mom!

Things are going great. We've gone out for lunch a few times and even went shopping.

Isaac hasn't left yet but I'm sure he will soon. I haven't seen him since the fight.

Ty and I are great. I love that dork to pieces.

~Aria

"So then this happened," Audrey finished, pointing to the mark on her neck.

She had just finished telling me about how Carter marked her last night.

They will make beautiful children. I don't know where that came from. Why am I thinking about children? And Carter making them, ew.

"That's so sweet," I replied, referring to her story.

"I know right," she squealed.

"So are you getting used to the idea of, you know, him being a wolf?" I asked.

"I mean I guess so it's just weird to think he is one." She sounded unsure like she couldn't quite put it into words, I know exactly what she is trying to say though.

"Have you met his parents?"

"That's what we are doing today. We are going to have dinner with them." She smiled.

"Ask Carter's dad about the ice cream truck story." I laughed.

"I will." She laughed.

* * *

Ty was in his office doing paperwork. In fact, he's been in there most of the day.

Audrey and I have been hanging out all day, but she and Carter just left for dinner with his parents. Damn Carter for taking my new best friend away from me.

I've only seen Ty like five times today, which is ridiculous! I lay on the couch and sighed. I really need to get a hobby.

I got off the couch and wandered into the hallway where I know Ty's office is. I opened the door and smiled when I saw Ty contently working on his papers.

"Hey gorgeous." Ty smiled, looking up.

"Hey psycho." I laughed.

"Still have that accent," he teased.

I rolled my eyes and went over to the office chair he was currently occupying and I straddled him.

"I guess I could use a break." He smirked.

"What are you even working on?" I asked, looking down at the paper he was just writing on.

"Boring pack stuff," he replied, grabbing my chin in his hand and turning my head so my eyes were on his again.

I smiled when I saw his eyes and leaned in to have my lips meet his. He smiled against my lips. He licked my bottom lip, and I didn't waste any time opening my mouth for him.

There was a knock at the door, making me pull away.

Tyson however leaned in again and our lips once again met.

I laughed and pulled away.

"Come in," I called, climbing off his lap. Ty pulled me back down though and I was now sitting on his lap a bit more properly.

Aiden walked in and looked a little frightened when he did. I looked up to see Ty glaring at him.

"Hey Aiden." I smiled, hoping to make him less scared.

"Hello Arrabella." He nodded in respect.

"What do you need?" Ty cut in.

"I need to know if you finished the paperwork for the Moonlight Pack and when the meeting will be," Aiden replied.

"Almost and it will be later tonight. Jason, Carter, you, and I can discuss the plan at nine sharp," Ty ordered.

"Alright thanks alpha, I will inform the others," Aiden replied then he left.

"Ty you nearly made him wet himself," I scolded, slapping his chest and standing up.

"He interrupted us." Ty pouted, reaching for me.

I stepped closer and he put his hands on my waist. I laughed because he's so damn cute when he needs to be this close to me; this is the one time it's like he needs me as much as I need him.

I sighed and pulled away from him.

"Come here." He pouted.

"No, you have to finish your work."

"I can take a break."

"It's seven thirty. You have an hour and a half until your meeting."

"It's seven thirty?" he asked, looking at his computer screen.

"Yes." I laughed.

"Did you eat dinner?"

"Yes, Carter made sure of it." I laughed.

"Good." He nodded.

"Now finish." I demanded, sitting on the couch.

"Wow, did we reverse roles today?"

"Nope. I'm tougher than you." I smirked.

"What?" He laughed.

"I am and you listen to me," I pointed out.

"Come here." He chuckled.

"No."

"No?" He repeated, getting out of his chair.

"Sit back down and finish your work!" I yelled as he ran towards me.

"Who's tough now?" Ty laughed, tickling me to death.

"You!" I shouted.

He chuckled and threw me over his shoulder.

"TY!" I squealed."

I can do my work with you on my lap." He chuckled, sitting me down. "Besides I haven't seen you all day."

"Okay fine," I replied, snuggling into him.

He started writing more things down but I was dozing in and out; being in Ty's arms made me feel safe and warm.

Not long later, I heard the door open and Ty welcome whoever entered.

"She fell asleep?" An amused voice asked. I smiled and opened my eyes.

"Shut up Carter." I yawned. I noticed Jason and Aiden also in the room and looked over at Ty's computer screen. It was nine so they were supposed to be having a meeting.

"I'll just lie down in the couch," I added, getting off of Ty's lap.

"Okay princess, try and go back to sleep if you're tired." Ty added.

"This might be intense for her Tyson. You sure she should be in here?" I heard Carter ask.

I sat down on the couch and waited for Ty's answer.

"She's fine. She's half asleep, and this won't interest her." I heard Ty answer.

I lay down and looked up at the ceiling. I actually think I did want to hear this.

"So I think I found the solution," Ty demanded going into full alpha mode. I turned my head to look at him; I don't really ever hear him act this professional or powerful. He never directs his alpha voice towards me, and it doesn't work on humans I guess.

"So Audrey told you the last she saw her was here?" Ty questioned. He's probably pointing to a map. *Wait. Audrey?*

"Audrey?" I asked.

Ty glanced over at me, and his face softened.

"It's okay Ar go back to sleep." He smiled.

"Why are you talking about Audrey?" I asked, ignoring him.

"Ty maybe this is too much for her," Carter replied.

"Carter, what's wrong with Audrey?"

"Nothing she's fine."

"So what's wrong?" I asked in confusion.

"Nothing baby," Ty replied.

"Don't lie to me."

Ty got up and walked over to me. He grabbed my hands and helped me stand up.

"I think you might sleep better in the bedroom," Ty said.

"No, I'm staying in here," I replied, ripping my hands from his.

"Okay babe, then please let us handle this," Ty pleaded.

"Okay." I sighed, sitting back down.

Carter smiled at me, and I knew he is silently thanking me for being concerned about Audrey.

"Audrey said that's why she's scared of wolves so it has to be them," Carter continued.

"If she thought it was a wild animal she probably thought it killed her, but it was probably the girl's mate," Aiden added.

"Exactly so this isn't going to work because whoever her mate is he isn't just going to hand her over," Ty added.

"Why would that make Audrey scared of wolves?" Carter questioned.

"There's probably more that she hasn't told you yet," Ty said.

"If she did find her mate though and that's it, why hasn't she called or wrote?" Carter asked.

I remember talking to Audrey about this. She told me she was scared of wolves and dogs.

A wolf must have done something to someone she cares about! That has to be it. But then Carter's question is valid. Why is meeting your mate something you can't write or call about?

Unless this girl didn't want a mate, and she was scared of wolves too.

"Maybe her mate kidnapped her," I said without thinking, so I slapped a hand over my mouth.

"Wait, what?" Carter asked.

"Nothing. Boy I'm tired. I think I'm going to go on up to bed," I replied, standing up. I just embarrassed myself in front of four wolves. I don't even have a clue what they were talking about and yet here I am adding in.

"Arrabella," Ty demanded.

I looked at the ground and sighed.

"Audrey, did one of her family members go missing?" I asked.

"Yes, her cousin a month ago. Do you know where she is?" Ty asked.

"No," I replied.

I heard him get up and I waited keeping my eyes glued to the floor.

"Arrabella," Ty demanded, lifting my chin up.

"I just thought that if her cousin's mate found her, then he would want her so he took her, and she thinks she's been kidnapped."

"That's an idea. If Addie was kidnapped by her mate she's probably trying to get away from him, making

his wolf crazy and forcing him to make her stay with him."
Ty smiled at my idea.

"Aria, you could talk to Addie like you did Audrey
and help her?" Ty added.

"I don't know Ty."

"Babe, you were great with Audrey."

"Okay but first you have to make sure that was
what happened."

"Gladly." He smirked, grabbing me and pulling me
over to his desk. He once again sat me on his lap and then
he picked up the phone and dialed a number.

"Hey Alpha Jeff, how've you been man?" Tyson
greeted.

"Great my Beta Carter's mate Audrey is looking for
her cousin Addie. Is she with you guys?"

"I see. Well that's understandable," Ty replied. He
paused and glanced over at me.

"Yeah Audrey's just worried. Can you put Paxton
on the phone?" Ty asked.

"Thanks," he replied.

"Hey Paxton," Ty greeted.

"So I hear you found your mate," he replied.

"It just so happens that Addie's cousin Audrey is
my beta's mate," Ty explained.

"Yeah Audrey's been worried about her, hasn't
heard from her in a while," Ty replied.

"It just so happens that my mate Aria has a way
with words." Ty smiled and pecked my lips.

"Yes, that would work for us. I think this is going to be good for her." Ty smiled.

"Thank you." Ty smiled. He hung up the phone and sighed in content.

"Well boys case closed. They aren't killing random humans. Addie is their Beta Paxton's mate," Ty explained.

"We are heading down there tomorrow," he added.

"Great. Can Audrey come?" Carter asked hopefully.

"Of course." Ty shrugged.

They then filed out of the room, leaving Ty and me alone.

"Are you sure you're comfortable with this?" Ty questioned.

"Hell yeah." I smiled, leaning in and pressing my lips to Ty's.

I may not know what I was going to say to Addie tomorrow but being able to help these girls have made me finally feel like this is where I'm meant to be and most definitely what I'm meant to be doing.

Chapter 34

Dear Diary,
Today I'm helping Audrey's cousin Addie.
I really hope this goes well.
~Aria

"Babe you're going to do great." Ty laughed.

"I know." I nodded. I couldn't help drumming my fingers on the cup holder.

"Seriously." Ty chuckled, grabbing my drumming hand in his.

We drove up the driveway of a mansion, much like ours, and then the car stopped.

"Here goes nothing," I sighed, getting out of the car.

A man came out of the house, smiling at us.

"Nice to see you again Tyson, and you must be Aria." The man smiled.

I nodded shyly and smiled.

"I'm Paxton."

"Nice to meet you."

"Addie is up in our bedroom. Shall I take you up?"

"I want to see her!" I heard someone say from behind me. I turned to see Audrey with Carter trying to soothe her.

"Is that the cousin?" Paxton asked.

"Yes," Tyson answered.

I walked over to Audrey and gave her a smile.

"Aria you found her!" She smiled and pulled me into a hug.

"Yes, and remember when you found out about wolves?" I asked her.

"Yeah of course," she replied.

"I need to go talk to Addie so she understands all this, then you can see her okay?"

"Okay."

Carter shot me a thank you glance. I walked back over to Paxton and Ty.

"Ready?" Paxton asked.

"Yep." I smiled.

He led me up a winding staircase to a long hallway. This house seems so big.

Paxton seemed like a nice guy. He had blonde hair and sky blue eyes; he's pretty adorable, like a puppy.

"She's a little upset."

"It's alright."

"She will probably yell when I walk in the room," he added sadly.

"It's okay."

He opened the door and a girl resembling Audrey with blonde hair and brown eyes was sitting on the bed.

"Addie this is Aria," Paxton introduced.

"I don't want to meet any more wolves," she sniffled.

"No sweetheart, she's human," he replied.

I watched her eyes light up as she ran over to me and hugged me.

"You're human?"

"Yes." I laughed.

"I'll be back later." Paxton chuckled.

"When did you get here?" she asked.

"Today." I shrugged, sitting on the bed.

She sat next to me and gave me a small smile.

"Do you know why I'm here?" I asked.

"No."

"I'm here to talk to you about mates."

"You are?"

"Yeah." I smiled.

"Do you have a mate?"

"Yes, his name his Tyson."

"Why aren't you mad?"

"Why would I be?"

"For forcing you to be with him."

"Do you know how you feel when you touch your mate? The sparks, the butterflies?"

"I guess."

"They feel a thousand times more towards you."

"Really?"

"Yeah and I was mad that Ty kept being a werewolf from me, trust me, but it's that moment when you look into your mate's eyes and you know that it doesn't matter about their past or yours, it's the future."

"I know, but I miss Audrey and my mom."

"Paxton will let you see them." I laughed.

"No, he won't!"

"Listen I know this may sound weird to you but he is protective of you. I guarantee if you open up to him and let him be your mate he will stop holding you hostage. Mates will do anything to make one another happy." I smiled.

"I do feel the sparks when we touch." She admitted. "Plus, I miss him when we are not together."

"You guys are meant to be. You just have to let him be your mate, or boyfriend if you're more comfortable with that label."

"But he is my mate. Doesn't it scare you that they are wolves?"

"It used to but Ty will never hurt me."

"How do you know?"

"You know they are really strong and fast right?" I asked. She nodded. "You should feel so safe when you're with Paxton because he would threaten anyone who would even look at you funny."

"I know but they are wolves." She obviously couldn't get over that.

"Why does that bother you so much?"

She looked down and played with her hands. She then looked up at me and sighed.

"When Audrey and I were little we took a walk in the woods together. We lived together with her mom because my parents weren't really ready to be reliable for me. I have always called Audrey's mom my mom because she raised me, anyways we went out in the woods. We heard fighting and Audrey wanted us to be detectives and see what was going on. There was a guy and a girl fighting. The girl was crying and telling him she was running away and not coming back to the house. The guy started yelling and then he snapped her legs. She screamed so loud that Audrey started crying. The man then looked over at us, and before we knew what was happening instead of a man standing in front of us it was a wolf. Audrey and I ran so fast back to the house, and since that day we have never gone near a dog or anything close to one."

"That's why you're scared?"

"Yes, I thought if I yelled at Paxton or ran away he would break my legs so I could never walk again and then I'd have to be with him forever," she sniffled.

"Listen I don't know what kind of pack that disgusting man is from but that is not how our packs work, trust me. I have run away from Ty multiple times and the worst that happened was that he carried me back to wherever it was he wanted me. But trust me on this when I tell Ty to stop or to put me down he stops immediately with no questions asked."

"Thank you," she cried. I leaned over and gave her a hug. She sniffled and then we pulled away.

"So give Paxton a chance okay?"

"I will." She smiled.

"Now I do have something to tell you." I grinned.

"What?"

"Audrey is downstairs right now with her mate Carter." I smiled.

"She has a wolf mate too?" Addie nearly screamed.

"Yes." I smiled.

"Let's go see them!" she screamed, grabbing my hand and sprinting down the stairs with me.

* * *

Tyson

Aria has been upstairs for a while now. Audrey sitting on Carter's lap makes me want my princess on my lap.

Paxton sure is anxious.

"Yes, she's going to tell her why she hates wolves so much!" Paxton waited for the answer. I listened as well. I can't believe how good Aria was with people.

I saw Audrey stiffen when Paxton said that and Carter noticed it too and asked her why she was nervous.

I listened in on the story Addie was telling Aria and nearly got out of my seat. What kind of person breaks his mate's legs?

I hope this story doesn't frighten Aria.

"That's why you don't like wolves or dogs?" Carter asked Audrey.

"Yeah," she whispered.

"Why didn't you tell me?" Carter asked her.

"After my talk with Aria I didn't care about what I saw that day in the woods. I knew you wouldn't hurt me."

Carter smiled and kissed her lips.

"Babe you can tell me anything," he replied.

I tuned them out however and smiled when I heard Aria telling Addie that the packs they were in aren't like that at all. I am so proud of my girl.

I love her more than she will ever realize.

* * *

Arrabella

We were on our way home and I was still smiling.

The way Addie and Audrey hugged made my heart swell. I never had a sibling or one I could hug, and they were like sisters, it's so amazing.

"You seriously made her love Paxton." Tyson smiled.

"No, she already did. I just made her realize it." I laughed.

"You're amazing babe."

"Thanks Ty." I smiled. I couldn't get the story out of my head though. I mean would a mate really break their mate's legs?

"Are you okay?" Ty asked.

"I was just wondering about this story Addie told me."

"I can't believe that, babe don't worry about it, that pack must be some kind of cult."

"I know but I thought mates could never hurt each other."

"I didn't think it was possible but his wolf must have been pushed too far and he thought the only way to keep her near was to break her legs. I mean that's not even a solution though because she would have never looked at him the same."

"What if I pushed your wolf too far," I whispered.

"Arrabella you never have to worry about that. You know I would never do that, don't you?" I looked into his eyes and knew it was dumb; Ty can't even tickle me without being careful not to hurt me.

"I know." I smiled, leaning my head on his shoulder.

Soon we were pulling back up to the house; it felt good to be home.

Chapter 35

Dear Diary,
My talk with Addie was a total success.
It felt good to help her out.
~Aria

My relationship with Ty has been better than ever these past few weeks. It was already July and I find my summer flying by! Ty and I have been a little more intimate lately I guess you could say.

I'm pretty sure I'm in an emotional state, and I love Ty more than I ever could, so I think I'm ready for us to fully become one, or mate, or just have sex whatever you want to call it.

Ty is just so sexy lately. I just want to kiss him all the time. After the whole Addie matter it's like a weight has been lifted off his shoulders, not to mention Isaac hasn't tried to contact me since our fight.

I don't know, it's like his eyes are sparkling more and lips are more kissable; I must be going crazy.

I heard Carter say that we are all just in summer heat or in other terms this is when wolves are most on edge with it being the end of spring. I guess I'm just catching the vibe from Ty or something.

Anyways Addie and Paxton are doing great now. Addie has let a lot of her walls down and even came to visit us last week. Paxton keeps thanking me for all I have done to help his mate. Honestly, I did it for Audrey, but I also love bringing the wonderful world of wolves and mates into people's lives. I mean mates are just so special and not everyone finds their mate.

"Are you trying to make me attack you?" Ty groaned.

"What?" I asked, turning my head towards him.

We are currently lying out in the grass just watching the clouds the go by.

"You've been in deep thought for the last ten minutes." He chuckled.

"Sorry." I giggled.

"You're so beautiful," he whispered, rolling over and on top of me; however, none of his weight was on me.

I smiled up at him. His hair was getting longer and I think I like it better that way; it has the whole shaggy look to it, making me want to reach up and scruff his head. His eyes are piercing down into mine, making me never want to look away.

"I love you." I smiled.

"I love you, and I love when you smile when you see me. I like that I can make those dimples of yours appear." He winked.

"You're a psycho," I mocked.

"Only for you," he teased. I smiled and closed my eyes as his head inched closer to mine. Instead of planting his lips on mine like I had thought he started planting small kisses all over my face.

"TY!" I laughed, opening my eyes.

"What?" he asked innocently.

I pushed at his chest and then stood up.

"If you run away," he started to say.

"If I run away what?" I mocked.

"I will capture you and never let you go."

"Haven't you already done that?" I teased.

"Take that back," he joked, moving towards me.

"RUN THERE'S A PSYCHO ON THE LOOSE!" I screamed even though we were the only ones out there besides Audrey and Carter who were on the porch swing.

They both laughed in amusement at us as I raced past them and into the house. I ran past the living room and was planning on going into the garage but Ty was now in front of me with his arms crossed.

I spun around but I felt two strong arms around me, caging me in.

"HELP!" I laughed as Ty picked me up and carried me upstairs.

"No one can hear your screams." He chuckled.

He placed me in the bedroom and shut the door.

"I love you so much babe and you are so sexy," I started to enumerate as he backed me into a corner.

"What else?" he asked in amusement.

"Um you're the strongest person alive and you are really fast," I squealed as his hands made contact with my hips.

"I'm not going to tickle you." He chuckled.

"Yay you're the best." I laughed.

"But I am going to hold you prisoner forever." He smirked.

"Deal." I laughed.

He pecked my lips, which turned into the hottest make out session yet; I don't know how this boy has such a great effect on me.

* * *

"I can't believe you have never seen fireworks!" Ty nearly shouted.

"I can't believe you have," I said defensively, even though I could.

"Well it is Fourth of July and so after tonight you will not be able to say that anymore." He smiled.

After a long drive we were at a small river. Ty laid out a blanket and told me this was going to be the best show ever.

We lay on the blanket and not long after fireworks erupted in the sky. I gasped. *This is not like anything I could have ever imagined! This was amazing.*

It all ended too soon.

"I don't know what was better, the fireworks or your face when you saw them," Ty whispered, rolling on top of me.

"That was the best thing I have ever seen."

"We can come again next year babe." He chuckled.

"Really?" I asked hopefully.

"We can come every year as long as you want to keep coming." He smiled.

"Thank you, Ty," I whispered.

"I love you." He chuckled.

After the drive home we headed upstairs and I changed into a tank top and short shorts; it was hot!

I walked out of the bathroom and sat on Ty's stomach.

"Are you trying to get me worked up?" He chuckled.

"Yes."

I think I am ready for this. I am ready for Ty. I know I am. I love him so much and I know he has been waiting for a long time to have me; he just hasn't said anything because he doesn't want to push me. Needless to say, I have been with Ty for a while now and I want him.

"Aria, are you sure?" Ty asked in shock but I knew he was ready to rip out of his clothes. I slid off his stomach and nodded grinning.

"You want to? You're sure?"

"Yes Ty, I love you and I'm ready."

"You need to tell me if you feel any pain, and I will stop."

"I will, promise." I smiled.

With that he beamed at me and then rolled on top of me. I attacked his lips while he slipped off my tank top.

He moved his lips down to my neck where my mark was making me moan.

This is a night I will never forget. Ty had taken me to see fireworks for the first time and now I feel fireworks all over my body. Right when I knew I had all of Tyson I felt a swarm of pleasure that I can't even put to words.

It did hurt, a lot for the first thirty seconds probably, but after those thirty seconds I know why I had made this decision. I love Tyson and I know for sure he is my first and last.

* * *

I woke up feeling amazing. I looked over and blushed when I saw my nude body pressed against Ty's nude body.

I slipped out of his reach and grabbed shorts and my tank top that had been thrown on the floor last night and went into the bathroom.

After changing and going to the bathroom and I climbed back into bed with Ty. I cringed a little at the pressure as I sat back down.

"Are you okay?" Ty asked.

"Yes." I blushed, turning my head the opposite way.

"Don't turn your pretty little head away from me." He chuckled, kissing my flushed cheeks.

"Are you sore babe?" he asked in concern. I looked at him and my blush deepened.

He asked that question as casually as if he was asking about the weather.

"A little," I admitted.

"Then you my princess stay here." He smiled, slipping on a pair of sweatpants.

Ty came back with two plates of waffles.

I smiled as he handed me my plate and he sat down with his.

"Thanks babe." I smiled, eating up, I am starving!

All I know is that I wouldn't want to be anywhere else but here eating waffles with my gorgeous mate after the most wonderful night of my life.

Chapter 36

Dear Diary,

Last night was amazing.

Ty and I "mated."

Carter and everyone can tell and apparently, I'm glowing.

I don't care though because it is just proof that he is mine

and I am his.

~Aria

"So the girls win," I declared.

We are currently sitting on the couch in the living room arguing over watching *Rise of the Planet of the Apes* or *The Last Song*.

"How? Carter and I both voted for this and you two voted for that, so it's a tie," Tyson replied.

"We are going to cry," I threatened, crossing my arms over my chest. Audrey glanced over at me and imitated my body language.

"Are you kidding me?" Tyson groaned.

"Nope." I smirked, and Audrey smirked at Carter. I've taught her well.

"How about if we watch *Rise of the Planets of the Apes* now, we can play night games tonight, and then watch *The Last Song* before bed?" Tyson reasoned.

Audrey and I looked at each other. It was a fair trade and when Audrey shrugged her shoulders I took that as confirmation.

"Okay deal." I nodded.

"Yes boys win!" Ty shouted.

I flicked my middle finger at him, making him smirk.

"Whoa babe maybe later," he replied chuckling. Carter burst out laughing and my cheeks turned flame red.

"Tyson Dalton!" I shouted.

"Love you babe." He winked.

* * *

It was now dark out and we are about to play night games. Ty is finishing up a phone call in his office and then we are going to play.

Some of the other pack members are joining us as well.

There is going to be a bonfire and we are going to play games like "Ghost in the Grave Yard" which is just and intense version of hide and seek in the dark with way more running.

Ty came out looking a little conflicted but his face softened when he saw me.

"Ready?" he asked.

"Ready." I nodded, but winced slightly at the pain in my stomach.

"Are you okay Ar?" he asked.

"Yeah I just have a stomachache, I'm fine." I smiled.

"Alright let's go." He nodded, grinning down at me and grabbing my hand.

After an exciting round of Ghost in the Graveyard Tyson was the tagger. I ran off as fast as I could and hid behind a tree.

In all honesty I knew Ty would find me first and attack me.

He has been holding onto my hand all night long and hiding with me. Somehow Carter managed to tag him though.

I felt two strong arms wrap around me, making me laugh.

"Tyson you can't just sneak up on people."

He grunted in response. I got a bad feeling all of the sudden. I didn't feel the sparks right now when we were touching and his arms didn't feel as strong or safe.

"Ty stop dragging me. Where are we going?" I asked.

"ARRABELLA!" I heard someone call. It was Tyson.

"TY?" I screamed.

A hand was slapped over my mouth and before I knew it I was being shoved into a van.

I screamed and screamed until I realized who was driving.

"Isaac what the hell?" I shouted.

"You wouldn't return my calls."

"What are you talking about?"

He then parked the van and climbed over the seat and into the back with me.

"I kept calling and calling and Tyson said he would tell you I called."

"He didn't tell me." I whispered, mostly to myself.

"I didn't mean to kidnap you Ella I swear. I just needed to talk to you."

"Okay but Ty's going to be pissed."

"I just want to let you know I'm sorry, I'm sorry for everything. For our past and for coming across as a maniac," he sighed in frustration.

"I know Isaac, I just think we are both different now than when we were little kids."

"Exactly which is why I wanted to call you and tell you I'm so happy that you found Tyson, and I'm going to move back in with my mom and I wanted to say goodbye and hope we keep in touch."

"We will Isaac and you're going to find someone great." I nodded.

"Thanks Ella." He smiled.

"Now Ty is probably looking for me." I worriedly told him.

Just then the van door flew open and I was being pulled out.

"Hell yes we are looking for you," Carter growled, hugging me and pulling me out of my seat.

I looked over and noticed Ty ripping Isaac out of the van.

I ran over to them and pushed at Ty.

"What did you do to her?" he asked.

I almost groaned in frustration I don't know if Ty actually thinks I'm in danger right now or he's just being jealous!

"Nothing man."

"Tyson stop!" I screamed.

He glanced over at me, and Carter pulled me back a little.

"Carter let me go," I calmly said.

"Let her go," Ty confirmed.

"Did you not just hear that conversation?" I asked.

"I heard you worried and telling him I was looking for you," he replied, glaring at Isaac.

"Let him go Tyson," I snapped.

The sharpness in my voice must have hit him because he let go of Isaac.

"I'm sorry Isaac," I said.

"Bye Ella." He waved, getting in the van and driving away.

"Aria?" Ty asked.

"I don't want to talk to you right now," I replied, walking away.

"You don't even know how to get back," Ty pointed out, appearing next to me.

"I can figure it out."

He stopped and stood in front of me.

"I'm lost Ar. Isaac kidnapped you and I'm the bad guy?" he asked.

"How many times did Isaac call?" I asked.

Understanding dawned on his face but it quickly turned to anger.

"Aria that scum doesn't need to talk to you."

"Is that really why you didn't tell me?"

"Yes."

"I can make that decision for myself Tyson," I groaned.

"You're better off without another man who hits you," he replied, standing in front of me and looking into my eyes.

"Ty he just wanted to tell me goodbye and that he was happy I found you."

Shock flashed over his face.

"Really?"

"Yes, he's going to live with his mother again."

"I was just trying to protect you."

"I know babe. I'm sorry I yelled at you." I sighed.

"I deserved it, and you can be pretty scary," he teased.

"I know babe." I laughed.

After that we walked back to the house and went up to the bedroom, and let me tell you the makeup sex was better than ever.

* * *

Carter

"Aria you're a brat," I teased, letting her put in *The Last Song*.

"I'm not a brat. You just think that because you're a jerk," she remarked in her very "Aria" way. I rolled my eyes and let them wander to Audrey who was in the kitchen getting popcorn. Since Aria somehow got kidnapped from a bunch of wolves last night we didn't watch the chick flick with them, which is why we were all sitting here on a Thursday afternoon about to watch *The Last Song*.

I looked over at Tyson and Aria, who was already on Tyson's lap, and snorted just loud enough to bug Aria.

"Carter you're a child."

"Okay whatever you say princess," I mocked, using the name Tyson always called her earning me a warning glare from Tyson.

"From the boy who believed the ice cream truck was out of ice cream when it played music," she sarcastically remarked. *I can't believe this girl spent most of her life not talking. I mean she never misses a beat.*

"Come on babe!" I called to Audrey. I missed her, and Tyson and Aria cuddling made me want Audrey in my arms even more.

I love her so much. I just don't know when the right time to tell her would be.

"Hold on," she called, glancing back at me with those light brown eyes of hers.

I sighed just for dramatic effect, plus I knew it would get on Aria's nerves as a bonus.

There's something different about Aria. I can't quite get my finger on it though. I mean she smells different for sure but that's probably from finally mating with Ty. If Tyson doesn't notice anything then it probably is nothing.

Audrey then came skipping over in obvious excitement about the movie we were about to waste two hours of our lives watching!

But the look on her face right now is the reason I'm sitting here about to give two hours of my life I'll never get back.

I already know I'll be watching my angel more than the movie.

"Carter can you stop staring at Audrey and press play?" Aria mocked, interrupting my thoughts.

"I can't help it. She's beautiful." I shrugged, making Audrey blush, score. I love her blush.

"I can't help that the remote is way over there, so press play," Aria teased. *Wow she is really getting good at comebacks.*

"You are the little sister I never wanted," I mocked, pressing play.

"You are the boy about to watch a two-hour chick flick," she reminded. I rolled my eyes and pulled Audrey closer to me.

In most ways Aria basically is my little sister. She sure acts like one and I sure do take the big brother role seriously, especially after I heard about what happened to her real brother. I mean Aria sure had a tough life but you would never guess that looking at her today.

I kissed Audrey's head making her smile up at me. *Man I love this little family of ours.*

Chapter 37

Dear Diary,

Ty and I are constantly well you know in bed.

I love him so much, and getting to know him on this level is amazing.

~Aria

"Babe where is the nearest bakery?" I asked.

"I don't know five miles from here."

"I need a chocolate cupcake!" I pleaded.

"Okay princess. I'll send someone." He chuckled.

"Yes! Thank you!" I shouted. I can already taste the warm chocolate cake melting in my mouth.

* * *

Five cupcakes and three bags of Doritos later and I am still hungry.

"Babe what is up?" Ty laughed.

"I don't know but look I've grown a pouch." I laughed, lifting my shirt up and showing him the stomach I have slightly developed. It's weird though because it's more like a bump and not fat.

"I think it has a heartbeat." I laughed, holding my hand to it. I felt a slight pound from the inside and gasped.

"Babe, feel it!"

Ty put his hand on my tummy and nearly wet himself. The smile on his face was bigger than any smile I have ever seen.

He then scooped me up in his arms and carried me to the nurse's room.

"Hey I remember this room." I laughed. That seemed so long ago.

"Hey can you check something for me?" Ty asked.

"Of course." She smiled.

Ty whispered something to her, making her grin.

"What?" I asked.

"I'm just going to place this on your stomach quickly dear." Nurse Sherry smiled.

"Okay." I shrugged.

"Look up on the screen. That there is your baby

"I'm pregnant?" I screamed.

"Yes ma'am. You're one month along." She nodded.

"Ty we're having a baby!"

He nodded; I pulled him in for a hug and cried. I'm carrying Tyson's baby, a little miracle.

I bet the baby will have his brown eyes!

"I love this little thing so much already," I sobbed, rubbing my stomach.

"You are going to be a great mommy Ar." Ty smiled.

"Are you kidding? You are going to be a great daddy." I grinned.

This baby was just extra proof of our love.

* * *

My mom is ecstatic that she is a grandma! Audrey is also excited about the baby. She helps me come up with names and we talk about how cute he or she is going to be all time.

Ty is more protective than ever because the first few months of a baby with wolf blood is crucial.

Ty tells me that it will be in our baby's blood; that it doesn't mean the baby will be a wolf but it will have a mate. But our child could be a wolf.

"Ty, I'm fine," I sighed, standing up to use the bathroom.

"I know Ar, but you need to rest."

"Walking is good Ty," I protested, waddling to the bathroom.

"The baby is growing fast babe. We have to be careful."

"You stressing me out isn't helping," I sang, sitting on the toilet. I didn't even care that Ty was in the bathroom with me.

He shut the door and rolled his eyes. *Man it felt good to relieve my bladder.*

"All I'm saying is you need to let me help more." He pouted.

"Okay babe."

"Our boy has to be healthy and strong like his daddy." Ty grinned.

I snorted and stood up from the toilet and washed my hands.

"Well since she is a girl your point is invalid." I shrugged.

Ty and I have been on this for the past two months! He thinks we are having a boy for sure but I knew in my heart that it was a girl.

"Regardless you need to rest." Ty smirked, lifting me up and carrying me to the bedroom.

"Ty, this isn't necessary," I groaned, sitting up.

"Babe we can't take chances," he replied, grabbing my hand. He then flipped on *The Last Song,* making me smile.

"Babe, babe she's kicking, aww she must have heard *The Last Song*," I cooed.

"He's telling you to change the channel." Ty smirked, touching my stomach and rubbing it.

"Hi baby, it's your daddy," he cooed, kissing my tummy.

"And your mommy whom you like better," I added, placing my hand on my stomach.

"I can't argue with that." Ty shrugged.

I laughed and kissed him.

I can't believe we are parents!

* * *

"Ty, Ty wake up," I sobbed. *My stomach hurts so badly!*

"What, what's wrong?" Ty panicked.

"My stomach," I cried.

"NURSE!" Ty screamed.

The nurse came racing into the room.

"She's in a lot of pain," Ty growled.

"Bring her down alpha," Sherry said in panic.

Ty scooped me up and ran down to the hospital room. He placed me on the bed and held my hands. I leaned my head into him, groaning in pain.

"What's wrong with my baby?" I cried.

"Shh," Ty soothed.

"Please help my baby," I cried to Sherry who was racing around the room.

"Please," I sobbed.

* * *

It has been two hours now. Sherry gave me painkillers that are safe to take during pregnancy and now she is running her final tests.

"What seems to have happened is your baby just hit a growth spurt. You have now reached three months. The baby is perfectly healthy." She smiled.

"Really?" I smiled.

"Yes." She smiled.

"Why is Aria feeling so much pain?" Ty asked. *Had he been crying?*

I took his hand in mine for comfort.

"Aria, being as little as she is, will feel a little more pain during the growth spurts because you have quite the little chunker in there," Sherry pointed out.

"Our baby's a chunker?" I laughed.

"Yes, it is." Ty chuckled.

I laughed and leaned my head against him; our baby is healthy and that's all that matters.

Chapter 38

Dear Diary,
We will find out the baby's gender today!
~Aria

"Fourth month." I smiled, kissing Ty; we only have two more to go after this. This pregnancy is flying by but I can't complain. I just want to hold my baby in my arms and kiss its head.

Our baby will be fully developed at six months in my womb because of the wolf blood.

Today we find out if it is a boy or girl, which is a relief because I'm tired of referring to the baby as "the baby" or "it."

"I can't wait until I prove you wrong." Ty beamed.

"I can't wait to teach you that I'm always right," I replied.

I walked into the room with a smile.

"Ready?" Sherry smiled.

"Ready." Ty and I both grinned.

Regardless of gender, it will be the most loved child in the world.

However, words can't describe the feeling that ran through me when Sherry said the words "It's a girl."

"A girl?" I shouted, tears running down my face.

"Yes, and a healthy one at that." She nodded.

"I told you." I sobbed, socking Ty in the arm.

"She's going to be a daddy's girl." Ty smiled but a few tears escaped from his eyes as well.

"Aww babe, a little me running around." I laughed.

"I wouldn't want it any other way." He chuckled.

At that moment I truly felt complete. In two months Ty and I would have a daughter, and man would she be the most spoiled girl in the world with two parents who love each other and her to no end.

* * *

"I'm not doing that." I groaned.

"Come on. That's a cute name," Ty protested.

"I know what it's like to have a boy middle name as a girl. I'm not doing that to her."

"What name?" Carter asked, plopping down on the couch.

"I'm not telling you because you are going to side with Tyson," I sighed.

There have been a lot of name ideas floating around lately. Everyone and I do mean everyone had ideas and suggestions: names with meanings, cute names, celebrity names. I'm happy that the pack members have their ideas and Emmalee and my mother have theirs, but at the end of the day it's our decision.

I can't say I never thought of putting our names together. I mean it would have meaning and everything but I haven't heard a name that clicked yet. I think when I hear the perfect one that will forever be my daughter's name. I will just know.

"As the baby's favorite uncle ever I should have a say." Carter pouted.

"You're a pain." I laughed.

"Tell him." Ty pushed.

"Kayla Dalton James Benson," I muttered. Ty really liked this name but I'm not sold on the name Kayla, and I definitely didn't want her to have a boy name as a middle name, let alone two.

"Kaya? Who came up with that?" Carter asked.

"KAYA!" I shouted. [k-uh]

"What?" Carter asked slightly taken aback.

"That's the perfect name." I smiled. In that moment, with his lack of focus, Carter came up with the perfect name: Kaya.

"I'm confused," Carter announced.

"She said Kayla." Tyson chuckled, placing emphasis on the *l*.

"Oh, well Kaya's cute." Carter shrugged.

"I think Kaya would be perfect." Tyson agreed.

"But she is not having two middle names especially James," I replied.

"But then the name will have meaning." Ty commented.

Carter rolled his eyes at us and then patted my stomach.

"Your parents are crazy Kaya, I'll talk to you later," Carter cooed, leaving.

"Psycho!" I called after him.

Ty picked me up and placed me on his lap. He started playing with my hair, making me relax.

"Why?" he asked.

A simple word, yet I knew exactly what he was talking about.

"My dad's middle name was James."

He thought about it for a minute and nodded.

"Okay we won't use it." He chuckled.

"How about Alee?" I suggested. [Aly]

"Alee?" he asked.

"Yeah because your mom's name's is Emmalee and my mom's name is Aleeah so Alee is in both of their names."

"Kaya Alee Benson," Ty confirmed.

"Do you like it?" I asked.

"I love it." He grinned.

"Great." I smiled. Finally, the perfect name and it did have meaning.

I cannot wait to call my daughter Kaya Alee Benson, a name I will never grow tired of.

* * *

"I just love feeling her kick," Audrey gushed.

"I know. It's just proof that there's a baby in there." I laughed.

"Did you ever picture yourself as a mom?" Audrey asked.

"I've always wanted to be a mom but I never pictured myself with a guy or even being pregnant."

"You wanted it to be a girl though." She smiled.

"Yeah I just want to be able to do the fun mother-daughter things and I'm sure Ty and I will have another one down the road."

"I'm sure you will, and one thing's for sure, Kaya is going to be beautiful." She smiled.

"Thanks. What about you and Carter?" I asked.

"What?" She blushed.

"Any baby making practicing going on?" I laughed.

"No." She groaned.

"It's okay the boys are out buying a crib. They can't hear us." I laughed.

"I know but no we haven't," she whispered.

"Yeah? Well you guys are just so cute together," I gushed.

"Thanks." She laughed.

"Girl, quit blushing. The psychos are back." I laughed, seeing them approach the door. Ty was carrying a huge box under his arm.

"Why are you blushing?" Carter smirked, kissing Audrey.

"You will never know," I cut in, bouncing up to Ty.

"I want to know." Ty pouted but he kissed me anyways.

He set down the box, giving me a look of the picture on the side.

"You found a white one." I grinned.

"Of course I did." He smirked, flexing his muscles.

"That has nothing to do with finding a crib," I scoffed.

"Yes, it does," he scoffed back. I laughed making him grin.

"I found you a bed Miss Kaya," Ty added, leaning down to talk with my stomach.

I laughed and pushed at him because I wanted to hug him. He chuckled and then wrapped me in his arms and kissed my head.

"I love you," he mumbled into my hair.

"I love you too," I mumbled into his chest.

* * *

We were now lying in bed watching *She's the Man*.

I was in deep thought and not really watching the movie.

I mean I want to tell Kaya that her daddy saved me but I don't know if I want her knowing all the details of my life.

I want her knowing that you always have to stand up for yourself and not let anyone push you around. I'm so scared and I haven't even brought her into the world yet.

I just never want her getting hurt.

Mostly I want to be the kind of mother like Emmalee, Ty's mom. I want to take her shopping and be there when she has her first crush. I just can't wait to be there for her.

I just never had a role model like that. I really hope Kaya will want to do these things with me. I want to be able to connect with her more than anything.

I know the connection when I talk to her and she kicks but when she's actually here I hope I can reach her like a mother was supposed to be able to do.

"You okay Ar?" Ty asked, ripping me out of my thoughts.

"Yeah." I smiled however I didn't look at him.

"Aria." He demanded.

I looked over and then back at the movie.

"Arrabella." He sighed, grabbing my face.

"What?" I laughed, pushing at his hands. He let go of my face, and I stared into his brown eyes.

"You want to tell me what's been going through that brain of yours for the past half hour?" He chuckled.

"Nope," I mocked.

"Yep," he teased.

"I was just thinking about Kaya."

"What about her?"

"I was just thinking about how I don't really know how to be a mom," I sighed.

"What? You are going to be a great mom."

"No Ty, I mean I didn't have a mom growing up so I'm not going to know what I'm doing," I groaned.

"Aria, I've seen you with the babies in the pack and how you are with talking to people like Audrey and Addie. You are going to be a natural." He soothed.

"You think so?"

"I know so." He grinned.

"Thanks babe." I laughed.

I snuggled into him and closed my eyes. Maybe I will be a natural.

Chapter 39

Dear Diary,
It's almost time for Kaya to arrive!
I can't wait to see her.
~Aria

"Where are we going?" I asked.

"You'll see." Ty chuckled.

He had his hands over my eyes. He took his hands off and I rolled my eyes.

"You led me through the house to come to the living room?" I laughed.

That is until Ty flicked on a light and a booming "SURPRISE" hit my ears.

I looked at the scene in front of me and tears started forming in my eyes.

There was a big banner above them saying 'Congratulations, It's A Girl.'

There were pink balloons and streamers everywhere!

I saw Carter and Audrey and Carter's parents. I was surprised to see Paxton and Addie. Then my eyes found Ty's parents and my mom.

There were also some other pack members I still don't know too well yet. I did however recognize Jason and Aiden. Also, I remember Jason's mate Catalina; I talked to her a while back and she is really nice.

"You guys," I sobbed.

A collective "Aww" resounded, making me laugh at myself for crying.

I punched Ty and then hugged him.

"You're a dork," I mumbled.

"I know babe." He chuckled.

Everyone wanted to come up and congratulate me. Ty would be making an announcement and I would tell everyone the name we chose then.

I got various gifts, well Kaya did.

Carter and Audrey got Kaya a purple teddy bear that said to Kaya on the bear's stomach and love Auntie Audrey and Uncle Carter on its back. Now I know Carter isn't Ty's brother but neither Ty nor I have siblings and so Kaya will now have an uncle and aunt, a crazy uncle but a good one that will love her. Also, when Carter and Audrey have children it will give Kaya the opportunity to have cousins!

My mother made Kaya a blanket; it was purple, pink, and yellow.

Ty's parents gave us a year's supply of diapers, a bunch of clothes, and pacifiers.

Addie and Paxton brought us a baby swing.

We also received a lot of stuffed animals, bibs, a high chair, and a lot of different mats, a playpen, and a camera. I know for sure I will use that camera and take as many pictures as possible, but hey you only regret the ones you don't take.

Ty stood up and then helped me up, and we made our way to the front of the room.

"We would just like to thank everyone for coming, also thank you for all the generous gifts. It's really great to know we are bringing our daughter into such a wonderful house, pack, and family. Aria is going to tell you the name we have chosen for our daughter." Ty grinned.

"Well her first name is Kaya and some of the credit for that name goes to Carter's hearing deficiency," I started. The crowd chuckled and I saw Carter pout. "Her middle name Alee spelled A-L-E-E because the name Alee is both in Ty's mom's name and my mother's name."

"So Kaya Alee Benson," Tyson announced.

Everyone clapped and nodded in agreement with the name, which made me smile because I love our baby's name.

After that we had cake and a lot of the people left.

My mom and Ty's parents, who I now know live in a house about mile from here straight back in the woods, stayed to help. My mom also stayed to help clean up.

"Aria, sit down. We got this," Emmalee scolded.

"Alright," I sighed, slowly sitting down.

My mom smiled and sat next to me.

"I am so proud of you," she sobbed, hugging me.

"Thanks mom." I smiled.

"What did Tyson mean when he said pack?" she asked.

"It's how they refer to themselves because there are a lot of people living here," I made up on the spot. *Wow that was pretty impressive.*

"Oh okay." She chuckled.

"So Isaac left then?" I confirmed.

"Yes, he is back living with his mom." She nodded.

"Good." I sighed in relief.

"I need to steal Aria away for a quick second." Ty smiled.

"Alright." My mom beamed.

"What's going on?" I asked as Ty helped me up.

"Just come on." He chuckled.

I followed him out. He helped me sit down in the grass and then I saw it, fireworks erupting in the sky. They were all white.

"Fireworks!" I beamed.

"Look." He chuckled.

"They say something?" I shouted. I didn't even know you could do that!

I read it out loud.

"Will you marry me?" I read. I was taking it all in when Ty pulled me to my feet and got down on one knee.

"Ty!" I gasped.

"Arrabella James Middleton you are the love of my life. I've loved you since the day I saw you in English class reading Twilight. I love the way your green eyes sparkle when you get excited and I love when you smile and your dimples show. I love everything about you. We are going to have a beautiful daughter shortly and I can only hope she will be as smart and kind hearted as her mother. Arrabella will you marry me?" Ty asked.

I nodded and then finally found my voice again.

"Yes." I laughed. He stood up and slipped the gorgeous ring on my finger.

"I love you Ty," I sniffled.

"I love you baby." He chuckled.

I cannot believe I am engaged to Tyson Benson!

* * *

Ty and I decided to have the wedding later on and have a long engagement. We want Kaya to be part of the wedding.

Also, I don't want to be pregnant during that time! Ty said it could be small or big. I told him to invite the entire pack so no one feels left out. Wolf weddings are different because the day Ty and I met he knew we would be together forever.

My mom cried when I told her the news. She's so happy for me.

"Babe where are the bottles?" I asked.

"I got it." Ty smiled, grabbing them from the sun room and stocking them into the cabinets.

"Thanks babe!" I called from the couch in the living room.

"Hey Aria." Audrey smiled, sitting on the couch next to me.

"Hey are you taking a break?" I laughed.

Audrey is moving in today! She has a lot of stuff! When I say a lot, I mean like Carter had to make two trips from her house to here just to transport everything.

"I am. Carter is still working." She shrugged.

"How long until he comes looking for you?" I scoffed.

"I give it," she started to say.

"Aud!" Carter called.

"Until now." She laughed.

"Yeah babe?" she asked.

"What's this?" he asked, holding up a football sweatshirt.

"That would be my friend's sweatshirt I never returned." She shrugged.

"Guy friend?"

"Yes Carter," she sighed.

"Who is he?"

"Carter stop. We were best friends in middle school. He's away at college now." She rolled her eyes.

"Well you wore it a lot." He pouted.

"Well look whose sweatshirt I'm wearing now." She pointed out while pointing to Carter's Vikings sweatshirt.

"That's my girl." He smiled, picking her up so she was straddling him.

"Okay bye." I called, standing up from the couch and walking into the kitchen.

I sat on the stool and watched as Ty stacked the bottles in the cabinet.

"Hey princess." He smiled.

"Hey Ty," I sighed, resting my chin on my hands.

"You tired?" he worriedly asked while searching my face.

"I'm tired of being pregnant. I just want the little chunker out." I pouted.

"I know babe. Soon enough she will be here."

I smiled up at him. He's right, soon enough Kaya would be in my arms, and I can't wait until she completes our little family.

Chapter 40

Dear Diary,

We are getting Kaya's nursery ready today!

~Aria

Ty showed me that the door on the left side of the room is actually a small room meant for the alpha's first born. We are painting it purple. There is a crib with purple bows and Kaya's name on the wall. It's perfect. We also have a cradle in our room for the first few months.

I can't wait until she is actually here and I can hold her and kiss her tiny head. I can only imagine the way she will look. I'm hoping she takes most of Ty's features.

"OH!" I screamed and fell to my knees.

"Aria!" Ty shouted, racing over to me.

"I think my water just broke!" I yelled.

Ty scooped me up and ran me down to the hospital room.

"Okay Aria, how bad is your pain?" Sherry asked.

"Out of ten a nine point five," I groaned. I can't even begin to describe this pain.

"Okay I will give you a shot." She nodded.

"Wait it's a week early!" I panicked.

"She's ready now." Sherry smiled.

"I'm not ready!"

Am I ready to keep a human being alive? I've never had experience with babies or even children. I mean I love kids but keeping one alive? What if I mess up? What if Kaya doesn't like me?

"Shh, it's okay babe. You are you are going to be a great mother, I promise."

"It hurts," I sobbed.

"I know baby, you're doing great," Ty sniffled, holding onto my hand.

* * *

Six hours later

"Push!" Sherry encouraged.

"I am pushing," I groaned.

"Come on until ten."

I made it to it to seven seconds. *Why is this so hard? Come on Arrabella you have to do this.* "You can do it Ar!" Ty soothed.

"I got this." I nodded.

I made it to ten.

"Did it work?" I asked.

"We've got the head. You need to push until I tell you to stop," Sherry added.

"Okay." I nodded.

"NOW!" She shouted.

I pushed as hard and long as I could. When I heard the crying my heart stopped. That was my daughter: half Tyson and half me.

Ty and I made this little girl.

Ty cut the umbilical cord, and Sherry cleaned her off.

"She weighs seven pounds two ounces," she announced, wrapping Kaya in a pink blanket and handing her to me.

"Hi Kaya, I'm your mama," I cried.

"I love you so much," I sobbed.

I looked over at Ty to see him looking at us in awe through his tears.

"That's your daddy," I cooed.

Ty smiled and kissed my head.

"She's perfect," he whispered.

"Hi little Kaya," he greeted, putting his finger in her tiny hand.

Kaya yawned and opened her little eyes. I gasped they were stunning. She had Ty's vibrant brown eyes with a small green sunburst.

I was now sobbing. This is my daughter. I've imagined her so many times but never this perfect. She's so beautiful. Her little oval shaped head and pudgy cheeks that made her look like she's pouting. She already had brown hair covering her little head. She was just perfect. I already love her more than words can describe.

This is the moment, you know "that moment" that you read about and see and movies. Nothing prepares you for the moment you see your baby's face—the face you've imagined a million times. I could stare at her forever.

"I have never seen eyes so beautiful."

"Alpha, the blood is human." Sherry smiled.

"Thank you." Ty smiled.

"You wanted her to be human?" I asked.

"I just wanted her to be whatever she was meant to be." He smiled.

Honestly, I didn't really care if Kaya was human or not. I'm just happy our little chunker is healthy.

"I love you." I grinned.

"I love you too." He smiled.

* * *

"Kaya." I laughed.

She was sticking her tongue out and all around.

"Get that tongue in there," I cooed.

She continued to amuse herself so I held her while finishing packing the diaper bag.

"Are you ready to see grandma?" I asked Kaya.

We are going to visit my mom today. It's been two weeks since Kaya was born and my mom is dying to see the perfect child I've been describing over the phone. My mom thinks that I was already seven months pregnant at the baby shower so she thinks Kaya is a perfectly healthy human, which she is, Kaya just happens to have a small amount of wolf blood in her. Plus I looked seven months pregnant during the baby shower so everything fell into place perfectly.

I told her about Kaya's brown eyes with green in them. She's so excited to hold her first grandchild. I'm so happy my mom and I patched things up and she can be a part of Kaya's life. After all it was my mother who gave me my green eyes and now her granddaughter has a small amount of green in her eyes but her eyes mostly look like her Daddy Ty's.

"Ready?" Ty asked.

"Yep." I smiled. He grabbed the bag and led me to the car. I put Kaya in her car seat and made sure she was buckled in properly.

We drove to my mom's apartment and my mom was waving at us excitedly through the window. I smiled and waved back. I got out of the car and grabbed Kaya from the back.

My mom was waiting for us at the door.

"Hey mom!" I called as we were walking up the steps.

"Hey, let me see her," my mom cooed.

I laughed and carefully handed Kaya to my mother as I entered the apartment.

"Oh!" My mom swooned.

Kaya looked up at her grandma. Kaya is always looking up at people with those eyes of hers. She loves looking into people's eyes in fact she gets fussy when you don't maintain eye contact; she's sure the center of attention right when I walk in the room with her.

After visiting with my mom, who spent the entire time gushing over our beautiful child, we drove back to the house.

"Your mom sure loves her." Ty chuckled.

"Everyone who lays eyes on her does." I laughed.

"Why wouldn't they? She's perfect," Ty said.

"Aww, are you a proud daddy?" I mocked, pinching his cheeks.

"I made her, so yes," he teased, wiggling his eyebrows.

"You're a psycho." I laughed.

"Am I Ar, am I psycho?" he questioned, putting an accent on the word psycho.

"Ty, I don't say it like that."

"Sorry princess but you do." He chuckled.

I rolled my eyes at the dork. Poor Kaya will have to deal with this embarrassing dork as a father, well at least she has two parents who love her and each other. What more could a girl ask for?

Chapter 41

Dear Diary,

Kaya is six months old today! Wow already half way to one. She's amazing. She lights up the room. She laughs at everything and loves me. She is such a loving and happy baby.

It is the best feeling in the world when she places her small head on my shoulder.

Ty and I are better than ever too. Kaya just completes our little family so amazingly. Ty and I are starting to plan for the wedding! We're thinking we will get married in August, which is only two months away.

~Aria

"Say mama," I encouraged.

"Mmmm." Kaya giggled.

"Well you got the first letter right," I cooed.

"Say dada!" Ty called from his desk.

This just made Kaya shift her attention from me to him. When he looked over at her and smiled she lifted her arms up and started bouncing in place.

I laughed and picked her up. She snuggled her head into my shoulder and I kissed her small head.

We were right about her dark hair. She got it from Tyson. Her eyes however remained a mix of Ty's and mine.

"I'm going to put her down for a nap," I told Ty.

"Alright babe, but then come back." He pouted.

"Okay, turn the baby monitors on," I called, leaving the room.

There is pretty much baby monitors all over the place in this house. However, on Ty's computer we can see and hear Kaya.

I placed her in her crib and watched as she snuggled into her blankets and shut her eyes.

"Night Kaya, love you," I whispered, shutting the door to her room. I then walked out of our bedroom and then went back downstairs.

"Where's Kay Kay?" Carter pouted from the couch.

"I just put her down for a nap." I laughed.

"Fine," he grumbled. Carter loves being an uncle to Kaya or Kay Kay as he calls her.

I walked back into Ty's office.

I love seeing Ty at his desk. His eyebrows are scrunched together because he's deep in thought. He looked up at me making me smile and shut the door. I walked over to him and sat on his lap.

I then pulled up Kaya's camera in her room to see if she was alright. She was sound asleep already holding onto the bear Audrey and Carter had bought her.

She is so perfect. She looks so innocent in her sleep; she looks just like Ty when he sleeps. She even moves her lips up in down like Ty does.

"She's fine love." Ty chuckled.

"I know, she looks like you when she sleeps." Ty looked at the computer and rolled his eyes.

"I don't look like that."

"Yes you do."

"Oh really?"

"Yeah, besides how would you know? You can't see yourself sleep." Instead of fighting back, Ty grabbed my face with his large hands and then ducked his head down so his lips made contact with mine.

I was a little surprised but I was kissing him back a second later. He smirked against my lips.

So that is why he kissed me, so I would shut up. Well this doesn't mean he won. I pulled away quickly knowing it would take Ty a minute to recover and I sprinted. I sprinted so fast through the house you would never know I had a baby six months ago. My body really snapped back quickly.

I ran up the stairs and went right and ran down to Carter and Audrey's room. I barged through the door and saw Audrey sitting on her bed getting her shoes on.

"Whoa, hey Aria." She laughed.

"Where are you going?" I asked still out of breath.

"I'm going on a walk with Carter. Why are you out of breath?" she asked.

"I just ran all the way up here," I panted.

"You're crazy." She laughed.

"Arrabella!" Ty demanded.

I looked up to see him in the doorway.

"Keep your voice down. You'll wake the baby up."

"Yeah too bad she's all the way on the other side of the hallway and can't hear us." He smirked.

"She can hear us, and you're lying right now," I teased.

"Come here."

"Say please."

"Are you kidding me?" He chuckled.

"Nope."

"Please."

I ran over to him and hugged him around the waist.

"You're so tall Ty you make me feel like a child." I laughed.

"You are a child."

"Joke's on you then because that means you're engaged to one," I said into his chest.

He chuckled making his chest rumble while he softly chucked. I love being in Ty's arms.

* * *

The wedding was only one month away!

Audrey and I have figured out the basics though. We are having purple, pink, and yellow roses. Then Ty and the Reverend will walk down the aisle, followed by Emmalee and Dalton. Then Audrey and Carter will walk down pulling Kaya in a white painted wood wagon covered with rose pedals; she will be our flower girl.

Then lastly my mother will escort me down the aisle. We decided that Audrey and my mother would wear purple dresses; Carter will wear a purple tie. Then Emmalee will wear a light pink dress, and Dalton will wear a light pink tie. Then Ty will wear a black suit with a white shirt and cream tie and then Kaya will wear a cream dress. I of course will be wearing a white wedding dress that Audrey and I found last week. My wedding dress is perfect and I can't wait to wear it!

After the ceremony the reception will be held out back that will have tables and chairs and a stage for live music. Tyson and I will have our first dance and then Ty and Kaya will dance along with the other father and daughters at the wedding. But most importantly that will be the day I become Arrabella James Benson.

Also, I invited Isaac. I told Ty and he wasn't even mad. In fact he said it would be a great idea! I mean Isaac and I have had our ups and downs but he was my best friend growing up.

"Mmmm," Kaya sounded, swinging her bear around.

"Mama." I laughed, kissing her head.

She smiled up at me. I am sitting on the floor with her looking through every song ever!

I am in charge of picking the song for Ty and my first dance! Audrey and I thought it would be a great surprise; but at this point it will be a surprise if I ever find a song!

I groaned and stood up, swinging Kaya around my hip.

"Let's go find Auntie Audrey," I told Kaya.

I walked to Carter and Audrey's bedroom and peeked through the doorway. They were on the bed playing an intense round of Uno.

"I hate to interrupt your game," I sarcastically started to say. "But I need Audrey's help." I pouted.

"Aww don't pout kid. What's wrong?" Carter asked.

"Carter I'm a mother, not a child." He laughed and stood up and took Kaya from my arms.

"Yeah right," he scoffed, throwing Kaya up a little and catching her.

"Kay kay," he sang, bouncing her. She laughed and grabbed onto his shirt.

"Talk to mama." Audrey smiled, patting the spot next to her on the bed.

I rolled my eyes and sat down.

"I can't find a song," I sighed.

"Well, what do you think about when you think of Tyson?"

"I don't know, love." I shrugged.

"What else." She laughed.

"That he helped me." I listed. Then I thought of all the things I love about Ty.

"What do you love about him?" she asked.

"His brown eyes, they're so light and vibrant and he always knows how to make me feel better. At night when he pulls me into him I feel so safe and comfy. He's like my best friend but way more. He's a great dad to Kaya." I went on. Everything, I love everything about Tyson.

"You're so cute," Audrey gushed.

"Stop." I laughed.

"Up and down," Carter sang, bouncing Kaya around.

Up and down what kind of song? Wait a minute! Ups and downs, that's it!

"Carter you're a genius!" I shouted.

"What?" he asked.

"God Gave Me You." I smiled.

Audrey's face lit up.

"That's perfect!" She screamed.

"It's a good thing Ty is out otherwise you two would have ruined the surprise, and yes I am a genius," He dramatically stated.

"You're on a roll babe first with Kaya's name and now with a song," Audrey mocked.

"I'm on a roll!" Carter sang to Kaya.

I rolled my eyes at the two. I'm so glad I have the perfect song; it describes our relationship perfectly.

Chapter 42

Dear Diary,

This is it, my wedding day.

I will become Arrabella James Benson in two hours.

~Aria

Audrey is helping me get ready.

I'm close to a panic attack.

"Kaya please don't," I begged as Kaya started pulling on the cord to the curling iron.

I picked her up and sat her on my lap. Audrey was curling my hair like crazy!

Kaya leaned her head into me and sighed.

I haven't seen Ty all day and I miss him. We aren't allowed to see each other the day of the wedding. So the first time I will see him is when I am walking down the aisle.

"I'll give Kaya to the boys," Audrey suggested, picking her up.

"Okay, tell Ty-," I started to say.

"Nope no communication."

"Bye Kay Alee!" I called, blowing her a kiss.

She clapped her hands, making me smile.

I looked at myself in the mirror. I remember the first day I met Ty. I didn't have a clue how much he would mean to me. I sure as hell never thought I would have a baby with him and be getting married to him.

"TYSON NO!" I heard Carter shout. Not in a mad way, in a Carter way. Tyson was probably about to get his way. I laughed at the thought.

Audrey came in and shut the door and locked it.

"What's going on?" I asked.

"Nothing." Audrey smiled. I knew she was just trying to not make me worry.

"I heard Carter shout." I laughed.

"Ty wanted to see you." She shrugged.

"Why what's wrong?" I asked, getting out of my seat.

"Nothing he's just going to have to wait," she scolded, sitting me back down.

"I miss him." I pouted.

"Yeah and he misses you so much he's about to break wedding traditions."

"I'm marrying a werewolf. I don't think wedding traditions apply here."

"Well you're human so it does apply here." She laughed.

"You're crazy," I scoffed.

"Okay, close your eyes and mouth. Time for your makeup." I rolled my eyes but obeyed. I can't wait until I'm walking down the aisle.

* * *

"You're good?" Audrey asked for the millionth time.

"Yes." I nodded, placing Kaya in her wagon.

I took a few deep breaths making Carter glance back at me. I nodded in assurance to him. I haven't had difficulty breathing in over a year and the idiot still gets worried.

"You look beautiful," my mother gasped as she joined me in the lineup.

"Mom." I smiled, giving her a hug.

"Look at Kaya." She smiled. Kaya looked up at the sound of her name and her little face brightened up when she saw her grandma.

"Hi baby!" my mom greeted, leaning down and kissing her head.

"This is it Ella, your wedding day." My mom smiled while a few tears escaped.

"Mom, don't start crying." I laughed, trying to hold back my own tears.

"You're just such an amazing women Ella, you really are."

"Thanks mom," I replied, hugging her again.

"Okay Ty and the Reverend are out there," Audrey informed.

"Aria we are walking out in thirty seconds but I wanted to come back here and tell you I'm so happy Tyson found you. You make him so happy and you already fit perfectly into the family. Kaya's gorgeous and you're gorgeous," Emmalee started to cry a little.

"Thank you, Emmalee." I smiled, hugging her.

"Dear we are walking down the aisle in ten seconds." Dalton chuckled, wiping away her tears.

Tyson is like Dalton like that. I love the way Emmalee and Dalton look at each other.

"We're happy you're joining the family Arrabella," Dalton added, smiling at me.

"I'm glad too." I smiled.

Dalton doesn't talk much. He's one to just sit back with a smile on his face; you can tell he's a very content man.

Before I knew it, Audrey and Carter were getting ready to walk and then it would be me and my mother.

"See you out there." Audrey smiled.

"Don't trip," Carter mocked.

I shook my head and waved.

"Smile Kaya," I called. She started clapping, making me laugh.

Carter pulled her along in her wagon.

I waited and I heard the bride music start playing. I took a deep breath and held onto my mother's arm.

The aisle came into view along with the crowd, but most importantly Ty came into view.

I beamed at the brown-eyed boy I have fallen completely in love with. Ty looked at me in awe.

A few tears slid down my face as I looked from him and over to Kaya who was looking at me.

I smiled at her as well and then shifted my attention back to Tyson.

Our eyes continued to stay locked all the way down the aisle. We finally made it to him and then my mother handed me over to Tyson.

I was completely lost in Ty's eyes the entire time.

"Tyson will now read his vows to Arrabella," The Reverend announced.

I smiled at Tyson and waited.

"Arrabella," he started to say. It wasn't in his Ty way. He wasn't teasing me because he knew I hated when people called me Arrabella, the way Ty said it was sincere. It was like he was demanding my attention.

"The first time I saw you," he went on. "You were at your locker on your first day of school." I remember that day so well.

"You didn't even shoot me a glance either." He smirked. I smiled at him, wanting so bad to just kiss him.

"Then I saw you in English reading Twilight. You were so into the book that I didn't even want to disturb you. You are an amazingly strong person, and I only hope our gorgeous daughter Kaya grows up to be exactly like you. I wasn't me before I met you; I let my temper take control of me almost every day. Now I barely ever lose my temper. I love waking up to your green eyes every morning. Ar, I don't know how you do it but you make me fall in love with you all over again every day. So Arrabella, I vow to not lose my temper. I vow to be as patient and kind hearted as you are. I vow to be a great husband and father every day. I vow that I will spend the rest of my life falling even harder for you every day. I love you." I let my tears spill over my cheeks. Ty used his thumb to wipe them away quickly. Then he put his hands back in mine.

I smiled up at him and took a deep breath.

"Tyson ever since I saw you in English I knew I was never getting rid of you," I started to say making the crowd erupt into quiet laughter.

"I got lost in your eyes like I still do to this day," I went on. "I was at a low point when you met me. I would go through everything I went through again just because all of it led me to you. I have never connected with anyone like I do with you and I'm so happy I get to wake up to my best friend every morning. So Tyson, I vow to love you every second of every day. I vow to be the best wife to you and the best mother to our beautiful daughter Kaya. I vow that we will spend the rest of our lives making each other laugh. I love you." A few tears escaped Ty's eyes, making me want to cry again.

"Tyson do you take Arrabella to be your wife?" The Reverend asked.

"I do." He smiled, slipping the wedding band onto my finger.

"Arrabella do you take Tyson to be your husband?"

"I do." I smiled.

"I now pronounce you husband and wife. You may kiss the bride!"

The crowd clapped, and Ty pulled me to him. We kissed for about ten seconds and then Ty took my hand.

"Ladies and gentlemen for the first time I present you with Tyson and Arrabella Benson!" He announced.

Ty and I walked down the aisle. *I'm officially Arrabella Benson!*

Ty and I are waiting outside. We had to be announced and then we would walk in and have our first dance!

"Don't be nervous," he whispered.

"I'm not," I whispered back, looking up at him.

"What's the song we are dancing to?" he asked, smirking.

"Wouldn't you like to know?" I teased.

Our names were then announced and Ty and I walked to the dance floor just as "God Gave Me You" by Blake Shelton came on.

Ty gasped a little under his breath and then we made it to the dance floor and he pulled me into him smiling like crazy.

"What?" I whispered.

"I love this song." He chuckled.

I beamed up at him and listened to the words, the words that described our relationship almost perfectly.

"I've been a walking heartache," the song started.

"I've made a mess of me

The person that I've been lately

Ain't who I wanna be

But you stay here right beside me

Watch as the storm blows through...

And I need you

Cause God gave me you for the ups and downs

God gave me you for the days of doubt

And for when I think I've lost my way

There are no words here left to say, it's true...."

Ty kissed me at the end of the song making me smile against his lips.

After our dance the father daughter dance was announced and Ty had picked the song for it. I have no idea what song is coming on.

Every father and their daughter get to dance for this one, I however am not dancing, mostly because I just want to watch Ty dance with Kaya.

The song started playing and I knew exactly what song it was right away, "My Little Girl" by Tim McGraw.

"Gotta hold on easy as I let you go," the song started.

Ty was swaying and singing the words softly to Kaya. I

started to videotape them because I want to show Kaya it one day. Ty really is a great dad.

"Gonna tell you how much I love you, though you think you already know.

I remember I thought you looked like an angel wrapped in pink so soft and warm.

You've had me wrapped around your finger since the day you were born.

You're beautiful baby from the outside in.

Chase your dreams but always know the road that'll lead you home again.

Go on, take on this whole world.

But to me you know you'll always be, my little girl.

When you were in trouble that crooked little smile could melt my heart of stone.

Now look at you, I've turned around and you've almost grown.

Sometimes you're asleep I whisper "I Love You!" in the moonlight at your door.

As I walk away, I hear you say, "Daddy Love You More!"

You're beautiful baby from the outside in.

Chase your dreams but always know the road that'll lead you home again."

You'll always be, my little girl," the song finished.

Ty kissed Kaya's cheek and walked over to me. I put down the camera and smiled at the two. I can't believe I get to call them family.

* * *

"You'd better not!" I warned as Ty and I cut the cake. I didn't want him smashing cake in my face!

"I won't." He promised.

He came through and neither of us smashed cake in the other's face even though I wanted to do it to him so bad!

"Everyone grab a piece!" I shouted.

Carter of course was first in line, making me roll my eyes. That's when I noticed Isaac. I smiled and went up to him.

"You made it." I grinned, hugging him.

"Yeah of course," he chuckled. "The way you two look at each other is amazing."

"Thanks."

"Kaya is adorable."

"Yeah and she knows it." I laughed.

"Hello Isaac," Ty greeted, walking up to us.

"Hello Tyson, congratulations I'm glad Ella found you." "Thanks man." He nodded.

Kaya stared at Isaac. She loves meeting new people. I grabbed her out of Ty's arms.

"Isaac this is my daughter Kaya," I introduced.

"Hi Kaya," he cooed.

She smiled and reached for him.

"Do you want to hold her?" I asked.

"Sure." He shrugged, grabbing her.

He bounced her around making her smile.

I'm glad Isaac and I patched things up.

* * *

"That was one hell of a night." Tyson grinned, scooping me up bridal style and carrying me into our bedroom.

"I agree." I laughed as he lay me on the bed.

"What is it people do on their wedding night?"

"I don't know care to show me?" I teased.

"I sure would Mrs. Benson." He smirked.

I don't know what the future holds. All I know is that I love Tyson Benson and whatever happens as long as I'm with him I'm happy.

Chapter 43

Dear Diary,
I'm officially Arrabella Benson!
Everything about the wedding was amazing!
I love Tyson so much.
~Aria

"Mmm," Kaya tried again.

"Come on angel," I encouraged.

"Babe, she's ten months old," Ty reminded, handing her a bottle.

"I know," I sighed. "I just want her to say mama." I pouted.

"I know princess." He chuckled, pulling me onto his lap. I laughed and turned my head up and pressed my lips to his. He moaned against my lips, making me smile.

"Ahh!" Kaya squealed. I laughed and pulled away. The girl sure demands her attention.

"I'm sorry Kaya." I laughed, getting off Ty's lap and placing Kaya on my lap.

I kissed her head. *I can't believe she will be one in two months!*

* * *

Dear Diary,

My baby's a year old!
We are having a little party in the backyard.
My mom is coming and bringing her boyfriend Krieg. I'm really excited to meet him; he sounds so nice.
~Aria

"Where is my birthday girl?" I sang, walking into Kaya's room. She was standing up, waiting for me in her crib.

"There she is!" I smiled.

"Ahhh!" Kaya squealed.

"Hi baby," I sang, lifting her out of her crib.

"Are you ready to get dressed in your pretty dress?" I asked her.

"Mmm," she replied.

Kaya would be wearing a pink and green dress. The green really brought out the green in her eyes.

I then put on her party hat and tiny shoes that matched the dress.

"You're ready for your party." I smiled.

"Hey girls." Ty walked in and kissed my head, helping me up.

"Who's the prettiest birthday girl?" Ty asked Kaya. She pointed to him, making us both laugh.

Ty took her, and we walked downstairs. I am wearing a long pink and purple dress.

Ty is in a green button-down shirt and dark jeans.

"Kay Kay has arrived!" Carter shouted. Kaya squealed at the sound of her uncle.

"Where is he?" Ty asked her. Kaya searched around.

When she saw him, she pointed and started bouncing.

"Hey Aria!" Audrey called, putting the candles on Kaya's pink cake.

"That looks amazing Audrey!" I smiled.

"Thanks." She beamed.

We walked out back and I went over to Emmalee and Dalton to give them a hug. Of course, Emmalee wanted to gush over Kaya's dress and Dalton wanted to know if Ty and I were practicing to make Kaya some siblings.

I saw my mom with a handsome man. He had light brown hair and hazel eyes.

"Hey mom!" I greeted.

"Hey honey." She smiled.

"You must be Krieg?" I asked.

"Yes, it is very nice to meet you Aria." He nodded.

My mom seems so happy with Krieg, which makes me happy.

"Where's the birthday girl?" My mother asked.

"With the boys, I'll go grab her," I replied, walking over to Ty and Carter.

They were singing some kind of remix of the belly button song to her.

"Hey psychos I need to borrow my child." I laughed.

"Okay." Ty laughed, handing her to me. Carter pouted, making me roll my eyes.

"Is your mom here?" Ty asked, walking with me.

"Yeah and Krieg."

"Of course." He nodded.

"Here she is," I told my mom, handing Kaya to her.

"Krieg this is my husband Tyson," I introduced.

"Nice to meet you Tyson," Krieg replied, giving Ty a handshake.

"She sure is a beauty," he commented, tickling Kaya.

"Thanks." I smiled.

* * *

"Happy birthday to Kaya. Happy birthday to you." We all sang, making Kaya clap her hands.

Ty and I got Kaya a bracelet. It had a small heart on it. She loves looking at it. We put it on her wrist, and now she won't let us take it off!

A year really flies by. Soon my little girl will be walking and talking. I can't wait to watch my amazing girl grow up; let's just hope it doesn't happen too fast.

* * *

Four months later

"TY IT'S REALLY HAPPENING!" I yelled from the living room. Carter, Audrey, and I were currently watching *Sofia the First* with Kaya, and Ty was in his office.

Ty was in a second later just as Kaya advanced toward the television.

"Kaya!" I cheered.

She turned around and gave me a huge smile. She then advanced toward me and I held out my hand to her. She held out her little arms and made her way over to me.

She grabbed onto my hands, and I pulled her onto my lap.

"You did it baby!" I sobbed.

Ty then picked her up and threw her in the air and caught her, making her smile and look at him through those long eyelashes of hers; she could win anyone's heart with just a glance.

"You did it angel," he whispered, kissing her cheek.

She laughed and blew him a kiss back.

Carter walked over to her and held out his fist. She gave him a fist pump. Carter insisted we teach her the fist pump instead of the high five.

"Auntie Audrey is so proud of Kay Kay." Audrey beamed at Kaya while walking over Ty and Kaya. She tickled Kaya's tummy.

She then pointed to Audrey's stomach, making her lift up her shirt to show Kaya where her cousin was.

Audrey was three months pregnant!

They only have to wait another month to find out the gender. Carter proposed to Audrey the week before they found out about the baby. They are waiting for the baby to be born until their wedding.

Carter says he wants a boy but I think he secretly wants a girl. Of course, Audrey and I both want it to be a girl!

How cute would it be for Kaya to have girl cousin as her best friend?

It finally feels like everything is falling into place.

Chapter 44

Dear Diary,
Audrey and Carter are having a girl!
They are still deciding on the name.
Kaya is now one and a half and still hasn't spoken; I think
even Ty is starting to worry.
~Aria

"How about Ava? That's cute," I suggested.

"Ava is cute," Audrey agreed.

"I like Taylor." Carter pouted.

"You only want to name her Taylor so it can be Kay Kay and Tay Tay," I pointed out.

"It would be cute."

"He's too much," Audrey mocked.

"Mmm," Kaya insisted from Ty's lap, letting us know she wanted my attention.

"Mama," I told her, looking at her.

"Ahh!" She pointed to the steps.

"You want to race?" Ty asked.

She clapped her hands, sliding off Ty's lap and to the stairs.

"One, two, three!" I called while Ty and her crawled up the stairs. It was pretty amusing to watch Ty slowly climb the stairs on his hands and knees just to let his daughter win.

"Winner!" he announced, making Kaya squeal.

"WIN!" She pronounced loud and clear.

"Did she just say win?" I nearly shouted.

"Win," she declared.

"Are you serious Kaya? That's your first word? You hang out with the boys too much." I laughed, taking her out of Ty's arms.

She pointed to Audrey's belly so I sat her next to Audrey.

"Yes Kay, baby cousin is in here," Audrey cooed, taking Kaya's hand and holding it to her stomach.

"Can you say baby, Kaya?" I asked her.

She shook her head.

"Win." She laughed.

I tickled her making her squeal. I then lifted up her shirt and blew on her stomach, making her giggle. The doorbell rang and Carter shot up.

"Pizza's here!" Carter announced.

He set the pizza on the table. I took one whiff of it and felt nauseous. I set Kaya on the couch and ran to the bathroom. I got there just in time before hurling into the toilet.

"Aria?" Ty asked, running to me and holding back my hair.

"What brought this on?" he asked.

"I don't know. One smell of that pizza and my nose just–," I stopped short and we were both looking at each other the same way.

"You don't think I'm–," I started to say.

"Pregnant?" He beamed. "Let's find out."

We walked into the hospital room and the nurse, Sherry, brought up an ultrasound.

"Congratulations, baby number two is one month along." She beamed.

I looked up at Ty who was beaming. I can't believe we were having another baby and Kaya's going to be a big sister!

* * *

"Where are we going?" I asked for the millionth time.

I am already two months pregnant, and Kaya will be two in three months! She is talking so much now. It's amazing!

"Kaya has daddy lost his mind?" I asked her.

"No mama."

I know Ty is carrying her in one arm. His other hand is over my eyes.

"Okay, say it Kay Alee," Ty prompted.

"Surprise!" she yelled.

Ty took his hands away from my eyes, and we were standing in front of a little house. It was perfect!

"Ty."

"You know how my mom and dad live in a house other than the pack house?" he asked.

"Yes." I nodded.

"Yeah they live right behind those trees but this one is ours." He beamed, gesturing to the adorable house.

"Ours?" I questioned.

"Yeah the pack house is right there. I walked you around for a while so you'd be confused," he mocked.

The pack house was literally forty steps away but our house had about four trees in front of it, just enough for our privacy but we would still be close to the pack.

"I love it!" I squealed.

"Great because our bedroom and Kaya's wouldn't really work with our second chunker on the way." Ty chuckled.

"I love you." I laughed.

"I love you too. Now let's move in!" he shouted. I laughed and took Kaya inside the house.

When Ty said let's move in he meant Kaya's stuff and our clothes. The house was already furnished.

It was the most amazing little place ever!

There was a living room with a kitchen off to the side, then the upstairs where there was the master bedroom and two other bedrooms. There was a bathroom attached to every bedroom! Then there was a basement with another bedroom and bathroom, a playroom and a family room.

This house is perfect!

Ty had already had Kaya's room painted purple, and the baby's room remained white since we didn't know if it's a boy or girl yet.

After getting everything moved in I put Kaya down for her nap. We set up the monitors and then I sat on the couch in the living room with Ty.

"I love this house." I smiled, kissing him. He pulled me onto his lap so I was straddling him.

"How's our chunker?" he asked, rubbing my stomach.

I laughed and then Ty's face changed.

"What?" I asked.

"Audrey just went into labor," he replied.

"What, oh my gosh." I panicked.

"It's okay."

"No, they don't even have a name picked out yet."

"Babe, trust me everything is okay." Ty doesn't want me worked up because it's not good for the baby or me.

I nodded.

"Here look what I brought." He smiled, holding up *Twilight.*

"You're a dork." I laughed, sliding off his lap so he could put it in.

All there's left to do is wait. I can't wait to see my niece. I'm sure she will be perfect.

* * *

Ty and I walked into the room. I sat down next to Audrey and sat Kaya in my lap.

In Audrey's arm was a beautiful girl wrapped in a soft pink blanket.

"She's perfect," I gushed.

"Thanks, she has my brown eyes."

"Baby." Kaya pointed.

"Kaya that's your cousin," I whispered.

"Cousin?" Kaya repeated.

"Did you decide on a name?" I asked.

Audrey looked up at Carter, who was looking at Audrey and his daughter like they were the most important things in the world, and he gave her a nod.

"We decided to name her Tiana," she started to say.

"That's so cute," I gushed.

"But her middle name Aria." She smiled.

I sat there for a moment as it dawned on me.

"Why?" I asked.

"Because you would kill us if it was Arrabella." Carter joked.

I rolled my eyes at him.

"Because you helped me not be afraid to stand up for myself. Not be afraid of new things, like wolves. We would be blessed if Tiana is half as amazing as you are," Audrey explained. A few tears escaped my eyes and I hugged Audrey.

"Thank you." I smiled, putting my finger in Tiana's hand.

"Baby," Kaya cooed, putting her hand on Tiana's stomach.

"That's your cousin, Tiana," I told her.

"TT." Kaya smiled.

"TT Aria." Audrey smiled down at the beautiful child. They are going to make great parents.

* * *

Tomorrow is the day Ty and I find out our baby's gender!

Tiana is already two months old and Kaya will be two next month.

"Baby," Kaya sang, touching my tummy. We are in the living room in the pack house. Audrey is upstairs napping, and Ty is in the shower over at our house.

"Your brother or sister is in there Kay Kay," I told her.

"Tiana?"

"No, Tiana is Auntie Audrey's baby."

"Tiana you're fine," Carter cooed while changing her diaper. The girl hated getting her diaper changed.

"Carter quit traumatizing her!" I called.

"Not helping!" he called back.

I laughed and set Kaya next to me on the couch. I turned on Little Einstein's and got up to get some food.

"Ar, please tell me Kaya walked over here by herself," Ty groaned walking in the door.

"Okay. Kaya walked over here all by herself," I mocked.

"I'm serious babe, you should be resting."

"Ty please chill for a second." I laughed.

He rolled his eyes, picking me up and putting me in a chair.

"Okay, now what do you want?" he asked.

"A salad please." I yawned, placing my head in my hands.

"Mama!" I heard Kaya call followed by little footsteps running on the tiled floor.

I lifted my head up when I felt her little hands on my legs.

"Hi angel." I smiled, lifting her onto my lap.

"Daddy." She smiled when she saw him.

"There's my angel." Ty smiled back.

"Where you go?" she asked, holding up her hands.

"I was in the shower baby," he replied.

"Shower?"

"Yes, the shower." He laughed.

"Daddy look!" She demanded, lifting my shirt up to show him my stomach.

"Well who's in there?" he asked her.

"Baby."

"A baby is right." He nodded.

"Look!" She repeated, lifting her shirt up to show him her tummy.

"What?" He chuckled.

"It's my belly button!" She shouted, pointing to it.

"It sure is." He smiled.

"Mommy got one." She smiled, showing Ty mine.

"Daddy has one too," he told her.

"What?" she asked, climbing on the counter.

He grabbed her and lifted up his shirt.

"Belly button!" she squealed.

"It would seem so." He laughed, tickling her stomach.

She laughed and pushed at his hands.

"Want to help me make mommy's salad?" he asked her.

"Sure." She shrugged.

I laughed at that too. You sure could tell they were father and daughter.

Kaya really started talking a lot last month; she realized it earned her more attention when she did. Now we can never get her to stop!

Tomorrow we find out if the baby is a boy or girl, and honestly, I will be ecstatic either way.

Chapter 45

Dear Diary,

Ty and I are all moved in!

Today we find out the gender of the baby!

Our room in the pack house is still the same except most of the clothes are gone. Plus, Kaya's room is almost completely empty.

I love our new house though, and all the space. We still spend a lot of our time at the pack house though!

~Aria

"Alright are you ready?" Sherry asked.

"Ready," Kaya replied. She was on the floor coloring in her Scooby-Doo coloring book.

"Yes." I laughed.

"Okay well you've got an even bigger chunker here," she started to say.

"Of course." I smiled.

The nurse stopped short and smiled hugely at the screen.

"It looks like you have the next alpha in there. It's a boy," Sherry announced.

"A boy." I smiled.

Ty beamed at the monitor and then at me.

Tears fell from both of our eyes, and Ty kissed my head and rubbed my tummy. Right when Ty put his hand on my stomach our son started kicking.

"Kaya come feel your brother kick," I told her. Kaya got up and climbed on the bed.

I placed her hand on my stomach and she grinned.

"Brother." She squealed.

"That's right baby." I laughed.

Our family just keeps getting better and better. Soon we will have two wonderful children.

* * *

"Carter." Carter smirked.

"I'm not naming him Carter!" I laughed, throwing a pillow at Carter.

"Oh switch around Ty's name and have it be Dalton Tyson," Audrey suggested.

"I don't want him having the same name as my dad. It's frowned upon in the alpha line." Ty shrugged.

"What?" Audrey and I both asked.

"The boy should take the father's middle name." Ty shrugged.

"Great so his middle name is Tyson. Now all we have to do is figure out the first name." I laughed.

"Something strong yet cute." Audrey nodded.

"Exactly!" I nearly shouted, but what?

Ty and Carter busted out laughing.

"Strong yet cute? You two are ridiculous!" Carter choked out.

"Ty it's not ridiculous." I pouted.

"Of course not princess." Ty soothed, sobering up.

He was trying not to upset me since my emotions were already all over the place.

I sighed. Why is naming a child so difficult?

"Forget it, we'll think of something eventually." I sighed, walking upstairs.

We are in our own house. Audrey and Carter are over quite frequently.

I walked into Kaya's room and smiled when I saw her sitting up in her crib.

"Ma-mama!" She squealed, standing up and reaching her arms out to me.

"Well hi pretty girl!" I sang. "Guess who's here Kay Kay?" I asked her.

"Uncle Car and Auntie Audy?" She sang. *She's so damn cute!*

"You are correct angel." I smiled, lifting her out of the crib.

"I go?" she asked.

"Yes, we are going downstairs." I laughed.

"Kaya will walk," she told me.

"Okay baby." I laughed, setting her down. She ran out of her room and down the stairs.

"UNCLE CAR!"

"Kay Kay is that you?" Carter asked.

"It's Kay Kay!" she screamed, racing over to him.

He laughed and picked her up onto his lap.

"Where's Daddy?" she asked.

"In the kitchen." Carter told her.

"With baby TT?" she asked.

"Yes, with Auntie Audrey and TT."

I smiled at the two and then took a picture and went into the kitchen.

Ty was getting Kaya's sippy cup filled and Audrey was warming up a bottle for Tiana.

"Babe, sit down please." Ty groaned, taking my hand and leading me out of the kitchen.

"I feel fine babe," I sighed.

"Uncle Car, Little Mermaid," Kaya demanded.

I laughed and sat down next to them.

Ty sat on the other side of me.

"Daddy!" Kaya smiled, climbing on my lap and reaching for the sippy cup.

"Here angel," he replied, giving her the cup.

"Thank you, Daddy!"

"You're welcome. Here sit with Dad so Mom and brother have enough room," he told her, pulling her onto his lap.

She snuggled into him and he kissed her head.

Audrey came in with Tiana and a bottle and we all watched *Little Mermaid*.

I felt myself dozing off and let my head fall on Ty's shoulder.

The last thing I remember was Ariel waking up to Eric on the beach.

* * *

"Wake up mama." I heard Kaya demand.

"Sit on her legs Kay Alee." I heard Ty prompt.

Then Kaya was sitting on my legs.

"Rawr!" I shouted, sitting up and tickling her.

"Ahh!" She laughed.

Ty came over and helped Kaya off me and then helped me off the couch.

He then led me over to the table where he had made spaghetti and meatballs.

"Wow Ty this is amazing." I smiled.

"It's nothing babe." He laughed, pecking my lips. He then lifted Kaya onto her highchair and then sat next to me.

"Daddy sunshine?" Kaya smiled.

"You want to show mama?" Ty chuckled.

She nodded her head crazily in excitement.

I looked at Ty in question.

"I've got sunshine," he belted out. "On a cloudy day, when it's cold outside I've got the month of May, and I'll bet you say what can make me feel this way." Ty sang and then pointed to Kaya.

"My girl." She laughed.

"We're talking 'bout," Ty sang.

"My little girl," Kaya sang.

"My girl," Ty added.

I laughed and clapped at the two.

"You two are crazy." I laughed, reaching up and tickling Kaya in her highchair.

"I think you two should be in a father-daughter band."

* * *

"I want Daddy to tuck me in!" Kaya called.

"Okay Kay, he's coming!" I called, going into her room.

I kissed her head and she remained standing.

"I love you Kaya Alee." I smiled.

"I love you mama." She grinned.

"Daddy's here!" Ty announced, handing Kaya her teddy bear.

"Daddy!" She squealed, holding up her arms.

I smiled and stood in the doorway, because I will never get tired of what happens next.

"There's this girl I know," Ty started to sing. "Her name is Kaya Alee. She is her daddy's girl, or so she tells me so. I love her with all my heart that she has a part of. Kaya likes to play, play, play all day, under the sunshine or in the pouring rain, she just likes to play. Oh she loves her mommy too. She and her mommy like to play Barbies. But Kaya's a daddy's girl at heart; she has a part of my heart that will always be hers. Oh Kaya Alee daddy loves you so, daddy loves you so," Ty finished, placing our daughter in her crib. Kaya was already almost asleep.

"I love you Kaya," Ty whispered.

Just as Ty was leaving Kaya shifted.

"Daddy, love you more!"

Ty smiled and shut the door.

"Really Ar, you cry every night," Ty mocked, taking my hand and wiping away my tears.

"I love that song," I sniffled.

"I am talented," Ty teased, wiggling his eyebrows. Ty came up with that song all on his own. He actually has a pretty decent voice as well.

We walked into our room and I climbed into bed.

"Shoot I have to pee!" I shouted, going into the bathroom.

"Crazy!" Ty called.

"Love you too babe!" I laughed from the bathroom.

I walked out and climbed back into bed. I lay down next to Ty, and he pulled me as close to him as my stomach would let him.

He still buried his face in my hair though, and took in a deep breath; I will never get tired of this.

Chapter 46

Dear Diary,
Ty and I have narrowed down our list to five names!
In no particular order:
1. Mason
2. Eric
3. Andrew
4. Carson
5. Hunter
He will be here in one month, and we have already painted
his nursery navy blue!
I can't wait for my second chunker to enter into the world.
~Aria

"Come on Daddy!" Kaya shouted.

"I'm coming Kaya!"

Today we are going to my mom's. My mom was so excited when I told her that I was pregnant with her second grandchild. She thinks I'm already eight months along.

"Ty how long does it take?" I shouted.

"It takes some time!" He shouted back. I laughed and then took Kaya's hand.

"Meet you in the car!" I called.

I walked Kaya out to the car and buckled her into her car seat. Ty finally came out of the house.

We sent Ty back upstairs to get Kaya's stuffed unicorn. Carter and Audrey had given it to her for her second birthday and now it has to go everywhere with us.

We drove to my mom's and she was already opening the door as we were pulling into the driveway.

Ty got out of the car and got Kaya out of her car seat and I slowly got myself out of the car.

"Ella you look great!" My mom smiled, approaching us.

"Thanks mom." I smiled, hugging her.

"How is my grandson today?" she asked.

"He's pretty calm today!" I replied.

"NANA!" Kaya screamed.

"Kaya Alee!" She beamed, taking her from Ty.

"Nana look!" Kaya grinned, holding up her unicorn.

"What is that?" she asked.

"My unicorn!"

I shook my head at the crazy child and followed my mom and Kaya into the house.

"Where's Krieg?" I asked her.

"He's at work." She smiled. She and Krieg are pretty serious and are always together when I talk to my mom on the phone. I'm happy my mom found a guy as great as Krieg.

"Kaya who is in Mommy's tummy?" My mom asked Kaya.

Kaya raced over to me and sat on my lap and lifted up my shirt.

"Brother," she told my mom.

"What do you think his name should be Kaya?" Ty asked her.

"Unicorn!"

I laughed and kissed her head.

"We'll keep that in mind." I told her.

After visiting my mom we headed back home. I wasn't feeling too good so Ty put Kaya down for a nap and I headed into our bedroom.

I walked in and opened my bag to find the medication the nurse had put me on.

That's when I noticed my diary. It wasn't to the left by my blanket, which I never moved; it was placed on top of it.

I thought back and I know I put it in its place.

Ty walked in and I turned around.

"Ty did you go in my bag?" I asked.

He looked a little torn and then sighed.

"Yeah," he whispered.

"Why?" I asked already growing mad.

"I'm sorry Ar," he whispered.

"You read my diary, didn't you?" I asked.

"Only like the last few pages."

"What the hell Ty, why?" I snapped.

"I just wanted to know why you were still writing in it. I thought something might be bothering you," he honestly replied, advancing towards me.

"Then why didn't you ask me?" I asked, taking a step back.

He looked hurt by this but I don't care at the moment. *How could Ty do this? He knows what I put in there isn't for anyone else to read.*

"Because Ar, you never want me to know what you are writing."

"You don't trust me?"

"I do Ar, come on." He groaned, taking a few more steps toward me.

I took a step back and watched as his face crumbled with slight regret.

"You come on Ty. I would have never done that if it were your diary. You don't see me reading through your emails or anything on your desk in your office."

"I know babe, I'm sorry. I just worry about you."

"Then ask me!"

"Okay Ar, I messed up. I'm so sorry. I promise I will ask you next time."

"Ty I wish I could believe that but you know that if I would have said I was fine you would have still looked through it," I said, walking past him.

He knows it's true. Ty is persistent when it comes to stuff like this.

"Where are you going?" He called after me.

"Pack house, don't follow me. Stay with Kaya," I demanded, walking out of the house.

I made it to the pack house and walked up to our bedroom.

"Whoa pregnant woman coming through!" Carter smiled when he saw me.

"Thanks Carter I wasn't aware," I mocked.

"What's wrong?" he asked, following me into my room.

"Ty and I had a fight. I'm just going to go to bed okay?"

"Alright night," he replied, shutting the door. Carter is just as protective as Ty so I know it's killing him that I didn't tell him about the fight. I'm just too tired to talk about it anymore.

It's weird being in this room again lying in this bed, the bed that I had to convince Ty to sleep in with me the first night I stayed here. I smiled at the memory and then dozed off.

* * *

I woke up to a baby lying next to me.

"Hi TT Aria!" I sang. She smiled and looked up at me. She looks just like Audrey with her blonde hair and big brown eyes.

"She wanted her Auntie." Carter shrugged, entering the room.

"I bet she did," I cooed, sitting up and pulling her onto my lap.

"So what happened?" Carter asked.

"Tyson went through my diary."

"That idiot," he dramatically said, successfully making me laugh.

"Your daddy is silly," I told Tiana, tickling her tummy making her laugh. I love this kid's laugh. It's so much like Carter's, just more angelic and not as annoying.

"Listen Aria, if Ty did that then he's obviously worried about you."

"I know Carter but nothing's wrong and he didn't even ask me about it," I sighed.

"Aria you wouldn't have told him anyways," Carter protested.

"There's nothing to tell," I sighed, playing with Tiana's small hands.

"Yeah okay, go talk to him."

"Okay psycho." I smirked.

He rolled his eyes, taking Tiana and helping me stand up.

"Did you decide on a name yet for my nephew?"

"Not yet." I shrugged.

Tiana held her arms out toward me.

"Sorry TT, but I have to leave you with the crazy guy," I told her.

"Okay you're done," he teased, leaving the room.

"Bye." I laughed, following him out of the room.

"Talk to Tyson," he called as I walked down the stairs.

I walked out of the pack house and back over to our house.

I walked upstairs to find Ty giving Kaya her bath.

"Mama!" Kaya squealed when she saw me.

"Hi angel!" I smiled.

"I'm taking a bath."

"I see that baby, good job," I told her.

"Are you okay?" Ty asked, lifting Kaya out of the bath and wrapping her in her fluffy pink towel.

"Yeah."

"Mama you okay?" Kaya mimicked.

"I'm great now that I've seen my angel." I smiled. She laughed and wrapped her arms around my legs.

"Come on let's pick out some pajamas," I told her.

After getting Kaya ready for bed I left the room so Ty could sing to her.

I went downstairs and saw Ty had left a plate of chicken and potatoes in the fridge for me. I grabbed it and heated it up in the microwave. I sat down and started eating.

Ty walked in the kitchen a few minutes later.

"Thanks for leaving my plate."

He sat down next to me and angled himself right in front of me.

"What's wrong?" he asked.

"You went through my diary Ty."

"I'm so sorry for that, but why are you still writing in it?"

"It's something I like to do Ty. For a long time that was all I had to put my thoughts in and feel like they mattered."

"Do you still feel like that?" he asked, already getting angry.

"Of course not Ty." I laughed.

"Then why?" he asked.

"Why does it bother you so much?"

"Because sometimes I feel like you like telling your thoughts to that thing so much, and then I never get to know them."

"So why didn't you just tell me that?" I asked.

"Okay, and I was curious as to what you were writing in it," he admitted.

"I'm not scared for you to see what's written in there but it's just the fact that you didn't just ask me."

"I know, I'm sorry Aria." He apologized.

"I forgive you Ty." I smiled.

He beamed back and gave me a peck on the lips.

"How's the chunker?" he asked.

"He's gotten chunkier."

Ty chuckled, shaking his head.

I can't wait for my second chunker to enter the world, knowing he has a great dad and an amazing but crazy aunt and uncle.

Chapter 47

Dear Diary,
Our son is coming any day now!
His room is ready and it's all Kaya talks about.
~Aria

"Unicorn," Kaya suggested.

"We can't name your brother unicorn," Ty told Kaya, lifting her onto the couch.

"Mama." She pouted, looking up at me in hope.

"Can you pick from the names we told you?" I asked her.

She sighed and shook her head. She then slid off the couch and started jumping up and down.

"Potty!" she shouted.

Ty then lifted her up and practically ran to the bathroom with her, making me laugh. We are currently trying to potty train Kaya.

I got up and made my way to the bathroom to see Kaya sitting on her little pink toilet.

"Mama, look!" She smiled.

"I see. Can you go potty?" I asked her.

"I did," she proudly said, standing up.

"KAYA! Good job baby!" I encouraged.

"Ice cream!" she shouted, running into the kitchen.

I laughed and followed after her.

My genius husband Ty told Kaya if she went potty in her toilet then she would get ice cream.

So that's how it's nine in the morning and I'm scooping Kaya ice cream.

"Here you go angel." I smiled.

I went over to put the tub of ice cream away when I felt a huge pain shoot through my stomach. The ice cream slipped through my hands, making Ty appear in front of me immediately.

"Ar?" He questioned.

I grabbed his arms to steady myself.

"I need to go see Sherry." I groaned.

In less than a second Ty had scooped me in his arms and was ushering Kaya out of the house.

I was on the hospital bed in a minute.

"How is your pain?" Nurse Sherry asked.

"It just started, maybe a five," I replied.

I remember how it felt with Kaya but this pain is almost more intense.

"Ar what's wrong?" Ty asked.

"Nothing," I replied dismissing the fact.

"Arrabella!" he demanded.

"Ty." I sighed, covering my face with my hands.

It hurt so badly and I don't know if I can do this.

"Where's Kaya?" I asked.

"With Carter and Audrey." I removed my hands and nodded.

"Aria?"

"This pain is more intense than with Kaya, but don't freak out," I warned.

Ty still shot Sherry a look that made me want to roll my eyes.

"Well I believe your son is a wolf and since you are human it's going to be more intense than with your human daughter Kaya. I will go get you the shots," she replied.

I nodded and Ty grabbed my hand and kissed it.

"You can do it Aria."

"We don't even have a name." I worried.

"We'll know when we see him." Ty smiled.

I nodded and with that I went through the most intense pain of my life, but when I saw my son's little face it was all worth it.

This little face I've dreamed of for the past six months is finally here in my arms. I've been staring at him for the past two minutes just taking it all in.

He's beyond perfect. He's got Ty's beautiful brown eyes and my light brown hair.

He's a big chunker though, weighing eight pounds and six ounces. Sherry confirmed that he is a wolf.

Ty's face is priceless right now.

The only thing that made this moment better was when Kaya came racing into the room.

"Brother?" she asked as Ty lifted her onto the bed.

"Yes Kaya, can you say hi to your baby brother?" I asked her.

"Hi brother!" She smiled, kissing his head.

"So Kaya, did you think of the names we told you?" I asked her. She nodded her face turning serious, well as serious as a two-year-old's can get.

"Carson." She shrugged.

"Carson?" I asked.

"Uh-huh like Uncle Car." She shrugged.

I pieced it together for a moment. How is it that a two-year-old can put together what a bunch of adults can't? Carson is the perfect name. It is a combination of Carter and Tyson.

"How are you so smart?" I asked her.

She giggled and I looked up at Ty for confirmation.

"Carson Tyson Benson it is," he confirmed.

"Yay!" Kaya clapped, beaming at her little brother.

"I love you brother!" There was a knock at the door and then Carter and Audrey came in, Audrey holding Tiana.

"Hey." Audrey smiled.

"Hi." I smiled.

"He's gorgeous!" She gushed, taking in Carson's face.

"I heard Kaya the wise named the baby half after her favorite uncle," Carter gloated.

"You're her only uncle." I snorted.

He playfully glared at me and then looked down at the little boy in my arms.

"I wanted to name him after you though. I didn't even think of the Carson thing." I laughed.

"Really?" he asked, half mocking and half sincere.

"Yeah because if it weren't for you I don't know where Ty and I would be today." I smiled.

"Thanks Aria." He smiled.

"Plus Tiana's middle name is Aria so we had to do something," Ty mocked.

I laughed. We really have the perfect little family.

* * *

"I didn't like the way he was looking at you," Ty persisted.

I groaned in protest. Ty and I are on date night. We are at this really nice restaurant and of course Ty is positive that the waiter is into me.

It's been four months since Carson was born, and this is my first time away from him. Now I'm sure Audrey and Carter are doing great with Kaya and Carson but I'm still worried.

"Are you even listening to me?" Ty demanded.

"Yes Ty." I sighed.

"Babe, are you worried about Carson and Kaya?"

"Aren't you?"

"Yes, but they are in good hands."

"I know." I nodded.

"Besides you've left Kaya with your mom and my parents before." He soothed.

"I know." I sighed.

"Are you guys doing okay?" The waiter, Gilmore, asked.

"We're great," Ty said.

"Alright, enjoy your meal," he added, sending a warm smile in my direction.

"Did you not see that?" Ty nearly shouted, gripping his fork tight.

"Ty calm down. He was being friendly," I protested.

"Yeah too friendly," he corrected.

"Tyson."

"Okay, okay I'm done. Sorry."

"You're forgiven," I mocked.

After dinner Ty and I drove home and I practically ran inside our house. Carter and Audrey were snuggled up on the couch watching Avatar.

"How were they?" I asked.

Audrey looked over and smiled.

"They were great!" She replied, standing up.

"What about Kaya before bed?" I asked.

"She was fine. Carter sang her a song about how he's the greatest uncle." Audrey laughed.

"Aw Carter," I mocked.

"Thanks Audrey," Carter teased.

"Is Tiana with Carson?" I laughed.

"Yeah." Audrey laughed.

I walked upstairs with her to see Tiana and Carson snuggled together in his crib. Tiana's one already but she's a little thing. Carson is almost her size, and they are eight months apart!

Audrey lifted Tiana out of Carson's crib and then I kissed Carson's head. I then went in to Kaya's room and kissed her head. I followed Audrey downstairs and said goodbye to them, and then Ty and I went up to bed. Ty went into Carson and Kaya's room as well and then walked into our room.

"They're alive!" he declared.

"Shut up!" I laughed, smacking his arm.

"What? What was that?" he mocked, pushing me on the bed and lying on top of me.

"Psycho!" I laughed.

"You're psycho for marrying a psycho."

"I have to pee!" I shouted, pushing up at his chest.

"No you don't." He chuckled.

"TY!" I shouted.

He let me up and instead of going to the bathroom I raced down the stairs.

Ty was right behind me and he threw me over his shoulder the second I stepped foot in the living room.

"TY!" I laughed.

He carried me upstairs and then threw me back on the bed.

"Don't Ty!" I pleaded.

It was too late he was already tickling the crap out of me.

"Ty!" I laughed.

"Say you love me."

"I love you!" I managed to say through my laughter.

He stopped and I smacked him. He rolled his eyes and then turned out the light and lay next to me.

"I love you too," he whispered, pulling me into him and burying his face in my hair.

"Wait Ty, I actually have to pee now," I protested.

"Are you kidding me?" he mumbled but I could tell he wanted to laugh.

He released me and I ran to the bathroom. When I jumped back in bed Ty wasted no time pulling me into him again.

"And you'll still have to pee the second you wake up tomorrow morning."

"Shh." I smiled. I think I fell asleep smiling that night.

Chapter 48

Dear Diary,

My babies are growing up too fast!

Kaya just started kindergarten yesterday!

The children attended pre-k and then kindergarten through twelfth grade in the pack house for school.

Carson starts his first day of preschool today because he's now three!

~Aria

"So then I said I know Mrs. Kole, one plus two is three!" Kaya told me.

"Wow Kaya you sure are smart." I smiled.

"Yeah and that's how I got a gold star on my chart," she explained.

"I saw you had three." I nodded impressed by my little angel.

"Yeah one was for helping and the other was for raising my hand." She smiled obviously satisfied with her first day of school.

Kaya is a talker. So when she raises her hand in school it's a big deal because she tends to say whatever pops into that head of hers.

"Did you make any new friends?" I asked her, sitting down in the pack houses' kitchen. Carson gets out of preschool in twenty minutes.

"Yeah, I met a boy named Owen and we played together outside." She smiled.

"Oh what did you guys play?" I asked her.

"We played basketball."

"Well angel it sounds like you had a great day." I laughed.

"It sure does," Ty added in, walking into the kitchen.

"Daddy!" Kaya sang, sliding off her stool and racing over to him.

"Hi angel." He smiled, scooping her up.

"What is this talk I hear about boys?"

"I made a new friend." She shrugged.

"Owen Matthews." Ty nodded.

"Yeah and guess what Daddy?" She smiled.

"What?" He grinned.

"I beat his butt in basketball." She beamed.

"Well that deserves a victory fist pump!" Ty shouted, bouncing up and down pumping his fist in the air making Kaya laugh and throw her fist in the air as well.

"Mrs. Benson?" Carson's teacher, Mrs. Weber, asked.

"Yes?" I replied, turning around.

"Is there a problem?" Ty asked, walking over to us, Kaya on his hip.

"Well today Carson said a word that I don't want the other children learning," she explained.

"What was the word?" I asked.

She glanced at Kaya and then Ty nodded, giving her permission to say it in front of her.

"Shit," she replied.

"Carson said that?" I questioned, shouting a little.

"Yes." She confirmed.

I looked up at Ty in horror.

"I'm so sorry." I apologized. "We will talk to him tonight." "Thank you for informing us, Marie. I can assure you this won't happen again," Ty added.

"Thank you. You can come pick him up now. Class is over," she replied.

"I'll go pick him up," I said, walking away without waiting for Ty's response. I didn't want Ty to be too hard on him. I mean he had to have learned the word from us so it's our fault.

"Hi buddy!" I smiled, picking him up and swinging him around my hip.

"Mama." He smiled.

"How was your day?" I asked.

"Good and you know what?" he asked.

"What?" I questioned.

"I got to see TT outside." He smiled.

"You did?" I asked.

"Yeah." He grinned.

I walked back out to the kitchen and I could tell Ty was upset about the whole bad word situation but he needed time to calm down before we explained to a three-year-old why a bad word is bad.

"Let's go home," I said. Kaya ran up to my side and grabbed my hand.

"How was your day Carson?" she asked him.

"Kay Kay I saw TT." He told her as we started walking back to the house.

"When?" she asked.

"For recess."

"That's because she didn't turn four yet," she explained to him.

"Yeah."

We arrived back at the house, and I put Carson down for a nap. Then I put Kaya in her room, telling her to do any homework she has.

"Ty, calm down," I pleaded, walking back downstairs.

"Let's go talk to him."

"No, not until you're calm."

"I am calm, Ar." He sighed.

"No, you're not," I sternly replied.

"Arrabella."

"Tyson."

"Aria, I'm fine. Let's just go talk to him."

"I want you to listen to this song first." I shrugged.

"Why?"

"When I didn't talk music was the only way I understood things. The only thing that could make me happy or even cry, so I want you to listen to this song."

"Okay." I handed him the iPod with the song already on the screen. I wanted him to listen to the song "Watching You" by Rodney Atkins.

He played it out loud and I went into the kitchen to cut Kaya an apple, but I could still hear the song. I love that song.

> "Driving through town just my boy and me
> With a happy meal in his booster seat
> Knowing that he couldn't have the toy
> Till his nuggets were gone
> A green traffic light turned straight to red
> I hit my brakes and mumbled under my breath
> His fries went a flying and his orange drink covered his lap
> Well then my four year old said a four letter word
> That started with "s" and I was concerned."

"Hey Ar, Carson beats this kid. He's only three," Ty called. I laughed I could tell it was already helping.

> So I said son now where did you learn to talk like that
> He said I've been watching you dad, ain't that cool

I'm your buckaroo, I wanna be like you
And eat all my food and grow as tall as you
are
We got cowboy boots and camo pants
Yeah we're just alike, hey ain't we dad
I wanna do everything you do
So I've been watching you.
The song went on. I walked upstairs and gave Kaya the bowl of apples.

"Mom what does that word mean?" Kaya asked.

I looked at her and smiled then sat next to her. Kaya is observant. In fact, she's been able to focus in on conversations and respond since the age of two. She loves learning especially new words so I should have seen this coming.

"Well angel that word is a not nice way of saying shoot," I told her.

"Is it bad?"

"Yes, it's called a swear word," I explained.

"Oh okay." She shrugged, happy with my answer.

"Okay you finish up your homework and then come downstairs."

"Okay love you mama!" she called.

"Love you Kay Kay!" I smiled, heading back downstairs.

The song was just ending and I swear Ty had a tear in his eye. I also noticed he had goose bumps.

"Okay it's our fault." Ty sighed.

"Yes, but we still need to talk to him."

"Okay let's do this." He nodded.

We walked upstairs and into Carson's room. He was in his bed looking through a picture book.

"Hey buddy!" I smiled.

"Hi Mama!" He shouted, getting off the bed.

"Daddy and I wanted to talk to you about something," I told him.

"What?" he asked. I sat on his bed and so did Ty. I then lifted Carson onto his bed in between us.

"Today your teacher told us you said a naughty word," I started out.

"Do you remember what that word was?" Ty asked.

"Shit?" he asked.

"That's the one." I pointed out.

"Where did you learn that word?" Ty asked him.

"You and Uncle Car," he replied in a voice filled with so much innocence I wanted to hug him and never let him go.

I looked up at Ty about to slap him.

"Daddy said Carter's full of shit," he added.

"Well Daddy is going into time out because that's a naughty word," I told him.

Ty almost protested but the look I gave him made him get up and go sit in the corner.

"What does it mean?" Carson asked.

"It means you will get a time out if you say it, so don't," Ty said from the corner.

That made Carson look over at him, and then he started laughing.

I then started laughing too, making Ty chuckle a little but then fake glare at me.

I tell you sometimes I feel like I'm raising three children, four if you include Carter, but I wouldn't have it any other way.

Chapter 49

Dear Diary,

I am a proud mother today!

Today is the day Carson and Tiana found out they were mates! It's going to take some getting used to, but deep down we all knew.

Kaya and Owen just celebrated two years together, as mates. I can't believe it's been two years since they found out.

Kaya just turned seventeen and Carson will be turning fifteen in two months.

My babies are growing up fast but I love them more than ever.

~Aria

"Yeah, I get it Carson but you and Tyler don't have to be so annoying," I heard Kaya demand from the living room.

"Whatever Kaya, you're just mad because we are right," Carson retorted, and I could tell he was smirking.

"Enough. What's going on?" I asked.

"Tyler and Carson went in my room and freaked out when Mason and I were in there!" she explained.

"You know they are best friends," I scolded.

"Not when Owen finds out," Carson replied.

"Mom!" Kaya shouted.

"Listen, Carson I know you're protective of your sister, but you can't go this far, and Kaya you should be thankful your brother is looking out for you."

"Where has Owen been anyway?" Carson asked.

"Running border," Kaya replied like she was talking to a small child.

Tyler and Tiana then walked in the house, making me smile.

Tyler looks just like Carter. He is ten now and follows Carson around like a lost puppy.

"Need a break from your crazy dad?" I asked them.

"Definitely." Tiana smiled and then she ran over to Carson, hugging him.

"Hey T, tell Carson to stay out of my business," Kaya said.

"What did you do?" Tiana asked.

"Nothing," he mumbled.

I smiled. I love watching these four banter.

"Carson." She demanded.

"Fine, Kaya, I won't tell Owen." Carson sighed.

"Tell him what?" Tiana asked now interested in the matter.

"That she and Mason were in her room together," Tyler added.

"So what's the problem?" Tiana asked.

"Yes, what is the problem?" Kaya shouted.

"He likes her!" Carson stated as if it were obvious.

"He does not." Tiana and Kaya scoffed at the same time.

"I can hear all four of you from the Canadian border!" Ty shouted, walking through the door.

"Hey Dad!" Kaya and Carson smiled, while Tiana and Tyler said "Hey Tyson."

"Let me guess you're enjoying this?" Ty asked, his glistening brown eyes landed on me.

I nodded and ran over to him and hugged him.

He chuckled and then his eyes landed on his other girl, Kaya.

"You'll be happy to hear that Owen is on his way back," he told her.

"Really?" She shouted in excitement.

"Really angel." He smiled.

Her brown-green eyes lit up and she bolted upstairs while shouting "I have to change!"

"You're always beautiful angel!" Ty called up to her though it was no use.

Kaya is sure beautiful though. Her wavy brown hair dangles to her rib cage now; her eyes still the perfect combination of Ty's and mine. Her personality is bold like

Ty's and she still moves her lips up and down when she sleeps just like Ty. She's short like me. She only stands about five feet five inches.

Carson on the other hand is a mixture. He has my light brown hair and Ty's light brown eyes. He's already about five feet seven inches. He pouts like Ty too, and has a slight temper.

My little Tiana Aria is growing up fast. She looks just like Audrey. She has her blonde hair yet it's slightly darker than her mother's, and she has brown eyes like her mom.

Tyler is like Carter. He's a complete goofball. He has Carter's sparkly blue eyes and his mom's light blonde hair.

Owen came through the door, snapping me out of my thoughts.

"Hey Owen!" I smiled.

"Hello Arrabella and Tyson." He nodded in respect.

I love Owen but he needs to take it seriously when I tell him not to call me Arrabella!

"Owen!" Kaya shouted, running down the stairs and into his arms. Owen is the perfect mate for Kaya. He's loving, caring, and thinks she's the most gorgeous, intelligent, and perfect girl in the world.

I looked over at Carson giving him a warning glance. He rolled his eyes at me: a habit developed from my constant eye rolling, and took Tiana's hand and led her outside.

Kaya and Owen then also went the pack house leaving just Ty, Tyler, and me alone.

"I wish I had a mate." He pouted.

"Don't rush it Tyler. You're only ten." I soothed.

The poor little guy was always left by the older kids because Tiana didn't want her little brother around all the time when she was with Carson, and Kaya didn't want him around her and Owen all the time because she wanted alone time with him.

"You're going to find her one day and everything will fall into place," Ty added, glancing up at me smiling.

"Is that what happened for you guys?" he asked.

"Something like that." I laughed.

"What's so funny?"

"I didn't like Ty right away." I smirked.

"You did too," Ty said defensively.

"Nope."

"Oh, you didn't like me? Okay," he sarcastically replied.

"At least I didn't stalk you," I retorted.

"One time, that was one time at the grocery store!"

"I was talking about the time I fell off the swing!" I laughed.

"Ty you followed me to the store that one day?" I yelled.

"Well it's not like I just ended up there." He chuckled.

"Stalker!" I pointed out.

"You liked it," he replied, wiggling his eyebrows.

"You guys are psychos!" Tyler shouted over us.

Ty straightened up and then completely lost it.

"You taught your nephew how to say psycho!" Ty gasped through his laughing fit.

"What?" we both asked.

"You both say psycho with an accent." He chuckled.

We looked at him like he was crazy.

"Psycho?" Tyler asked, making Ty nod and laugh more.

"Forget him Tyler, it's cute," I replied.

"How old were you when you found Tyson?" Tyler asked.

"Ty was eighteen and I was seventeen." I smiled at the little cutie.

"Wow that's old," Tyler replied.

"What about my dad and mom?" he asked.

"Carter was nineteen I think," I replied.

"I hope I find my mate when I'm fifteen like Carson," he said.

"Good luck kid," Ty replied.

"You'll find her when the time's right. Now go on and find your dad. I bet he'll want your help in the training field." I shooed.

"I love being a wolf!" Tyler shouted, sprinting out the door.

I shook my head at the boy and smiled. Without wolves my life sure would be dull.

Epilogue

Dear Diary,

It's been a while. How've you been?

It's been five years since I've written in you. I guess I don't need to write down my thoughts anymore because I speak them now.

I wanted to say thank you. Thank you for being there when no one else was. Thank you for letting me write down everything I needed to get out. All the tears that hit the pages and the nights I didn't want to be alive anymore for a while you were all I had.

Now I have everything I ever wanted.

I have this diary to thank for that. Who knows what would have happened to me if I hadn't written down my thoughts. I wouldn't have had anything to give my thoughts too. For a while all I had was paper and pencils.

But what happened over the past five years?

First Kaya, she's twenty-one now. She and Owen got married when they were eighteen and at nineteen she became a mother to my first grandchild, a little girl named Aucten. She's two and a half now and you'll never guess what color eyes the little angel has, green. Just like her grandma and great grandma.

Carson and Tiana are next. They got married last year. Tiana just gave birth to my second grandchild and first grandson, little Andrew. Andrew is gorgeous. He has light hair and brown eyes. He's definitely a little chunker.

Tyler my crazy nephew is exactly as we thought, just like Carter. He's fifteen now and he found his mate last year. Her name is Amzie. She is a quiet girl with dark hair and pale blue eyes.

Also, you'll never guess who stopped by last year, Addie and Paxton. They are so cute together and have one son and two little girls. Mila and Mya are eight-year-old twins and Travis is seventeen.

My mom and Krieg got married! We see them about once a week, and they both love being great grandparents.

As for Carter and Audrey, Audrey is still my best friend in the entire world and Carter is still annoying as hell.

These past five years have been amazing and I can't wait for all the years to come.

~Aria

"I haven't seen you write in that for a while." Ty observed, entering our bedroom.

"Yeah I can't remember when I stopped."

"Na-nana!" I heard a little voice call.

"Aucten?" I called back.

"They're here!" Ty excitedly said, racing downstairs. I followed him and smiled when I saw Kaya, Owen, and Aucten in the doorway.

"Hey mom!" Kaya smiled.

"My angel!" I smiled, hugging her tight and lifting Aucten out of her arms.

"Nana!" She smiled.

"Yes, you're my littlest angel, aren't you?" I beamed at the green-eyed child.

"Angel," she sang, nodding her head making her beautiful light hair bounce up and down.

Then Carson came in with Tiana cradling our newest little man in her arms. Andrew is already bright and gives you his full attention when you talk to him and he's only one month old!

After the kids left I wandered back upstairs to find myself reaching for my diary once again. Once again, I opened it and then I flipped through it a little. I read the first page and the next. I read all the pages.

From my first entry of sorrows to my first entry of Ty, I read everything.

Dear Diary,

Ty did it. He made me laugh for the first time in nine years.

~Aria

I laughed at the memory. I laughed for the first time when Ty smartly commented, "I'm not a cat Aria."

Dear Diary,
I'm officially Arrabella Benson!
Everything about the wedding was amazing!
I love Tyson so much.
~Aria

The entry following one of the best days of my life:

Dear Diary,
Kaya is six months old today! Wow already halfway to one.
She's amazing. She lights up the room. She laughs at
everything and loves me. She is such a loving and happy
baby.
It is the best feeling in the world when she places her small
head on my shoulder.
Ty and I are better than ever too. Kaya just completes our
little family so amazingly.
~Aria

My favorite entry I have of Kaya:

Dear Diary,
Audrey and Carter are having a girl!
~Aria

The entry when I found out I was going to be an aunt:

Dear Diary,

Our son is coming any day now!
His room is ready and it's all Kaya talks about.
~Aria

I can still feel the excitement when I read this one.

My favorite entry still makes me smile; it was the entry after finding out about mates.

It read:

Dear Diary,

I have a mate. What is a mate? I don't know. I think it means friend. I don't have friends. I don't talk to anyone, besides you. I don't even write in school, people think I'm stupid. It's him, Diary. It's Tyson. I don't know what it is about him; well I guess I do know. It's everything about him. Everything he does makes me smile. It's him; he makes me want to talk. He makes me feel like me again. I want to talk to him, I really do, but I have to do what's best for me. He might even be what's best for me. I'm lost Diary... I need help or maybe a friend. If I had a mom I would ask her. If I talked I would ask Ty what he wants with me. If I showed emotions I would show everyone that Arrabella James Middleton is a real person with real thoughts and feeling. However, Diary I don't talk. I haven't talked since I was eight years old. You're the only person I talk to, or write I suppose. I don't know where I stand anymore; I'm just so confused...

~Aria

A single tear slid down my cheek as I closed the diary, the diary that had been through it all with me.

I put the diary on the shelf in our room and walked out.

I smiled to myself as I thought of how different my life would have been if it weren't for Ty and my diary. I'm so thankful for them.

I'm so glad I wrote all my thoughts down in that diary, the first thing to ever know my thoughts. The first thing I told about Ty. The first thing I gave my thoughts on mates to.

I confided in my diary before Ty.

The day I found out Ty was better than the diary,

the day I wrote Dear Diary, I have a mate was the day that changed my life forever.

THE END

Can't get enough of Aria and Tyson? Make sure you sign up for the author's blog to find out more about them!

Get these two bonus chapters and more freebies when you sign up at http://abbie-lynn.awesomeauthors.org

Here is a sample from another story you may enjoy:

A NOVEL WRITTEN BY
RANEEM
HASAN

Chapter 1

I was woken up from my peaceful sleep when I felt someone sitting on the edge of my bed while poking my arm every once in a while. I groaned and pushed my head deeper into my pillow. *Who on earth is disturbing my beauty sleep?* I growled to myself.

"Wake up wake up, sleepy head, sleepy head that's not your bed," an annoying voice sang.

I groaned and immediately knew who it was.

Adam.

Didn't he know that I'm not a morning person and don't like to be woken up? Well clearly, I have to remind him because no matter what I do, it won't get through his stubborn head.

"Adam! Leave me be!" I growled at him, and he only chuckled.

"Come on, Tiana. It's time to get up," he said while poking my arm even harder.

"No, why would I get up? It's summer break for God's sake," I told him while pulling my arm from his grasp and waving it around, trying to smack my hand in his face.

"Well, we have lots of things to do today. Your mom wants us to go to the market and grab a couple of stuff for the party tonight," he answered.

I opened one eye when he mentioned the party. Yesterday, we graduated from high school, and Adam, I, and a couple of friends went out to a bar. Today, my mom was hosting a party for us and for the rest of the pack members who graduated.

"I'll get up in ten minutes," I muttered and closed my eyes, trying to get back to sleep.

I sighed happily when I felt him get off my bed. I got comfortable and was about to welcome sleep with open arms when a moment later I jerked up and gasped for air. I was confused for a second until I saw Adam laughing his butt off while trying to gasp for air as well but in a different way. I was soaked in water, and my clothes were hugging my body.

"Adam!" I growled, interrupting his laughter, and immediately stood up. Adams' eyes widened in fear and with a hint of amusement when I took a step closer to him, and he gulped, putting his hands in the air in front of him.

"Hey, Tiana, you didn't take that seriously, did you?" he asked while laughing nervously.

"Adam! You are so dead!" I hissed and ran after him when he ran out of my bedroom door screaming like a five-year-old. I growled and ran up to him then jumped on his back and punched him in his arm several times.

"Help! Help! There's a crazy girl on the loose," he screamed but laughed hysterically.

"How." Punch. "Many." Punch. "Times." Punch. "Do I." Punch. "Have to tell you." Punch. "Never." Punch. "To wake me up?" Punch.

Of course, Adam just kept on laughing while trying to get me off of his back. "You do know that your punches aren't affecting me, right?" he asked.

"I don't care!" I yelled as I continued to throw lame punches at him. "You freakin dumped water on me!"

"Okay, okay, I'm sorry. Just get off of me!" he said while wiggling and trying to make me fall off of his back.

I sighed and punched him lightly in the head and jumped off his back.

He pouted and rubbed his head. "Geez, women, you're so violent." I just rolled my eyes, and he smirked, running his eyes over my body.

I looked down and blushed when I saw my shirt was see-through because of the water everywhere. I looked up at him and scowled, but he only grinned.

"Might as well clean up so we can go," he said while shrugging and walking away and into the kitchen. I looked around and saw no one was awake yet. Good, because I wouldn't want anyone seeing me like this.

Adam will so pay for this.

I rushed to my room, grabbed my clothes, and went in the bathroom, stripping out of my clothes and hopping in the shower. I turned on the water and started to wash my hair and body. As I was doing that, I was thinking about my years in high school. Time really does go by fast. It was just like yesterday when I was in freshman year, and now I was done. Done with all the drama and done with all the stress. I was planning on going to college but didn't know which one yet.

But for the meantime, I was planning to enjoy my break while I could. I turned eighteen a couple weeks ago, and that means I'm an adult now so I can do stuff I couldn't do before. Don't get the wrong idea. I'm talking about traveling the world. You can say my parents were always worried about me and never agreed with the idea of me traveling to new places, but since I'm eighteen, now I could convince them that I can take care of myself. Well, I hoped I could.

I finished scrubbing my body and turned the water off then got out of the shower. I reached for the towel and wrapped it around my body. I dried my hair with a hairdryer and dressed in my casual clothes then made my way outside the bathroom. I applied mascara then tied my hair into a high ponytail before walking down the stairs.

When I made it downstairs, I saw everyone sitting at the table, getting ready to eat their breakfast. My pack isn't the biggest nor the smallest pack. We all live in the pack house except for the alpha and the luna. They have their own house, but since our pack isn't that big, we all live in a big pack house that has enough room for all of us.

I went towards the big table and kissed my mom and dad on the cheek.

"Good morning, sweetheart," my mom said. "Good morning."

"How's my baby girl?" my dad asked. I smiled up at him and glanced at Adam who was across from us and looked back to my dad. "I'm fine. Just someone woke me up in an unpleasant way." Adams' eyes widened, and a smirk grew on his lips.

My mom turned over to Adam and gave him a pointed look. "What did you do this time?" she asked.

Adam shrugged while glancing up at me. "I didn't do anything. She just wouldn't wake up."

"He dumped water on me."

My mom and dad looked at Adam while he just laughed. "I told you, she wouldn't wake up."

I rolled my eyes at him and sat down on one of the chairs. Soon our breakfast came, and we all ate. After we were done eating, Adam and I had to go to the market to grab the stuff my mom needs for the party tonight. My mom insisted that she plan out the party and no one else. It's like she's planning a wedding or something.

I hopped into Adams' car, and once he got into the driver's seat, we took off. After a while of awkward silence, Adam decided to speak.

"You mad at me?" he asked and glanced at me then back to the road.

"No, just annoyed." I looked at him and shook my head.

"Well, sorry about that." He smiled at me and chuckled.

"Just don't do that again. Or I will do something you won't like," I murmured.

He smirked and glanced at me. "Like what? Throw punches at me?"

I scowled at him and shrugged. "No, like cut Adam Jr. off." I grinned as he gasped.

"How dare you say that?" he asked dramatically.

I chuckled and elbowed him in the arm. "Next time, think before you wake me up."

"Next time I'll wear armor," he said, and I glared at him. "But there won't be a next time." He assured. I laughed a little, and he smiled at me then turned his back focus to the road.

After a while, we reached the market and parked the car before getting out. We made our way to the market and started buying the stuff my mom wrote down on a list.

"So what's the first thing we should get?" I asked Adam. Adam took the list from his pocket and opened it.

"Food, she wants us to get food," he answered. I smiled at that. Food! The best thing that ever happened to me! Okay, before you think that I'm exaggerating, think again. Food is life.

"Then let's go!" I said and grabbed his hand, pulling him into the food section. I sighed happily and wiped a fake tear off while Adam just looked at me like I was crazy.

"This is my heaven," I told him. He nodded his head while chuckling.

"Yeah, I know. It explains those time when you would attack me over them."

I grinned at him, and we bought treats and drinks. After that, we went and bought decorations. After a while, I was so tired. All I wanted to do was go back to bed and sleep, but clearly, that was not going to happen.

"Can we take a break?" I whined.

He shook his head at me and continued walking.

"Come on. Adam. I'm tired," I begged.

He looked at me and gave me a knowing look, "No, we still have lots of stuff to buy." I huffed and crossed my arms.

"You're a guy! You're not supposed to like shopping," I pointed out.

He smiled at me and raised a brow. "Sexist much? Besides, who said I like shopping? It's just that you don't have any friends other than me to go shopping with."

I gasped at him. "What? I do have friends."

He shook his head. "Like your bed?"

I crossed my arms over my chest and sighed. Okay, maybe I didn't have much friends, but it's all this guy's fault. Whenever I would try to make friends, he would always ruin it, like telling them I'm weird and I'll go crazy on them, telling them a handful of lies.

"You're such a bully," I muttered under my breath, but of course because of our werewolf hearing, he heard it.

"Says the violent girl." We both laughed and smiled. Adam was the only friend who stood by me and never left my side, and for that, I'm grateful even though there were times I just wanted to strangle him.

After a couple of hours of torture, we finally stopped to grab a bite. Finally. We were carrying a ton of bags, but I, being the lazy person that I am, made Adam carry them. He didn't mind, anyway.

We sat on empty chairs, and Adam got up to order our food. I put my head on the table and closed my eyes for a bit but pulled my head back up when I saw from the corner of my eye a pack member who I barely knew sitting next to a boy while holding hands. I guess they're mates. Not many people find their mates, but for those who do, then they're lucky. At least, that's what they all say.

I heard that having a mate is the best thing that could ever happen to you, but somehow, I couldn't believe that. I mean, yes itis nice to have someone who loves you deeply and share your soul with, but I found that hard to believe. I didn't want a mate nor any guy. Not anymore that is.

I was cut out of my thoughts when Adam placed the tray of food in front of me and sat down. I lightened up, and at the right moment, my stomach grumbled.

"Dig in," Adam said, and I didn't need to hear that a second time to chomp on my food.

* * *

After eating, we drove back home with the shopping bags, but before that, I bought a dress for the party tonight. It's a simple white dress that hugged my curves.

We walked into the pack house, and my mom walked up to us with a smile on her face. "Thank you, honey. You too, Adam," she said.

"You're welcome, Mom," I told her. She smiled up at me, and a couple of people took the bags from us and walked away.

We excused ourselves before walking away.

Adam and I walked up to my room, and I took the dress out of the bag I was holding and placed it on my bed. Adam looked at it and furrowed his eyebrows. When I bought this dress, he was waiting outside the store, so he didn't see what kind of dress I bought.

"You're wearing that?" he asked and pointed to the dress that was on my bed.

I looked at him and nodded. "Yes, is there something wrong with it?" I questioned.

He crossed his arms over his chest. "Not really. It's just it's too short," he muttered.

I raised a brow. Here we go again, Adam was always complaining about the clothes I wear. Whether it's too short or too tight, he acts like an overprotective brother.

"I know, but it's not that short," I stated and showed him the dress. "See?"

He shrugged and scratched the back of his neck. "Um...I'll just go. Call me if you need anything," he said and walked out of my room. I shrugged and sat on my bed while admiring the dress.

The party was going to start at seven, and it was still three, so I had plenty of time to get ready. I decided to lie down on my bed and relax my eyes a bit before getting ready.

* * *

I snapped my eyes open when I felt someone shaking my arms.

"Tiana, wake up."

I looked up at the person and saw my mom standing above me with her arms crossed over her chest. "Mom? Is there something wrong?" I asked.

"Yes, there is. You have about an hour to get ready," she stated. My eyes widened, and I turned to the clock and saw it was almost six.

I looked up at her then got up from my bed. "It's okay, Mom. I'll get ready before the party starts."

She smiled at me and nodded before turning around but stopped and looked at me. "Just don't be late."

With that, she walked out, and I rushed to the bathroom and took a quick shower before wrapping the towel around me and drying my hair. I applied a little makeup and let my hair loose.

After that, I grabbed the dress, wore it, and looked at myself in the mirror, smiling. I looked good.

I looked at the clock and saw I still had ten minutes left, so I got out of my room and walked to Adam's room. I entered without knocking and saw Adam putting his shirt on. I wasn't embarrassed nor did I think much about it because Adam and I have known each other since we were babies, so I've seen him naked before and the other way around.

Once he was done, he looked at me and smiled. "Well, don't you look beautiful," he said, and I only chuckled at him.

"You look good too."

"Good? I look sexy," he stated, and I laughed.

"Sure you do."

He gasped at me. "For your information. Girls die to have a piece of my body," he said.

I rolled my eyes and sat on his bed.

He came up to me and sat next to me. "Well, thank you for the compliment," he said sarcastically.

I grinned and bumped my side into his.

He laughed while looking at me. "I meant it when I said you look beautiful," he said seriously.

I smiled at him and nodded my head. "I know. Thanks." I got up from the bed and walked towards the door but not before turning around and looking at Adam. "Let's go before my mom gets us herself."

He smiled and nodded. We walked out of his room and made our way downstairs. There were food and drinks everywhere. The lights were off, but there were colorful lights everywhere, and it gave the room a party feeling. Lots of teenagers were dancing to the music and eating food. I smiled and made my way to Mom and Dad and hugged them tightly.

"Thank you," I said, and Adam came up from behind me and said the same thing.

"Yes thank you, it's wonderful."

"Oh, it's no problem. Besides the pack needed a break and have some fun," my mom said. We nodded our heads, and I kissed both my mom and dad on the cheek.

"Have fun," my dad yelled through the music as we walked towards the dance floor.

"Let's dance." Adam grabbed my hand and pulled me further to the dance floor. We danced for a while until we were tired. Then we decided to eat a couple snacks, so we went to the food section.

We were about to eat when my parents came running towards us, and all of a sudden, the music was turned off.

My face turned into confusion, and I had a bad feeling that something bad was going to happen.

"Mom, Dad? What's wrong?" I asked. They both looked at each other's faces filled with fear.

And what they said next made my heart stop beating.

"We're under attack."

If you enjoyed this sample then look for
Mason's Impossible Prey
on Amazon!

Other books you might enjoy:

My Beloved

T.M Mendes

Available on Amazon!

Other books you might enjoy:

Daybreak Flatlined

Elle Arcie

Available on Amazon!

Introducing the Characters Magazine App

Download the app to get the free issues of interviews from famous fiction characters and find your next favorite book!

iTunes: bit.ly/CharactersApple
Google Play: bit.ly/CharactersAndroid

Acknowledgements

I would like to thank some people who have encouraged me to write this book:

First, I have to thank Wattpad. Without their platform I would have never thought to put my stories out on the Internet. By taking a shot in the dark with this amazing website I was able to reach millions of viewers with my stories.

Second, I have to thank the literary agent, AJ Dane, who made this all possible.

Thirdly, I have to thank my editor Michelle Yañez who made my story what it is today.

Lastly, I have to thank the amazing publishing company BLVNP for this incredible opportunity.

I also have to thank my family, especially my mom, who has always encouraged me to follow my dreams and pursue my passions.

However, I owe the greatest debt to my Wattpad fans to whom this book is dedicated. Through their encouraging comments and messages I was able to complete this book.

Author's Note

Hey there!

Thank you so much for reading Dear Diary, I Have A Mate! I can't express how grateful I am for reading something that was once just a thought inside my head.

As far as I can remember I have always wanted to have a published novel. Getting my work published is one of my greatest achievements as a writer. It is an indescribable feeling to finally have this story finalized. It is quite mindboggling to know that an infinite number of viewers will be able to read my words. I only hope that this book can help people find their voice. I hope that Aria's story will be an inspiration for my readers to never be afraid to speak up and stand up for what they believe is right.

I'd love to hear from you! Please feel free to email me at abbie_lynn@awesomeauthors.org and sign up at abbie-lynn.awesomeauthors.org for freebies!

One last thing: I'd love to hear your thoughts on the book. Please leave a review on Amazon or Goodreads because I just love reading your comments and getting to know YOU!

Whether that review is good or bad, I'd still love to hear it!

Can't wait to hear from you!

Abbie Lynn

About the Author

Abbie Lynn is a 20-year-old full time student. She lives in the United States with her six siblings and orange cat. Abbie enjoys traveling, shopping, and spending time with friends.

www.ingramcontent.com/pod-product-compliance
Lightning Source LLC
Chambersburg PA
CBHW021213260626
47172CB00002B/404

* 9 7 8 1 6 8 0 3 0 9 5 5 3 *